Photo credit: Meg Periton

Jan Dunning studied English and Art at university, where she set her heart on a career with words and pictures. The plot took an unexpected twist, however, when she was scouted at Glastonbury festival and became an international fashion model instead. Jan spent the next decade striding down the runway, flying around the world on photoshoots and startling her friends and family on billboards for Gucci, Garnier and Gap. Finally realizing she had more to say behind the camera, Jan trained as a photographer and art teacher and began writing fiction. She now lives with her family in Bath, dreaming up ideas in the studio at the bottom of her garden, with help from Misty, her cat.

Twitter @JanDunning1
Instagram @jandunningbooks

For Simon, Rowan and Meg, with love.

Published in the UK by Scholastic, 2023
1 London Bridge, London, SE1 9BG
Scholastic Ireland, 89E Lagan Road, Dublin Industrial Estate,
Glasnevin, Dublin, D11 HP5F

SCHOLASTIC and associated logos are trademarks and/or
registered trademarks of Scholastic Inc.

Text © Jan Dunning, 2023
Cover illustration by Johnny Tarajosu adapted by Scholastic
Cover © Scholastic, 2023

The right of Jan Dunning to be identified
as the author of this work has been asserted by her
under the Copyright, Designs and Patents Act 1988.

ISBN 978 0702 32375 1

Printed by CPI Group (UK) Ltd, Croydon, CR0 4YY
Paper made from wood grown in sustainable forests
and other controlled sources.

1 3 5 7 9 10 8 6 4 2

www.scholastic.co.uk

MIRROR ME

JAN DUNNING

■ SCHOLASTIC

"Art finds her own perfection within, and not outside of, herself. She is not to be judged by any external standard of resemblance. She is a veil, rather than a mirror."

OSCAR WILDE

"You don't take a photograph, you make it."

ANSEL ADAMS

Come closer.
Look, and listen.
Let me be your guide, your friend.
Don't turn away.
I know how hard it is —
how flawed you are — but trust me.
It doesn't have to be that way.

1

"Summer selfie! Who's with me?"

The girl bursts out of the cafe on the heath, nearly knocking me on to the grass. Saskia Farrow, of course. With two of her followers, Ruby and Lila, close behind.

Holding her phone at arm's length, Saskia poses like a model on a runway. The other girls squeeze into the shot beside her: a glossy three-headed beast. As Saskia shoots, they adjust their bodies and tilt their faces, their shiny, pouting lips forming tiny Os.

I stare.

How did they learn to do that?

"After some tips, Freya?" Saskia's eyes flick to me.

I move away, my face burning. We were friends once, me and Saskia, until she dropped me in Year 8, and got herself an upgrade. It was like she'd read some secret manual over summer, one that said which clothes and hair and nails were cool.

How was I supposed to know that stuff?

The girls grab a bench and cluster round Saskia's phone.

"Oh my God, delete! Delete!"

"I look awful. Try a filter on it!"

"That *is* with a filter."

"Another one, then."

"That's worse!"

They collapse with laughter.

"You look good though, Sass."

"Yeah, amazing."

"I know." Saskia tosses her head. "Maybe I'll make it my new profile pic. After I've cropped you guys out."

The other girls nod. "Definitely."

"Oh, yeah. You should."

I pull my hoodie tight, despite the heat. If Sam could hear this, he'd be cracking up. Still, there's no denying it – when you're perfect, you're powerful. No one contradicts Saskia. You can't argue with a face like that.

Where is Sam, anyway?

I squint through the cafe window, looking for Sam's lanky frame in the queue for slushies. The sunlight turns the glass into a mirror, throwing my own face back. Dodgy skin that never tans. Wonky nose, mousy hair. Even my

2

freckles aren't the cute kind — more like someone opened their Coke in my face. As for my eyes, they're completely forgettable. Sam's dad's paint chart would call the colour *Drizzle*.

Yeah, I know my side of the camera.

I dig into my bag. My fingers close around cool metal, and a smile spreads over my face. *My camera*. My sixteenth birthday present from Dad, and the most precious thing I own. I lift the camera to my eye. Already I feel better, safe behind the lens. When the world shrinks down to the tiny rectangle in my viewfinder, I forget about everything, especially myself.

I look for a shot, Dad's voice in my ear. *"Find your subject, then your frame. Think about the light."*

I zoom in on a feather, caught on a blade of grass. In my head, Dad smiles encouragement. *"Now check your focus — that's it. You've got the skills, Freya. You just need to find your voice."*

Whatever that means.

"Ready for my close-up!" Sam's face looms, bug-eyed in my lens.

"Hey! You're messing up my shot."

"Improving it, you mean." He preens his quiff.

I hide a smile. "You've been ages."

"Queue was long. The sun's dragged *everyone* out." He glances in Saskia's direction, and waves his slushy under my nose. "We can share. Let's grab a table?"

"I have to get back."

3

"Already?" Sam pouts. "We've not been here that long. I thought you wanted to take more pictures."

"I did. But I told Dad I wouldn't be late."

Sam pauses mid-slurp, as he clocks my meaning. "Wait. Back up. It's today? She's moving in *today*?"

I nod.

We walk towards the main road, my stomach fluttering. I don't know why – it's not like it's my first time meeting Bella. Dad introduced us two weeks ago when she picked him up for one of their "dates". I stood there, lost for words, as she smiled and shook my hand. Never in my whole life have I seen anyone who looks like that.

"Is she totally gorgeous?" Sam reads my mind.

"Well, that's kind of in the job description."

"*Belladonna Wilde*." He shakes his head. "It's surreal. She was massive, back in the day. You *seriously* had never heard of her? Sometimes I think you live under a rock. She's all over the old *Vogues* at Mum's salon, I can show you, if you like?"

"Maybe." I shrug. Sam's into that stuff, not me. He's always watching runway shows on YouTube or makeovers on TV. Fashion and me? Let's just say we're not a fit.

"I can't believe you'll be living with a model!"

I roll my eyes. "It's not for long. She's 'in between apartments', Dad says. She's only staying till she finds a new one."

We cut down an alley of pastel houses and I pause, framing the rainbow colours in my lens.

4

Sam leans against a wall. "Aren't you happy for him?"

"Dad? Sure. But it's early days. They only just met." I frown.

Two months ago, not that I'm counting. And he's been … different *ever since.*

"Hold still," I tell Sam, pushing away the thought. The sun has cast his shadow on the wall in razor-sharp profile. I grab the shot, and turn the screen around.

"Cool." Sam reaches for my camera. "Let me do you."

"No, thanks." I duck out of his way.

"Aww, Freya. Don't feel bad." Sam jogs to catch me up. "Not everyone can be as photogenic as me." He sashays down the alley with a smirk. "And there's always Photoshop. Have a word with your dad."

I stick out my tongue. "Newsflash. He's given that up."

We reach the bridge at the start of my road, where Sam usually cuts back to his flat. He shuffles on the kerb, clearly angling for an invite to meet Bella. I pretend not to notice. Today is going to be awkward enough without Sam there, acting the fanboy.

"I'll text you later. I want to download these." I nod at my camera. It's not even an excuse. I got some good shots today, and I want to print them out. I'm supposed to have a project to show when I start at sixth-form college.

"You'd better." Sam warns. "I want to know *everything*. Bella Wilde's an enigma these days. She's, like, famously private. Almost a recluse. She hasn't given an interview for years."

I nod. I've googled Bella too.

"I'm relying on you to find out all her secrets!" Sam grins.

"What if she doesn't have any?" I say. "Maybe she's just … ordinary." *An ordinary person who looks like that?* "I mean, she's dating Dad, isn't she?"

"You're probably right." Sam sighs. "She must be pretty down-to-earth. Your dad's the original Mr Nice."

Reluctantly, he saunters off.

As I open the front door, Kodak shoots out, her black-and-white tail a fuzzy brush.

"Hey, cat, what's up?" *Weird.* She never runs into the street. I chase her inside, and call down the hall. "Dad? I'm back!"

No answer.

Which isn't strange — usually he's at the camera shop till six. But he was finishing early today to help Bella settle in. Perhaps she hasn't arrived yet? Or maybe they've gone out?

I pad upstairs, my camera in my hand.

Then I freeze.

The sight steals my breath away.

Dad's bedroom door is slightly ajar, and beyond it there's a woman, standing with her back towards me, in front of a chest of drawers. She's wearing a bath robe, and gazing into a small, oval mirror on a stand. Her reflection is lit by the sun.

Bella.

It means "beautiful" in Italian. And she is.

6

Tumbling honey-blonde hair framing a symmetrical face. Huge eyes rimmed by long, dark lashes. The daintiest of noses and full rosebud lips.

I wait for her turn, to say hello, but she doesn't move. She can't have heard me come in. She's too absorbed, gazing into the mirror. It isn't ours; she must have brought it with her. The frame is dark and dainty, carved with twisting stems. So out of place next to Dad's Ikea pine.

Bella leans in further, her face pressed close to the glass. As she stares, I count the seconds. *Six … seven … eight…* Will she ever blink? Then she licks her lips. The intimate gesture makes me flinch.

I should go. Her beauty routine is none of my business. I've got photos to download.

But I stay where I am. My eyes are glued to her face. There's no other word except … *flawless.*

I wonder how it feels.

I lift up my camera. *One quick shot. She'll never know.*

As I press the shutter button, Bella clears her throat. I jerk down my camera, sweat prickling my forehead. Her lips are moving – she's whispering – but not to me.

She's talking to the *mirror.*

OK, that's definitely weird.

Her voice is a murmur, impossible to make out. Perhaps she's praying? Dad never said she was the religious type.

Goosebumps pepper my arms. For a second, the surface of the mirror seems to distort, rippling like pebbles in a pond.

No.

7

I blink, and everything's back to normal. The mirror is old, that's all. The glass is cloudy and cracked. *Typical Freya, overreacting.* I'm not a fan of mirrors at the best of times.

Bella has fallen silent. I stare at her perfect face. Her eyes are closed, and her cheeks are flushed. If it's even possible, she looks brighter, more vivid than before.

She stretches, and I jump. A floorboard creaks.

Bella spins around. "Freya?"

"Hi." My mouth is dry. I feel like an intruder, but that's silly. This is my house. Mine and Dad's.

"I didn't hear you there." Her face is hard to read. A citrusy scent reaches me as she comes towards the door.

"Where's Dad?" I ask, shifting uncomfortably. Her gaze is intense, like a spotlight.

"He went to get something for dinner." Bella's eyes land on my camera. She frowns. "Did you…?"

I flush.

"May I see?"

Without waiting for a reply, she lifts the camera from my hands. She scrolls through the images on the display: the pictures I took earlier on the heath.

"Goodness, you're quite the photographer." She blinks. "I didn't know."

I shrug.

"The thing is, Freya." Bella moves closer. "If you wanted to take my picture, you should really have asked me first."

"I know," I mumble. "I'm sorry."

"As we're going to be living together, we should respect each other's privacy. Don't you think?"

I manage a nod. I'm too mesmerized by her face. Her eyes are a shade of green I've never seen in real life, and her skin is like wax – not a single pore.

"It's OK. No harm done." Bella holds out my camera, like a peace offering. "Let's forget all about this and start afresh. Don't worry, I won't mention it to Nick." She smiles serenely.

I take my camera, and she gently shuts the door.

I stand in the hallway for a moment. My head feels strangely foggy. Pulling myself together, I stumble to my room.

Connect my camera to my laptop. Switch to image playback, ready to download.

Wait. What?

I stare at the screen.

It's blank. Empty. Nothing to import.

The photographs on my camera are all gone.

2

She did it on purpose, that's my first thought. She was angry that I took her photo without asking. She wanted to teach me a lesson. I needed those pictures for my project, and now they're gone.

Then I stop.

I'm not being fair. It's easy to press the wrong button and delete stuff by accident. I've done it a thousand times myself.

This was an accident, that's all.

It's surreal, eating dinner in our cramped kitchen with Bella there. Like a magical unicorn has wandered in off the grimy Camden streets. She's so poised and polished in her silky red blouse, like she's at some swanky restaurant, not sitting at our rickety old table that Dad rescued from a skip. And her dewy skin and glossy hair looks all kinds of wrong next to Dad's five o'clock shadow and wiry ginger mop.

They gaze at one another, ignoring me. Talk about a third wheel. But I can't blame Dad. I'm staring too. Bella's like a magnet. She sucks all the attention in the room.

"More wine?" Dad's hand trembles as he tops up her glass, droplets splashing on the posh tablecloth we only use at Christmas.

"Nick, this is wonderful!" Bella glows. "You're a lifesaver."

"We want you to feel at home, don't we, Freya?" Dad looks at me, so I nod.

"Well I do, so thank you. You too, Freya. For sharing your dad with me." Bella smiles and I smile back. True to her word, she hasn't mentioned our awkward meeting earlier. I guess she meant it, about starting afresh.

Dad's shoulders relax. He turns to me. "So, Snowdrop, tell us about your day."

Snowdrop. The nickname makes me flush.

"Snowdrop?" Bella's laugh tinkles. "How sweet. Where does that come from?"

"Oh, it's silly really." Dad becomes quiet, staring at his plate.

"My mum went into labour in a snowstorm," I say,

taking over. It feels weird telling a stranger, but in truth, I like this story — what I know of it, anyway. "We lived in Tokyo when I was a baby. My middle name is *Yuki*. It means 'snow' in Japanese."

I glance at Dad. He's focused on his fish.

"I didn't know you lived in Japan, Nick!" Bella perks up. "Do you know, I've never been? I'd love to hear more."

Dad clears his throat. "There isn't much to tell. We weren't there for long. We moved back to London after Tess … when Freya was one."

I hold my breath, wondering what he's told Bella about Mum. It's fifteen years since she died, but Dad barely mentions her, not even to me.

"Get any good shots today?" he asks, changing the subject.

"Nothing worth saving." I glance at Bella. Her face gives nothing away.

"Freya's a talented photographer," Dad says. "A chip off the old block." He laughs. "I'm kidding. She's better than me. Top of the class when she gets those exam results next month, I'll bet. A famous photographer one day."

I squirm hearing him speak my dreams out loud. "Dad, stop."

"Don't be modest," he teases. "You're good."

"I learned from the best," I say, and we share a grin. Bella is silent, sipping her wine.

"So…" Dad keeps the small talk going. "Have you and

Sam made any plans for the summer? Work's busy, I'm afraid, or I'd take some time off."

I bite my lip. He promised to help with my edits. Has he forgotten? "Just working on my project, I guess." I shrug. "It needs a theme, but I haven't decided what."

"How about portraits?" Dad lights up. "Maybe Bella would pose for you?" He winks. "Take advantage of having a professional in the house!"

There's a pause as Bella puts down her glass.

"I wish I could help, Freya." She smiles an apology. "But I'm afraid I try to keep my work and my personal life separate. I've got so many shoots booked this summer – you can imagine that I don't want to do it at home as well."

"Of course," Dad rushes in.

"That's OK," I say.

"Oh, but now I feel terrible." Bella pouts, prettily. "I know! Let's do something else, instead. Something much more fun! We could go shopping together, have a facial, maybe get our nails done?"

She beams like she's giving me a gift – and in a way, she is. Still, I put down my fork and slide my bitten fingernails into my lap.

"That's a very kind offer, isn't it, Freya?" Dad prompts. "I knew the two of you would get along."

I nod. My appetite has gone. I wait for a chance to make an excuse and escape to my room. It doesn't take long. As I push back my chair, Dad hardly looks up, too lost in Bella to pay much attention to me.

My phone is full of messages from Sam.

> *So what's she like?*
> *Freya, answer me! Is her hair naturally that colour?*
> *Is it true she used to date Leonardo DiCaprio?*
> *Are you BFFs yet? THIS IS TORTURE!*

I think before replying.

> **She seems nice.**

Send.

I keep typing.

> **But ... I'm not sure I trust her.**

I change my mind and delete it. He'll want me to explain, and I can't.

I don't know why I feel it, but I do.

I wake to an empty house. Dad cycles to the camera shop at eight. I suppose Bella must have left for a shoot. I linger on the landing, outside their bedroom door.

I have the strangest urge to see it − Bella's mirror. It was so odd and old-fashioned, not the kind of thing I'd expect to belong to someone like her. I suppose it's an antique; an heirloom, maybe. Not that she's mentioned family.

14

I twist the handle, but the door is locked.

Huh? Dad's never locked it before.

I send Sam a text.

> U around today?

> *Sorry. Helping Mum at the salon.*

I sigh.

The summer before college was supposed to be simple. Hanging with Sam, taking photos on the heath. Editing my project with Dad. But now Bella's here, things feel different…

Precarious.

Only one thing can cheer me up.

Camden Market.

I stand inside the entrance, drinking it in. I've been coming here since I was small, and I still love it just as much as I did the first time. The scent of incense tickles my nose, mingling with the stomach-rumbling smell of curry. A nearby sound system pumps out a thudding bassline, and all around, a babble of languages rises and falls, drowning out the drama in my head.

I watch as tourists flood the cobbles, crawling over bright stalls of slogan T-shirts, quirky jewellery and emoji cushions. It's easy to be invisible here. The whole world comes to Camden. I stand in the eye of the storm, soothed by the chaos, wishing I could capture it.

And I can.

I pick up my camera, savouring its weight. My fingers tingle at the thought of choosing my frame, picking my moment, triggering the shutter.

Today's plan is simple: a long exposure, the shutter wide open. Long enough for the crowd to become a beautiful, liquid blur. I set up my tripod and fix my camera in place. Then I go to work.

Everything drops away.

Concentration wraps me like a cloak. As I search for the right balance of colour and shape, there's no room in my brain for anything else. The process takes over.

It's magic.

Shoppers stream before my lens. I set the aperture, deciding how much light to let in, then pick my shutter speed: three seconds. There's still something missing, though. A focal point.

Then I notice the girl.

She's standing off the main drag. She's a few years older than me, maybe nineteen, or twenty – and rocking a colour-clashing look I'd never dare. Strong features are framed by a halo of tight black curls. She's still, except for her eyes, which dart about the crowd. *What's she doing?* There's no time to wonder. Clouds are gathering; my light's about to go. Anyway, she's perfect to focus on.

Click.

The sound of the shutter sends a thrill rushing through me. I take some more images, adjust my settings, just in case. A dozen shots later, I unclip my camera and scroll back, looking for good ones. *Yes!* Adrenaline dances through my veins. The market stalls pop with colour, the tourists form a river of movement, and the girl with the incredible Afro takes centre stage, pulling in the viewer.

"Nice."

I jump. She's standing beside me, her cool eyes studying my face.

"Thanks." I hug my camera to my chest and scrabble to put my tripod away.

"Wait. Can I see more?"

Her smile seems genuine. I turn my camera around, face heating as she scrolls through.

"Cool." She looks at me sidelong. "Any shots of you?"

"Me?"

"You know. Selfies, or…"

"No!" I splutter. "I mean … I'm better behind the camera."

She raises an eyebrow. "Which socials are you on?"

"I'm not," I say, thinking guiltily of the account Sam made me set up. "I mean, I am, but it's private. I only use it for messaging. I never post."

"OK." The girl looks bemused. My cheeks grow warmer. How can I explain? *I can't put myself out there. My pictures are for me.*

"Here." She hands me a card.

"I'm Jas. What's your name?"

"Freya," I mumble. "Freya Jones." *Does she work for a photography magazine?* My heart skips a beat.

"How old are you, Freya?"

"Sixteen."

"Still at school?"

"I just left. I start college in September."

Jas looks at me and tilts her head. "Would you be interested in modelling?"

"*Modelling?*" I echo. "You're joking." I swing round, expecting to see Saskia sniggering with her gang. This is something they would do.

"Not at all." Jas seems surprised by my reaction. "I'm casting for a shoot…" Just then, her phone bursts into life, cutting her off. She groans at the screen. "Sorry, I have to take this." She gestures to the card, still in my hand. "If you change your mind…" She starts to back away. "Get your mum to give me a ring."

The crowd swallows her up.

I stand there, taking deep breaths. It's not the modelling idea that's upset me, or even her assumption about Mum.

I'm angry with myself for thinking – even for a second – that anyone could be interested in my photos.

18

3

I lose the day taking pictures. It's late when I get in.

Dad and Bella are on the sofa, Dad's arm draped around Bella's shoulders. I clock the bottle of champagne on the coffee table, the two half-empty glasses. All at once, my meeting with Jas is the last thing on my mind.

"What's going on?"

My eyes zoom in on a little leather box. The glimmer of gold on Bella's hand.

"Oh, Freya!" Bella's eyes are shining. Her hair is tied back with a red headscarf. It makes her look girlish and young. "We have wonderful news!" She kisses Dad's cheek, scarlet lips grazing his shaving cut.

"*You got engaged?*" The room is spinning.

"I know it seems sudden…" Dad plays with a sofa thread.

"*Sudden?*" My mouth has fallen open. "You met in June. You hardly know each other! She's only staying a couple of weeks!"

"Freya, don't be rude." Dad rubs his eyes. "I can explain."

"Nick, darling, it's OK." Bella calms his fidgeting fingers with her manicured hand. "I totally get it; it's a shock. Please, Freya, come and sit down."

She pats the sofa. I don't move.

"The thing is…" Bella goes on. "The moment I met your father, everything fell into place. We have a connection. You know that cliché – 'when you know, you know?' – well, that's the way we feel."

I shake my head.

"It's like the stars have aligned!" She laughs. "It's absurd for me to look for a new apartment when you've both made me so welcome here. I feel as though I've come home." She beams like she's sitting on a throne, not our tatty old sofa, shredded by Kodak's claws.

I can't speak.

"Pour Freya a small glass, Nick. Let's toast the future." She turns his face to hers. "It's time to leave the past behind."

I frown. *What's that supposed to mean?*

"I don't want any champagne," I tell Dad. "How could you do this without talking to me?"

He doesn't get a chance to answer.

"Oh, Freya." Bella's face is full of sympathy. "I can imagine how hard this must be. I promise, though, nothing's going to change. I know I could never be your mother." Her eyes flicker. "But, together, I know we'll make a happy family."

"We *are* a happy family! Me and Dad!"

Her face falls. Dad looks pained. "Snowdrop..." He drags himself from Bella and gets up to give me a hug.

I jerk away. There's a flash of white as Jas's card flies from the pocket of my hoodie. It lands under the coffee table, down by Bella's feet.

"Freya, come on. Let's talk about this," Dad pleads.

"What's the point?" I snap. "Looks like everything's been decided. Have you set a date?"

He flushes. Nods.

"When?"

A pause, then: "August the fifth."

"Next year?"

A longer pause. "This year," Dad mumbles.

I gape. "But that's ... ten days away!" My brain is struggling to compute. "Is that even possible?"

Bella interjects. "The haste is my fault, I'm afraid. I rang the registry office, and as luck would have it, they had a cancellation. The press will descend if they get a whiff of this. It's better to do these things quickly, under the radar."

"We gave notice a little while back," Dad adds, his face

bright red. "On a whim, just after we met. I meant to tell you, Freya, honestly. Like Bella says, we *knew*. And at my age, you don't want to wait."

I roll my eyes.

"Oh, Nick, how romantic!" Bella teases. "And, darling, you're hardly old. Men are lucky, Freya. They only improve with age." I clench my jaw. "I can see you two need to talk. I'll leave you to it."

Bella goes to stand up, and as she does, she spots Jas's card. She picks it up and reads it with a frown. I wait for her to hand it to me, but she slips it into her pocket.

What?

"You know, Freya…" Bella pauses in the doorway, and looks me straight in the eye. "I do want to make this work. I'm not the enemy, you know."

The air feels suddenly charged. Her gaze is intense, almost hypnotic. Her skin is so smooth, I can't read the surface, and the symmetry of her face is like a sedative, sapping my strength. I'm falling, spiralling, drowning…

No.

I shake my head to snap out of it.

"I'm sorry you feel that way." Bella shuts the door. Her perfume lingers: that cloyingly sweet citrus scent.

What. Just. Happened?

Dad is oblivious. Miles away.

"Dad?" My vision blurs. "Dad, why are you doing this?"

He blinks, his focus back. He holds out his arms and I

22

give in. As he gathers me in a hug, I drench his shoulder in snotty tears. He makes a cubbyhole with his arm, and I burrow in.

"Sweetheart, I know this is hard to accept. It's been just the two of us for so long." He pauses. "That's how I wanted it, after…"

My tummy flutters. Will he mention Mum?

Dad takes a deep breath. "When Tess died, I made a decision. I decided to focus on you. I wanted to do everything I could to make up for … her not being there. I think I've done a good job." His eyes crinkle, and I squeeze his hand. "Your gran helped, too. Letting us move in here with her. Looking after you."

Pictures play in my mind. *A white-haired lady with tracing-paper skin.*

"And when you started at junior school, I got the shop job, so I could be around."

Dad in the playground at three-fifteen. A scruffy ginger beacon in a sea of mums.

"You're saying you gave up your dreams for me." I bite my lip.

Dad shakes his head. "I'm not sure I'd call retouching pictures for advertising agencies my dream."

"Your photography, I mean."

He shrugs. "That doesn't matter. You came first. But you're older now. Try to understand. It's been hard for me at times. And lonely."

I open my mouth, but he stops me.

23

"We're a great team, you and me. But we live in our own bubble."

I nod. With Gran gone, there's no extended family. Mum's parents died before I ever had a chance to meet them, and neither of my parents had siblings, so I don't have aunts, uncles, cousins. It really is just Dad and me.

"It's time to move on. Let other people in. There are things I can't give you, Freya. You need a female influence."

Like Bella?

"I never thought I'd feel this way again," he goes on. "Your mum was … unique. Special. I thought no one could ever live up to her."

"But Bella—"

He blushes and his freckles momentarily fade. "There's something about her. I don't know what it is, but she's managed to get under my skin. This is new for her too, you know. She's never had kids, she has no family. The fashion world is all she's ever known. But she says she loves me, and I love her too. Do you think you can give her a chance?"

The room tilts. *Perhaps he's right. I'm being unfair.*

But doubt gnaws my brain, like a maggot in an apple. Something doesn't add up.

What does poised, perfect Bella see in my down-to-earth dad?

I open my mouth to say that no, I won't give Bella a chance, that there's something about her I don't quite trust. Then I see his expression, so sweet and full of hope.

I can't do it.

Dad looks disappointed by my silence. "We're getting

married," he says, disentangling himself and standing up. "Bella's right. I need to focus on the future. This is a new chapter in my life, and I'm happy. I thought you'd want that."

As the door clicks shut behind him, I curl into a ball.

Of course I want Dad to be happy.

But why does it have to be with her?

Let me tell you about beauty.
Some say it lies in the beholder's eyes.
They're wrong.
I've seen how people flinch from flaws
and blemishes. Seen how babies gaze in
rapture at a well-proportioned face.
The truth is undeniable; I will show you
the enduring power of the pleasing form.
So don't despair. It's why I'm here.
Transform, conform – and
make my glamour grow.
Don't think too hard. I'll do
your thinking for you.
Submit to my ideal.
I have such perfect taste.

4

The stairs creak as Dad comes up to bed. I wait for him to knock and say goodnight.

His footsteps pass right by my bedroom door.

My insides feel like lead. I text Sam with heavy fingers. Typing the words makes them real.

Dad and Bella are engaged.

STOP IT.

It's true.

No. Way.
When's the wedding?

5th August.

THIS August?

10 days.

YOU'RE KIDDING ME.

I wish.

Sam video-calls, but I don't pick up. I can't trust myself to speak.

Talk tomorrow?

I can come over first thing x

I drag myself to bed, but my brain is wired. Sleep feels light-years away.

On the one hand, I get it. Dad's lonely, and Bella's gorgeous. At least on the surface.

So why does it feel like something's rotten underneath?

I think about her slipping Jas's card into her pocket. Why would she keep it? And why didn't I stop her?

I toss and turn.

There's definitely something odd about her. Almost creepy. When she turns her gaze on me, I can't think clearly. Any confidence I have just seems to … drain away. Dad's different around her too – so passive and weak. All this talk of the future, forgetting the past. Surely he can't be serious?

The past only means one thing.

Mum.

I turn on my light and reach up to my bookshelf. My fingers close around a silver frame. It's the only picture I have of her.

Tess White.

My mum.

It was taken on the day they got married. Dad's behind the camera – I can tell by her smile. I trace her features: intelligent brown eyes and short dark hair. She's nothing like Bella – not stand-out beautiful – but there's something striking about her all the same: a humour in her gaze.

I take my time, soaking up the image. I know every detail by heart – right down to the way the wind ruffles the hem of Mum's long, silvery dress. With its bell-shaped sleeves and gossamer cape, she looks more like an insect than a bride – but there's an elegance in the way she stands, the way she holds her head. A self-assurance. It's a quirky choice; not your typical wedding dress, maybe. But what do I know?

What *do* I know?

Only this.

They met in Tokyo, when Dad was starting out with his photography. Mum was travelling, he said. They got married quickly, just the two of them, and I was born the following January. But Mum died, a year later, a few months after my first birthday. A brain aneurysm, out of the blue. Dad brought me back to England, and that's where the story ends. I used to ask questions, but his eyes would cloud over and his voice would go mumbly. His heart was broken, I suppose. So I stopped asking.

At least he gave me this photo.

The memory washes over me.

I'm in a dark room with Daddy. A light glows dull and red.

Daddy's face looks like a monster's, but I'm not scared. I'm dancing up and down. I've come to Daddy's work. We took a bus past a big white skyscraper, right into the middle of the city.

"What are you doing, Daddy?"

"I'm going to print a picture."

He puts a shiny plastic rectangle in a little metal holder, and slides it into a tall black tower.

"Can I watch?"

"Actually, Snowdrop, you can help."

He turns on a light, and a picture pops up on the table under the tower. A man's hairy face makes me giggle. "He looks funny."

"It's in negative." Daddy twists a handle, and the man gets clearer. I can see every bristle in his beard.

The light goes off, and the picture goes away. Daddy puts some paper in its place. "See this paper? It's sensitive to light. Press the button, Freya."

I do. Back comes the face.

"OK, now bring the paper here. Drop it in this tray. Watch!"

My eyes grow wide. Under the water, the man appears, the right way round this time.

I clap my hands. "It's magic!"

Daddy laughs. "I think you're right."

I got the photography bug there and then. The smell of the chemicals, the glow of the safelight – I loved it all. Even though I've grown up with digital, I still like knowing the history, understanding how a camera works. And I loved Dad's workshop. There was a main room with lights and a curved backdrop wall, and the darkroom tucked away at the back.

Watching Dad work made me calm.

And the dark always made me brave.

"What was Mummy like?"

Daddy goes still and I panic. I've spoiled the magic, done something wrong.

"What do you want to know?"

I shake my head, forgetting he can't see.

"Why don't I show you instead?"

He rummages through a drawer, then slides a plastic strip into the frame. The tower light pings on.

"There."

31

My mouth falls open. I'm staring at a lady with sparkling eyes and short dark hair. Then black swallows her up, as Daddy puts the paper into place.

"You're in the picture too," he says, counting the seconds of light.

"Where?"

He drops the paper into the tray. There she is – Mum! – shimmering underwater.

Daddy's finger points to her curving belly. "You came along three months later."

Questions come tumbling out.

"Where was I born? What time was it? Did I cry? Did Mummy choose my name?"

"Enough," Daddy says finally, and his voice sounds funny. "Freya, love, that's enough!"

He pegs Mummy's picture on a washing line to dry. Then we lock his special workshop and run to catch the bus.

That was one of the last times I went to Dad's workshop.

Soon after, his darkroom work dried up. The world was changing, he said. He had to move with the times. He bought a digital camera and taught himself Photoshop at the kitchen table. It didn't take long before he started getting advertising work. He was amazing at retouching, though I remember him grumbling to himself: *"A good photographer should tell the truth."* He seemed happy when the shop job came up.

I turn over the silver frame with Mum's photo inside,

and slide the catches loose. The photo falls out into my hand.

In the corner, there's a crease.

Strange.

I rarely take it out, and I'm careful when I do. I try to smooth the crease with my finger, but it's no use. A sob catches in my throat.

It's only a photo, but it feels like a sign – that things are fragile, falling apart.

For years, I've told myself the past doesn't matter. That Dad is all I need. That I can't miss someone I've never known.

Now I'm not sure that's true.

Bella's arrival has made me realize. I'm missing a piece of my jigsaw. Not knowing my mum is like crossing a city without a map, or building a house without a plan. If I don't have the blueprints, how am I supposed to figure out who I am?

I slide my precious photo back inside its frame and look once more into Mum's eyes. *Who were you, really?* I've cobbled together a version from my imagination, but I need to know the truth.

I won't let Dad forget you.

If Bella is my future, the past feels more important than ever.

5

The display on my alarm clock glows 2:00 a.m.

I listen, trying to figure out what woke me. A siren, probably. Camden never sleeps.

At the foot of my bed, Kodak twitches in a dream. From next door comes Dad's buzzing snore.

Then I hear it.

Whispering.

I swing my legs to the ground and tiptoe on to the landing. The light from the street casts an orange filter on the walls. The door to Dad and Bella's room is closed. The whispering starts again. It's coming from the living room.

Clinging to the shadows, I pad downstairs. Halfway, I

stop. The living-room door is ajar, and through the gap, I can just make out our ancient sofa and the shadowy shape of someone lying on it.

I crouch for a better view.

Bare feet with glossy red toenails. Long pale limbs, bathed in the dim light. Bella's hair falls in loose golden waves around her shoulders, her collarbones curving under the straps of her nightdress. Mentally, I take a photo. She looks like a painting – one of the Pre-Raphaelites we studied last year.

Or she would, if she wasn't on her phone.

"I admit, I'm disappointed, Victor. Those pictures were important." She rubs her forehead. "It's another case of bad lighting, I suppose. If you'd stop sending me to work with amateurs…"

I frown. Is *Victor* her agent? Does she usually speak to him in the middle of the night?

Bella lets out a sigh.

"Anyway, it doesn't matter. I may have a solution… It turns out, he has a talent, one that could be useful to the project… Exactly. Best kept busy, I always say."

Her voice drops. I lean forward to hear.

"Yes … yes, things are progressing well. I just need a little more time. Everything will soon be under way…" She falls silent, pursing her lips. "I know, I thought it would be easier too, but these things … they have to be handled delicately. It's a question of access, building trust. That's why I decided to fix a date…"

35

I sink on to the stair. *Is she talking about the wedding?*

Bella tosses her head. "Of course I know what I'm doing... Think of it as a safety net... It tightens the legalities..." A smile crosses her lips. "It's a tiny inconvenience for everything I'll gain."

My fingers grip the banister.

There's a silence. Bella breaks it with a giggle. "I know … eating out of my hand. But if anything changes, I can handle it..." Her voice tightens and my ears prick up. "Hmm … that's a minor complication... And soon I'll have more authority, remember? No, she's more a nuisance than a threat."

My body feels hot and cold at once.

Upstairs, Dad coughs in his sleep. Bella's eyes dart to the ceiling. "I'd better go," she whispers. "But listen. We need to move quickly, we only have five weeks... You have the first image, so production can begin. Get a sample ready for press..." She stretches and sits up. "Be patient. There'll be plenty more soon... Yes, tell Raven to prepare the contracts. I need a team of people I can trust."

She hauls herself to standing. Panic spikes my veins.

I mustn't let her find me here.

Heart pounding, I creep back upstairs. I've just made it to the landing when Bella's last words reach me.

"It will *all* be worth it in the end … Oh, no. This is more than a comeback. This is a renaissance."

*

36

I'm sitting at a mirror framed by light bulbs, so bright they make my eyes water. Bella is standing behind me. In her hand is an old-fashioned comb. The creamy teeth are made of bone.

"Don't worry, Freya," Bella croons. "I'm going to make you perfect. Perfect for the wedding."

I try to get up, but I can't. I'm wearing a dress so tight and heavy I can hardly breathe.

Bella begins to comb. The teeth bite into my scalp. Droplets of blood scatter on the floor like beads. I look at myself in the mirror. With every stroke, my hair grows more and more knotted. Soon, it's a snarling nest of tangles. Blood is streaming down my face.

"Oh dear." Bella sighs, sadly. "I'm afraid there's no hope for you at all."

I sleep late and wake up aching, my pillow damp with sweat. I rub my eyes to push away the nightmare, but other fragments of memory come rushing back.

The wedding. Bella's night-time phone call.

Numbly, I get dressed. Something isn't right. I'll talk to Dad again, meet him in his lunch hour. Sam will be here soon. He'll help.

I head downstairs and stop short.

Dad is in the hallway, wearing a suit. The clock on the wall says eleven.

"Dad?"

He doesn't answer, fumbling with his cuffs.

"Dad! Why aren't you at work?"

He jerks around. "Freya! You gave me a fright."

"Why are you all dressed up?"

I glance down the hall and see Bella sitting at the kitchen table. She's wearing a cream blouse with a cherry-red pencil skirt, and she's scrawling in a book. "Nick?" she calls without looking up. "Darling, are you ready?"

Dad blinks, and his eyes finally focus on me. "Ah, yes. I changed my shift. Bella's agent called this morning. Victor. He wants to run something past me. We're meeting at the agency. I'm heading there now with Bella."

We both look at Bella; she is strapping on glossy black stilettos. Dark-red soles peep out from underneath, like she's stepped in paint, or blood.

Turns out, he has a talent. My tummy squirms.

"Dad, are you all right?"

"I'm fine," he says, rubbing his eyes. "Just tired. Must have drunk too much champagne. I didn't sleep too well."

"Me neither." I mutter.

"So go back to bed, Snowdrop." He kisses my forehead. "It's the summer holidays, you're allowed to rest."

Bella appears in the hall. "Morning, Freya. How are you today?" She turns to Dad without waiting for a response. "The taxi is on its way. Oh, Nick, darling, come here." She puts her notebook on the shelf, and adjusts Dad's collar, nose wrinkling at the cat hairs on his sleeve. "You really do need someone to take care of you."

I scowl.

A car blows its horn.

"Perfect timing," Bella sing-songs, kissing Dad on the nose. "You're all set. Let's go."

"Dad, what time will you be—"

"Sorry, Freya, we're running ever so late," Bella cuts me off, steering Dad through the door. She ushers him into the taxi. I wait for him to look back, but he doesn't.

He doesn't even blow me a kiss.

6

I'm still staring after them when my phone pings.

Sam.

On my way.

My shoulders relax. Sam will help to put things in perspective. Then I notice something.

Bella's notebook.

No, not a notebook – *an appointment diary*. Like an old-school agenda. It's chic, in soft maroon leather, with the gold-embossed year on the front. She left it on the shelf when she was fussing over Dad. She'll probably come back for it when she realizes.

If she realizes.

I listen for the purr of the taxi, but the street outside is quiet. My fingers hover above the diary. Last night's phone call has left me uneasy. What was Bella talking about? What do I know about her, really? Beyond the fact that she's famous and beautiful – nothing. Like Sam said, she's an enigma. Back in June, when Dad and Bella started dating, Sam sent me a link to her profile on the Façade agency website, and even that had barely any details. I know her height and her shoe size and her ridiculously tiny measurements. I know she exploded on to the fashion scene in the early 2000s, seemingly out of nowhere. But I don't know where she was born, where she grew up, who her friends are, what she loves.

None of the real stuff.

I know nothing about her, yet she's marrying my dad.

Bella's like a blurry photograph, impossible to make out. What if I could sharpen the image?

I pick up the diary and start at the beginning.

Surprisingly, the first five months of the year are almost empty; only a smattering of notes in Bella's curling handwriting and a whole bunch of entries, crossed out.

Spanish Vogue editorial
Italian Harpers Bazaar beauty
French Elle: cover try

In no time, I've reached June. My tummy tightens.

The night that Bella met Dad.

I remember him going to the exhibition – a retrospective by a famous fashion photographer, in some church-turned-gallery in Camden. Loads of celebrities were there. Dad never normally goes to stuff like that – the invite came out of the blue. He guessed it was because he'd done some retouching for the photographer, years ago. Anyway, he went along, and Bella was there – not just on the walls, but in the flesh. She walked up to him, introduced herself, and that was it.

I push away the image.

There are a few more entries in the diary for July. Odd phrases, meaningless to me.

Source suppliers / fabricators.
Speak to lawyer re: NDAs.
Plan teaser campaign.

And on today's date:

Thursday 27th July
Press / Media Strategy.

That's all. Nothing unusual. Typical model stuff, I guess.

I psych myself up before I turn the next page. I'm not ready to see the wedding marked in Bella's swirling print.

But for 5th August, an empty space looks back.

I lean against the wall.

Strange.

Bella rang the register office; you'd think she'd have made some note. Back in Year 8, when Sam had a crush on Harvey Williams, he drew this secret symbol – a swirly heart – in his school planner whenever Harvey spoke to him. I still tease him about it. Bella's getting married in just over a week, but you wouldn't know it from her diary.

It's like she doesn't care.

"It's a question of access, building trust … a tiny inconvenience, for everything I'll gain."

My hands feel clammy.

The rest of August is full of reminders: orders, briefings, castings, fittings. Blah, blah, blah.

Finally, I reach September, where there's only one entry, on the first of the month. A delicate drawing – intricate leaves surrounding an elegant letter N.

I breathe out. *N is for Nick.*

She was in a hurry. She got her dates mixed up. That's all.

The doorbell makes me jump. Shoving the diary back on to the shelf, I open the door to Sam.

"You nearly gave me a heart attack!"

"Sorry for the surprise visit," he deadpans, striding into the hall. "OK, Freya, spill. I *cannot* believe what I'm hearing. Your dad is getting married to Belladonna Wilde? Is she here? Am I actually going to meet her?"

"Not today," I say, side-eyeing his quiff. It's higher than usual and gelled almost solid. "So your effort's gone to waste."

Sam tuts and runs his fingers over his head. "I buzzed the back myself. What d'you think?"

"Looks the same to me."

He rolls his eyes. "You should let me cut yours. I'm getting good. Mum's boss got new scissors for the salon, Korean imports. We could ask to borrow them. I'll give you a crop."

"I need my hair."

"I know. For hiding." Sam musses it over my face. "Life's more interesting when you stand out. You should try it some time."

I follow him into the kitchen, not bothering to reply. We've had this argument before. Sam's always on at me to experiment with how I look. Not that he does himself – he basically lives in sportswear like every other boy from school. But fashion comes with way too many pitfalls – trends I can't keep up with, rules I'll never learn. Getting it wrong is terrifying. Easier to opt out.

Sam stuffs the toaster and hops on to the counter, doodling on our chalkboard while he waits. As usual, the drawings emerge from his fingertips like magic: Bella, a fantasy Barbie bride, leading Dad, a shaggy dog on a lead. And me in the background – a bowlegged bridesmaid in a hideous dress, hiding behind my camera and my hair.

"Not funny."

"Aww, you know I love you really." He grins, and I can't help grinning back. We're mismatched in a million different ways, but we bond over the creative stuff. Art for Sam, photography for me.

"You're related to fashion royalty," he says as the toast pops.

"Not yet." I scowl.

"Aw, you have to admit, it's cool!" He glances up when I stay silent. "I thought you liked her?"

"I said she seemed nice, but…"

My mind jumps to Bella on the sofa in the moonlight, talking into her phone. Her flawless face and perfect silhouette. As I tell Sam about it, my skin prickles.

"It was weird," I say. "She was talking to her agent, but it was the middle of the night. She was complaining about a photoshoot, and she mentioned some project. She's planning something."

"It sounds like work drama to me. No big deal." Sam shrugs.

"No." I shake my head. "There's something … *strange* about her. Intense."

"Well, all models are eccentric, right? Think what the attention would do to your ego."

"It's more than that," I insist. "She's got this … *presence*. It's like she's mesmerizing—"

"Of course she's mesmerizing! She'd be a pretty rubbish model if she wasn't."

"You're not listening! Dad's totally under her spell. She

only has to look at him and he does whatever she wants." I grow thoughtful. "I've felt it too. When she gives you her full attention, it's like … drowning. She's so beautiful … so *perfect*. You can't think or concentrate. You just give in. All your confidence slips away."

"Confidence?" Sam gives me a pointed look. "Look, I get it. She's intimidating. She's probably used to getting her own way. You'll soon get to know each other."

I shake my head. *He's missing the point.* "Something's going on. This engagement, it's way too fast. I–I'm worried she doesn't love Dad. I'm scared she's using him."

"Using him, how?"

I sigh. "I wish I knew."

Sam chews his toast. "You know what *is* weird? She's moved in permanently, right? Where's all her stuff?"

I look around the kitchen at our mismatched crockery and cluttered shelves. My old school timetable and Dad's work rota, pinned to the fridge. It's true. Bella said it felt like home, but there's nothing personal of hers here. No books, no pictures, not even a favourite mug.

"I suppose she'll have it sent on later. She did bring clothes, I guess. And an old mirror…"

"An old mirror?" Sam's ears prick up.

I realize I haven't told him – about Bella, muttering into the glass; how creepy it was. I stay silent. He'd just laugh or say I'm overreacting – and he might have a point.

"So where is it, this mirror?"

"Upstairs, in their room."

46

Sam's eyes spark. "Show me."

I hesitate.

"Don't tell me you haven't snooped around?"

"I promised to respect her privacy." I squirm, remembering the diary. "Anyway, the door is locked."

"No problem." Sam hops down from the counter. "And she's invading *your* privacy, marrying your dad. Don't you want to know more about her?"

Yes.

"What if she comes back?"

He winks. "We'll be quick."

For the longest time, I was forgotten.
Neglected and imprisoned — by those
who didn't know my worth.
Dust laid a carpet upon my form.
Spiders cast threads across my face.
My silver began to flake away.
It's true, I don't look my best these days.
How ironic!
But all this time, my ambition
never changed.

7

"Told you," I say, as Sam tries the handle.

"Wait." He digs into the back pocket of his jeans, pulling out a couple of hairpins. They must be from the salon. I watch as he expertly bends a pin and pulls off the tip in his teeth, then he slides it into the lock and starts wiggling.

"Hurry!" I urge. If Bella comes back and catches us, she'll be furious. But if she's got anything to hide, I need to know.

Finally, the lock clicks. Sam grins. "Multi-talented, me."

"It's there." I push the door open a crack, but Sam barges in. The mirror is standing innocently on the chest of drawers, Bella's scarlet headscarf covering the glass.

"Ooh. Creepy." Sam whips away the scarf. As the glass catches the light, the mirror seems to flash.

"What do you think?" Sam wraps the scarf around his head. "Am I giving off Audrey Hepburn vibes?"

"Put it back." I'm too jumpy to laugh. Even so, I find myself edging closer to the mirror, like I'm being pulled towards it, my legs moving of their own accord. "Can you feel that?" I ask Sam.

He's too busy striking film-star poses. "I wonder how old it is?" he says, angling the frame to get a better view.

"Who knows?"

I have the weirdest urge to look into the glass. It's so unlike me – usually I avoid mirrors at all costs. Sam's hogging the space though, so I stop side-on instead, running my fingers over the wooden carvings on the frame. A tangle of vines. The mirror itself is small and neat, and on either side are two wooden arms – also carved – attached to a stand at the base. The design makes the mirror seem to float, held up by twisting stems.

Creepy doesn't begin to cover it.

"I wonder where she got it?" I say. Sam doesn't answer. He's twisted the scarf into a turban and is posing again. "Sam, stop messing around!"

"Buzzkill." He huffs, unwinding the scarf and throwing it back over the glass. Instantly, I feel lighter, like a switch has been flicked.

"Think she'd mind if I try her perfume?" Sam picks up a small glass bottle, shaped like an apple.

50

I pluck it from his hands before he can douse himself. "Yes, I do."

"Never mind. Ooh, wonder what's in here?"

He pulls out a tiny drawer in the base of the mirror's stand. There's not much inside: a few coins, a credit card, another bottle, small and brown.

Sam snatches the credit card, so I pick up the bottle. It has a rubber stopper at the top, like something from the science labs at school. Essential oil, I suppose. The label's fallen off. I put it back.

"*Miss Belladonna Wilde,*" Sam reads the gold lettering on the credit card. "Reckon she'll change her name when she marries your dad?"

"Hmm. *Bella Jones?*" The words taste sour in my mouth.

Sam snorts. "Nah. Doesn't have the same ring."

I'm quiet suddenly, thinking about Mum. I know she kept her maiden name – White – when she got married, though I don't know why; Dad never said.

I take the card and put it back in the drawer with the bottle. A sudden citrus scent makes me spin around. I half-expect to see Bella standing in the doorway, but it isn't her, it's Sam. He's opened up the wardrobe and is rifling through the rails.

"Oh. My. God! Chanel, Gucci, Versace, Dior, Prada … she's got *everything.* And she's really into red, isn't she?"

I stare at Bella's slinky designer outfits pressed up tight against Dad's faded shirts and jeans. Maybe it's the sickly scent of perfume, but bile rises in my throat. "Will you stop touching things!"

51

"Ugh, you're no fun," Sam groans, but he shuts the wardrobe door.

"Let's go." I hustle Sam out of the room before he can interfere with anything else. Then I triple-check that everything looks the way it should. Flipping the lock, I pull the door closed. Finally, I can breathe.

"Freya! Come and see this!"

I find Sam in the bathroom with the cabinet doors thrown wide. "Look!" He gestures at the shelves.

"What?" I blink. Toothpaste, toothbrushes, shaving foam. Deodorant, shower gel, plasters… Nothing out of the ordinary. "I don't see anything?"

"Exactly!" Sam says. "Where are her products? Her make-up, her moisturizers, her serums? There was only perfume in her room, and there's nothing at all here. Don't you think that's strange?"

I frown. "Not everyone wears make-up."

"Sure, but she's a *model*."

I shrug. "She doesn't need it. She's perfect as she is."

"No." Sam shakes his head. "Bella must be … what? Early forties? The same age as my mum. And our bathroom cabinet is full of stuff. Hair dye, face creams, you name it. You know she never posts on social media either?"

"Who, your mum?"

He tuts. "No. Bella. Obviously."

"Well, neither do I."

"Maybe you've got more in common than you think."

I pull a face, but Sam is serious. "No, Freya. It doesn't

52

add up. A stunningly gorgeous forty-something model with no make-up or beauty products? An attention-grabbing designer wardrobe, but no social media showing it off? I've been digging, and I can't find *anything*. Even if she's super shy or down-to-earth, you'd think she'd have someone doing it for her. It's her business, after all."

Super shy or down-to-earth.

These are not words I associate with Bella.

The sound of a car makes me jump. I peer through the frosted windowpane. A flash of dark red, and the shape of a figure, moving on the street below.

"It's her!" I slam the cabinet door. My tummy swirls.

"So what?" Sam whines, as I drag him downstairs. "We weren't doing anything wrong!"

"Quick! Go out the back!" I grab my camera and push Sam into the garden, just as the front door clicks. Ten seconds later, we're through the gate and safely in the side street.

There are so many contradictions surrounding Bella.

They make Sam curious, but they only make me scared.

8

"What was that about?" Sam slows up, panting. "You're allowed to hang out in your own home, you know."

"It doesn't feel like home when she's there. Can't we go to yours?"

His shoulders sag. "Nah. My dad's got the day off."

"So?"

He chews his lip. "He's been on my back."

I look up in surprise. Sam's dad Tom is OK – more blokey than my dad – into football and the pub. I don't see him often, though, as he's busy with his painting and decorating business.

"What about?" I ask.

"He keeps saying I need to think about the future. You know – after our results."

I nod, no need to say what we both know. Sam might not be going to college in September. School's not really his thing, and he messed up his exams, or so he reckons. Art's the only one he's sure he'll get.

"He thinks it would help if I got a summer job." Sam sighs.

"You help out at the salon."

"Sometimes. But Mum's not the boss. It's not up to her." He squishes a weed with his toe. "Dad's weird about the salon, anyway."

"Why?"

He shrugs and heads off in the direction of the canal. I hurry after him.

"So what does he think you should do?"

Sam blows out a breath. "He mentioned a job next week. Needs an extra pair of hands."

"Painting, you mean? But you'd be good at that."

"Yeah." Sam turns sharply on to Chalk Farm Road and picks up the pace. "Yeah, I guess you're right."

"Freya Jones?"

The woman's voice is so piercing, it brings us to a halt. Coming out of the door of a trendy nail bar, looking coiffed and glossy, is Alyson Farrow, Saskia's mum, with Saskia, her mini-me, by her side. I haven't seen Mrs Farrow in years. Not since Saskia binned me as her friend.

"Hi, Freya!" Saskia flashes a smile that immediately puts me on guard. "Good to see you!"

I eye her cautiously. "Er … yeah. Good to see you too."

"What a coincidence!" Alyson exclaims. "Saskia and I were just talking about you, Freya!"

"Really?"

Saskia nods. "I was saying to Mum it's such a shame we stopped hanging out. We used to be good friends."

Beside me, Sam coughs.

"You must come over," Alyson chips in. "Saskia would love that, wouldn't you, darling?"

I wait for Saskia to laugh. "Totally." She smiles. "Any time."

"Okaaay…" I mumble. This feels like a trick. Sam pulls at my arm.

"That's wonderful!" Alyson actually claps her hands. She leans towards me, her voice a stage whisper. "I couldn't believe it when I heard. Is it true that your dad has been seeing Belladonna Wilde?"

"Come on, Freya, time to go," Sam mutters.

"Tell me, what is she like?" Alyson asks, ignoring Sam. "Where has she been all these years? I assumed she must have married a billionaire and moved to the Caribbean. Is she as gorgeous as ever? You know, during my twenties, I was obsessed with trying to look like Bella Wilde. I dyed my hair her exact colour and I was *always* on a diet, trying to get that teeny-tiny waist. It never seemed to work. You lucky thing, Freya. She'll tell you all her beauty secrets!"

"Mmm," I manage to say.

"Do you think she would put in a word for Saskia, at her model agency?"

"Come *on*, Freya." Sam's yanking my arm out of its socket.

"Sorry, Mrs Farrow," I say. "I really have to go."

Both Saskia and her mum look gutted. "Well, don't forget," Alyson calls after us. "Drop by anytime. You know where we are. And bring Bella too, if you like. The more the merrier!"

"Pathetic," Sam whispers in my ear.

We head to the canal and hang by the water's edge. My head is jumbled up with thoughts, so while Sam wanders off, throwing stones, I pull out my camera. Casting around for a shot, I don't have far to look.

Across the water, a swan is gliding by. With her pristine white feathers and elegant neck, she's crying out for a picture. I lift my lens and grab a frame.

"Lovely, isn't she? And she knows it."

The voice makes me jump.

A woman is sitting on a canal boat. Her long white hair is striking against her tanned skin. She laughs, deep creases forming at the corners of her eyes. They make her face look comfortable, lived in. The woman gestures to my camera. "Look closer. Beauty comes in many different forms."

"I don't know what you mean."

The woman only smiles, so I lift up my camera again.

This time I pass over the swan. At first, I can only see the murky swirl of canal water, then something else catches my eye. Turning my lens, I zoom in.

Wedged on the far bank is a nest, and among the greys and browns of twigs and branches, flashes of colour pop. Pieces of plastic, crinkled foil, shredded strips of cardboard – all sorts of odd bits of rubbish – have been carefully woven in. In the middle of the nest sits a bird, a thread of nylon rope in its beak.

I frame and focus and shoot. I don't know what type of bird it is – nothing as stunning as the swan, that's for sure. But sitting on the incredible nest she's made from all these worthless things, she looks like a queen on a throne. I smile at my pictures. They're better too.

I turn to thank the woman, but she's gone.

Sam only grunts when I show him. He's in a funny mood, and when his mum calls, asking him to collect his little sister Lily from holiday club, I'm almost relieved to see him go.

I linger at the canal a little longer, but my inspiration's gone. Soon, thoughts of Dad and Bella return. In nine days' they'll be married, and I'm afraid.

Afraid of Bella's intentions.

And afraid of Dad, closing the door on Mum for ever.

I have to convince him that he's making a mistake.

I'm sitting at the kitchen table, uploading today's shots on to my laptop when Dad comes in, humming. His copper hair is sticking up at all angles, and his suit jacket is flung over one arm. He's much more messy and relaxed than when he left this morning with Bella, and I perk up when I realize he's alone.

"Good day?" he asks, kissing my head.

"Not bad. Where's Bella?"

"Having dinner with Victor. We're not joined at the hip, you know."

I raise an eyebrow, but Dad doesn't notice. Pulling a beer from the fridge, he flops into a chair. His eyes twinkle. "So … Victor offered me a job."

I tense. "What kind of job?"

"At Façade, with the digital team. Only for a week, but if the work goes well, there could be more. I'll have my own office and everything."

"What about the shop? You said you were busy."

"They'll manage." Dad shrugs. "This thing at Façade is just a trial. The money's too good to turn down."

I take this in. "The digital team. You mean retouching? Photoshop?"

He picks at the label on his beer bottle. "It might involve a bit of that."

I click my laptop shut. "But … I thought you hated all that? I thought if you left the shop, you'd do your own photography again?"

Dad takes a long slug of beer. "Freya, my photography career is over. And I'm fine with that, but we still have bills to pay."

59

"What about Bella? She must be loaded."

He gives me a hard look. "I'm not asking her for money. Anyway, she's going through a quiet patch at work."

I'm silent, thinking of the diary entries, crossed out.

"Christ, it's no big deal!" Dad swigs hard on his beer again. "Cleaning up one or two images – everybody does it! I loved the darkroom stuff, sure. But times change. This is the way of the world."

The way of the world?

I push back my chair. "It's ... it's too fast."

"It's just a job!"

"I don't mean the job, I mean everything! Bella moving in. Getting married. You barely *know* her. What's the big rush?" I pause. "Don't you think it's strange?"

"Strange?"

"Yes! That someone like *her* would be with someone like *you*?"

I clap my hand to my mouth as Dad's face caves in. "Dad, I'm sorry ... I didn't mean—"

He blinks. "I told you already, Freya. I need a fresh start. I've spent too long living in the past."

"But you don't!" The words fly out before I can stop them. "You don't live in the past; you barely even mention it! I ask you questions, but you never really answer them. Why don't you ever talk about Mum? Why do you always change the subject? It's like you've got something to hide!"

Dad is very still.

"Is this what she would have wanted?" I whisper. "For you? And me?"

"We'll never know what Tess would have wanted." There's an edge to Dad's voice. "Because she's not here to tell us, is she?"

I stare at him. "It wasn't her fault she died!"

"No." Dad turns away. Placing his bottle on the table, he gets up slowly, like an old man. "I'm shattered, love. Think I'll head to bed. Switch the light off when you go upstairs."

I nod, unable to reply. It's only as he leaves that I notice – he's shaking.

9

For a week, I hardly see Dad at all.

Early every morning, he and Bella take a taxi to the agency, returning late in the evening the same way. I hunker in my room so I don't have to see them smooching and sharing cosy meals.

Sam sends photos from the job with his dad – paint-splattered selfies designed to cheer me up. It doesn't work.

At night, I lie in bed, dread pooling in my stomach. Nothing about this feels right – not the wedding, nor Dad's trial at Bella's agency. *"A good photographer should tell the truth."* That's what he used to say. Why would he change his tune?

It's not just that, though.

He's keeping something from me. Something about the past. Something about Mum. I'm sure of it. But there's no chance to discuss it – Bella's always there. She never leaves him for a second. I can't help feeling she's deliberately keeping us apart.

I bury my face in Kodak's black-and-white fur. Dad named her after his favourite brand of old-school photographic film. But that Dad is gone.

Since Bella came, he's changed.

It's like he's fallen under a spell.

Friday arrives too soon. Not even the smell of bacon creeping under my bedroom door can lift my spirits. I rub my eyes and remember.

The wedding. It's tomorrow.

My eyes land on a black cylinder sitting on my desk. *A camera lens?* It's not mine. I've never seen it before.

I find Dad in the kitchen, whisking eggs. He's alone.

A fry-up and a present: Dad's version of a white flag. My tummy betrays me with a rumble, but I keep my face blank. "Where is she?"

"Bella?" Dad asks innocently. "Sleeping off a headache. Don't disturb her."

I wouldn't dream of it.

"Big day tomorrow," he adds.

"Dad—"

"You found your present, then?" The subject change is swift.

I look at the lens in my hand.

"I discovered it in the attic," Dad says. "Bella and I were up there the other day, sorting through some things. It's an 85mm. Perfect for portraits. I used to use it on my old Nikon, but it should fit your digital. The low aperture will give you loads of light, while the background falls out of focus. That's the key to a good portrait. Why don't you try it out?"

I can't help smiling. "OK."

I dash upstairs and grab my camera. Back in the kitchen, I unscrew my zoom lens and fit the 85 mm. Looking through the viewfinder, I see what Dad means. Everything looks closer, more intense.

"Say cheese!" I thrust my camera in his face.

He sticks out his tongue and we both crack up. Suddenly, everything feels lighter. I wander around the kitchen, snapping anything in sight.

"You could set a timer to take self-portraits," Dad comments. "Or should I say *selfies*?"

I roll my eyes. "I'm good, thanks."

"You are." He ruffles my hair.

"Hey! I'm trying to focus!"

"Take another one of me."

He pulls a look he calls *Blue Steel,* and I giggle. It feels nice to mess around, the two of us. Like how it used to be. Dad's in a good mood: relaxed and funny. This is the perfect time to talk to him about—

"What's all the noise?"

I swing round, my camera still at eye level.

Bella is in the doorway. Even unwell, her beauty floors me. Her cheeks are flushed and her body is like liquid in a red silk robe. Suddenly, I'm hyper-aware of my too-short pyjamas and my unbrushed hair. I twist my focus ring and Bella's green eyes sharpen in the viewfinder. My finger hovers over the shutter button.

"Sorry, darling, did we wake you?" Dad kisses Bella's cheek. "How are you feeling?"

"Worse." She glares at me. "Get that out of my face."

"OK," I say, but messing with Dad has left me feeling giddy. Reckless, even. Quickly, I press the shutter button. *Click.*

Bella's face turns red. "Did you just take my picture?"

I don't answer.

"I thought we had an agreement." She lunges at me. "Give me your camera."

"No," I say, backing away.

"Freya, delete that picture now."

I look at Dad, who nods.

"Dad, *seriously?*"

"Come on, Freya. Bella's not well."

"O-K. I'll do it later." The scent of Bella's perfume mingles with the burning bacon, making my stomach turn. "I'm not hungry any more. I'll be upstairs."

Bella blocks my way. "Do it now, Freya. Tell her, Nick!"

"I'm sure if Freya said she would—" Dad's voice withers

65

under Bella's imploring eyes. She swings back to me and my swagger fades too.

"Fine." I switch to playback on my camera. Bella appears on the screen, wide-eyed and surprised.

I stare.

The image looks wrong, like the colours are diluted. Instead of warm gold, her hair is mousy-brown. Her cheeks aren't flushed, but wan and pale. Shadows line her eyes, not so much emerald, as murky green.

I've got my settings wrong. Or the light is odd. Or…

"We're waiting, Freya," Dad says.

Sighing, I press delete. "Done." I flip the camera around.

Bella turns without a word. The house shudders as she stomps upstairs.

"Could you not be more sensitive?" Dad says, banging the breakfast plates down.

I don't reply, too busy with my camera. The settings look fine. Nothing seems amiss.

I push away my eggs, my appetite gone for good.

Something wasn't right about that photo.

And I'm pretty sure that Bella knew it too.

I waited.
I'm very good at waiting.
It only takes one person to set
the wheels in motion.
One tremor to start a tidal wave,
one match to start a fire.
From the moment I saw her, I knew she
was the one: a dark-eyed, dark-haired
girl, with doubt in her downcast eyes.
I called to her, prepared to show her perfect.
I drew her to me. Easy prey.

10

August the fifth.

I pull back my curtains to a shimmering summer's day. Good weather feels like a betrayal. A vapour trail from a lone aeroplane is the only thing breaking the endless blue sky. I frame a shot: the white knife slicing the calm sea.

There. That works.

"Freya?"

My door clicks open. Dad peers into the room, his newly shaved face raw.

"Taxi's coming soon. Don't be late." He leaves me to dress.

I open up my wardrobe and drag out the first decent

thing I can find: a jumpsuit from last summer. I rarely buy clothes, can't remember the last time I wore a dress. The jumpsuit isn't smart, but Dad won't notice. I've got nothing to celebrate and no one to impress. I pull on my trainers and slip a sweater over my head, my urge to hide stronger than ever.

Dad's pacing the hall when I come downstairs. He doesn't look twice at my outfit, and luckily, Bella isn't here to comment. I saw her last night from my window, taking a taxi to Victor's place, where she'd arranged to stay the night. I noticed her mirror went with her, wrapped in a scarf and peeking out the top of her designer tote bag. It seemed ridiculous. I mean, surely Victor's got one in his flat?

Dad smiles. "All set?"

I climb into the taxi with legs of lead, wishing Sam were here to give me strength. Dad said he couldn't come – that Bella wanted to keep things "exclusive".

While Dad sits up front with the driver, I grip my camera tightly. The streets slip by, like a dream.

"We're here."

We've pulled up outside a large municipal building. Dark imposing windows, grey central steps. Carved into the stonework is a sign: ISLINGTON TOWN HALL.

Bella is nowhere to be seen, but I know better than to hope. She'll turn up. What Bella wants, she gets. Once more, I think of her late-night phone call.

What does she want with Dad?

A breeze whips ancient confetti around my ankles. To distract myself, I pull out my camera, zooming in on the tiny tornadoes: fragments of celebration, twisting in the dirt. I can hear Dad, cracking jokes with the taxi driver to hide his nerves.

"You see it on TV, don't you? The bride gets cold feet, the groom gets stood up, someone runs in at the last minute to stop the ceremony..."

My heart skips a beat.

Stop the ceremony. That's it. It's my only hope.

The only question is how?

Desperate thoughts circle in my head. I could stand up in the middle of it and say that Bella's using Dad. Only I can't be sure, and I certainly can't prove anything. Maybe I could say she doesn't love him? But even if everyone believed me, poor Dad would be so hurt.

I sigh. Who am I kidding? Nothing I can do at this point will make any difference.

"You look pale," Dad tells me, as the taxi drives away. "Reckon I'm the one who should be nervous. Don't you worry. It'll all be over soon!"

As we climb the steps, I come to a decision. Whatever Bella's intentions, Dad deserves better. I'll ... improvise. Make something up if I have to. As long as it stops the ceremony, I'll deal with the fallout later.

You're right, Dad. This will *be over soon.*

*

70

Revolving doors spit us into an empty lobby.

I glance around. "Where are the guests?" I know Bella wanted this to be exclusive, but it still seems odd. "Who's the best man? What about Bella, is she bringing any friends?"

Dad shrugs away my questions. "We didn't want a fuss."

A smartly dressed woman appears from a side door.

"Good morning. You must be Mr Jones. I'm Marjorie, the Superintendent Registrar." She shakes Dad's hand and turns to me. "And you're—?"

"This is my daughter, Freya," Dad says. "My fiancée is bringing our witnesses. They should be arriving soon."

Marjorie nods and leads us down a long corridor into a high-ceilinged room with plush pink chairs arranged to face the front. A felt-covered desk sits to one side, with a sign on top.

WARNING

Any person who knowingly and wilfully gives false information, or makes a false declaration to a registrar, for insertion in a marriage or civil partnership register, will be prosecuted for perjury.

I grip a chair, feeling faint.

"Are you all right?" Marjorie asks. "Would you like some water?"

"Yes, please."

A false declaration. My head is spinning. If I accuse Bella without proof, does that mean I'm breaking the law?

I lift up my camera to calm me down. Dad is busy pacing by the window. The more I zoom in, the more I notice – the room isn't as grand as it first appears. Cracks line the ceiling, the parquet floor is scuffed. Faded curtains surround dusty window frames. I like the shabbiness – it has a history, a past – but at the same time, it makes me uneasy.

It fits him, but not her.

Why would Bella get married here? Why would she marry Dad?

The door opens. Marjorie is back, her expression slightly dazed. In her hand is a glass of water, and behind her is Bella.

I gape.

Towering in stilettos and a long, carmine gown, Bella's hourglass shape defies belief. Feathers fringe her shoulders, and her hair is twisted up, emphasizing her long, slender neck. Golden tendrils frame her face and her lips are scarlet to match her fingernails. In her ears, ruby studs glisten like tiny drops of blood.

The effect is powerful, intimidating. She's like some rare, exotic bird.

A predatory one.

My resolve begins to weaken.

"Nick, darling." Bella kisses Dad's cheek. "So handsome! And Freya…" She appraises my jumpsuit. "Such an original choice."

A slim, tanned man enters the room, all angles in a sharply tailored suit. Salt and pepper hair falls into piercing blue eyes. Behind him, a woman in a short black dress and knee-high boots peers, unsmiling, from under her dark, blunt fringe.

"Victor! Raven! Come and join us." Bella beckons.

So this is Victor.

Giving a curt nod to Dad, Victor takes his place beside Bella. Raven hovers further back. Her haughty vibe makes me want to shrivel up.

Marjorie hands me my water. "Will you be taking pictures?" she asks, noticing my camera.

"Not during the ceremony," Bella cuts in before I can answer. "We want it to feel intimate, don't we, Nick? I'm sure there'll be time for photos later."

The ceremony begins.

Dad takes Bella's hand. Marjorie's voice becomes solemn as she reminds us of the occasion, the binding vows Dad and Bella are about to make. Blood is pumping in my ears. I sip my water, trying to stay calm.

Marjorie clears her throat. "And if any person present knows of any lawful impediment to this marriage, they should declare it now." She pauses.

Beside me, Dad is tense. Bella's eyes are fixed on the wall. Victor seems to be examining his pointy designer shoes. Raven stifles a yawn.

This is it.

I take a deep breath. "I..." The words fizzle out. Everyone turns to look at me and I shrink.

What am I doing? "Sorry to interrupt, guys, but the bride's not what she seems. I think she's bewitching my dad!"

I can't do it. It sounds utterly ridiculous.

Marjorie peers over her folder. "Did you wish to say something?"

"Uh…" My throat is parched. I take a sip of water and glance at Bella.

Big mistake.

She's staring straight at me. The force of her gaze seems to slash me like a knife. I stagger back, choking.

"Freya!" Dad reacts first, guiding me to a chair.

"Freya," Bella echoes. "Darling, are you all right?"

"Oh dear," Marjorie says. "Perhaps you drank too quickly? Take a seat and we'll carry on."

I feel dizzy, weak. My breath is coming fast. Something is wrong, very wrong. Another glance at Bella, and my courage crumbles completely. She's the embodiment of presence, power, perfection, while I'm nothing — an insignificant nobody.

A tiny smile flickers on her lips. "Are you sure you're all right?" she asks, her voice all concern.

I give a faint nod.

The ceremony resumes. My chance has gone.

Around me, the world turns blurry, as though everything is happening underwater. Mouths move, bodies gesture in slow motion, gold rings glitter in the light.

Into my mind swims the picture of Mum on her wedding day, her hand on the waist of her strange silver dress.

74

I'm losing her. She's floating away.

I blink back the tears threatening to drown me and surface as the ceremony ends.

"It gives me great pleasure to declare that you are now legally married," Marjorie announces.

Dad's mouth meets Bella's. She breaks the kiss first, pulling him to the desk. Fountain pens are produced. Signatures are scratched in a book.

And just like that, it's done.

11

There's no confetti.

The ceremony over, Marjorie ushers us to the lobby once more.

Outside, another party is gathered on the steps, waiting for the next marriage slot. Excited little girls in chiffon skirts are turning cartwheels. A woman pins a corsage to a bridegroom's lapel, while he lights a trembling cigarette.

I push past them all, feeling numb.

The flash stops me in my tracks.

"Bella! Bella! Over here!"

The paparazzo is lying in wait across the street, hidden behind a long lens. I glance at Dad and Bella. A second flash turns Bella rigid. A look of panic crosses her face, quickly replaced by fury. "Do something!" she hisses.

It's Victor who explodes into action, charging down the steps and spewing a torrent of French. The paparazzo legs it down the street.

"Bloody press," Dad mutters. "How did they find out?"

Bella recovers quickly. Brushing off Dad's arm, she struts into the traffic like a scarlet beacon and hails a cab. "*Kagami*," she says to the driver, motioning for us to get in. "Go ahead, darling," she tells Dad. "I'll join you as soon as I can." The door slams before he can reply.

"Where are we going? What's happening, Dad?"

Dad leans back in his seat. His eyes are glassy and he looks tired. "Don't worry, everything's fine. Bella booked a place for lunch. She'll take a different cab. If any more press are lurking, it'll throw them off the scent." He sighs. "She hates the attention, poor thing."

Kagami.

I've heard of it, of course. Saskia used to say she'd been. Snooty dress code, outrageous prices. Totally off limits to the likes of Dad and me.

Until now.

The entrance is a small wooden door on a tucked-away Soho backstreet. Dad gives his name to a bouncer-type guy who repeats it into his headset, scowling at my trainers. The door buzzes open, revealing a dark lobby and an iron staircase spiralling down below.

We descend into a cavernous basement. The space seems to go on for ever. Then I realize it's an illusion; there are mirrors covering every wall. I cringe at the kaleidoscope of Freyas everywhere I turn.

"Welcome." A woman in crisp overalls greets us. "May I take your coats?"

Dad hands over his jacket, but I wrap my arms around my sweater. Fifty mirror-Freyas do the same.

The woman smiles. "Ah, yes. *Kagami* means 'mirror' in Japanese."

I stare at the elegant place settings, the sunken tables. Finally, the penny drops. *This is a Japanese restaurant.* Except Dad doesn't eat Japanese food. He says raw fish gives him indigestion, but I'm not stupid. I know it must remind him of Tokyo, of Mum.

My shoulders tense. Why did Bella bring us here?

Dad goes in search of the toilets, while I follow the woman across the floor. Tealights twinkle, multiplied in the mirrors. I go to lift up my camera but the woman raises a hand.

"No photographs allowed."

So that's it. *No paparazzi risk.*

I scan the menu while I'm waiting. Swirling Japanese characters dance across the page, elegant but impenetrable. And the English translations are no help. *Sashimi Sake. Uni Gunkan-Maki.* Questions flood my brain: did Mum eat these dishes? Did she learn Japanese? Would we still live in Tokyo if she hadn't died? I twist the napkin on my lap.

"There you are!" Bella's heels ring out on the metal staircase. She's alone. Victor and Raven are nowhere to be seen. She takes her time crossing the room, enjoying the admiring glances of the other diners.

"Feeling at home, Freya?" she says, sinking into the seat opposite me. "Oh, I forgot. You won't remember Japan." Her wedding ring glints in the light. "Perhaps that's for the best."

"What do you mean?" I ask, but Dad is back.

"My gorgeous girls!" He slides next to Bella, an arm around her waist. "What are you chatting about?"

"The future," Bella replies, smiling. I'm too busy processing.

Has Dad told Bella something that he's been keeping from me?

A waiter appears at our table. "We've prepared the menu you requested, Ms Wilde. Perhaps you'd like to start with drinks? Champagne?" His eyes are glued on Bella, like Dad and I don't exist.

"Perfect," she simpers, and the waiter scuttles away. She turns to Dad. "We do have plenty to celebrate. Have you told her yet, Nick?"

"Later, we said." Dad looks uneasy. "Not now."

"What are you talking about?" I'm suddenly cold. An awful scenario has just popped into my head. Bella's not … *pregnant,* is she?

The waiter returns with three glasses on a tray. Champagne for Dad. Juice for me. Water for Bella.

No.

"To the future." Dad raises his glass. "To us."

Bella ignores the toast. "Darling, there's no point keeping Freya in the dark." She looks at him intently. "She'll have to know soon enough."

"Know about what?" I growl.

She beams. "About your father's new career!"

I let out a sigh of relief. *She's not pregnant.* Then I sit up. "Wait. What new career? The job for Victor?" I turn to Dad. "You passed the trial?"

"*More* than passed," Bella answers for him. "He's proved himself indispensable."

Dad shakes his head. "It's not a big deal."

"You're too modest, Nick." Bella turns back to me. "Your father's talented, Freya. He deserves success. Exciting opportunities. Don't you agree?"

"Of course," I say, confused. "But what about the shop?"

She laughs. "Oh, sweetie! You really think working in a camera shop is the career your father deserves?" She turns to Dad. "Nick is going to be part of my team. He'll be helping me on a project – something very special. Don't worry, Freya – this will all work out for the best. But I'm afraid we've had to make one or two arrangements."

"What arrangements?" I stare at Dad. He's slumped in his seat, not looking at me.

Bella pauses. "Arrangements for you."

"Bella, please!" Dad finally breaks in. His forehead is screwed tight, like he's struggling to concentrate. "We'll talk it through properly, later."

A swarm of waiters suddenly surrounds the table. Each waiter is carrying a wooden platter. Glossy slices of raw fish shine like brightly coloured jewels. My stomach heaves.

"Can someone explain what's going on?" I say, barely controlling my voice.

"In a minute. I … need to … get some … air." Dad stands, swaying on his feet. As he stumbles to the exit, I frown. Surely he's only had a few sips of champagne?

Bella doesn't even bother to watch him go. Picking up her chopsticks with ease, she expertly plucks a sliver of salmon from the plate in front of her. I stare, hypnotized, as she slips it between her lips.

Not long ago, that fish was swimming free. Now it's sliced up on a plate.

She takes her time, swallowing slowly, her emerald eyes locked on mine. The air between us feels thick, like glue.

"Your father has always put you first, Freya. He's put everything on pause for you – his ambitions, his dreams. But things change. It's time to move on. With my help, he'll fulfil his true potential. There's no easy way to say this…" She smiles sadly. "You may not mean to, Freya darling, but you're holding your father back. It's time you gained some independence, discovered your own voice, your own path. So we came to a decision…"

"What decision?" I whisper.

"Boarding school. You'll love it, I know."

12

"No!"

I struggle to my feet, knocking over my glass. A sticky tsunami swamps the fish.

"Freya?" Dad is back, looking pale but more alert. He reaches for my arm. "What are you doing? Don't go. Nothing's been decided yet."

"That's not what it sounds like!" My head feels foggy and confused. I clamber up the metal staircase, gulping back tears, and push past smirking Headset Guy, out on to the street.

The fresh air hits me. I run.

On to Oxford Street, weaving through the shoppers

with their bulging carrier bags, then Tottenham Court Road, dodging the bucket shakers and newspaper stands. Someone shoves a leaflet in my face:

YOU CAN CHANGE YOUR LIFE TODAY!

If only.

A bus pulls in at Goodge Street station and I throw myself on board. One look at my face and the driver waves me through. Habit guides me to the top deck, where I slump in the front seat. We always used to sit here, whenever Dad and I went to his workshop. I'd make him pretend to drive the bus.

Dad.

Thinking about him sets me off again. Dad would never send me away. Yes, he's talked about me "finding my own voice", or whatever. But not like this! This is Bella's influence, it has to be.

And it feels unstoppable.

When I finally get home to an empty house, my tears have turned to anger. Lying on the doormat, as if it's been waiting for me, is a glossy brochure for somewhere called Brendon Hall School for Girls, in Devon.

It's addressed to *Freya Jones and Guardian*.

I tear into the plastic. All I see are fields and forests and grey stone buildings, hundreds of miles from London and Dad and Sam.

83

I flick through the pages with a growing sense of dread. There's not even a photography course.

How could Dad agree to this?

I lean against the door. He knows how important my photography is to me. The old Dad would never go along with this.

A loose piece of paper floats to the ground. I pick it up and read.

Dear Ms Wilde,

Further to our conversation, I'm delighted to confirm that we have a last-minute place for your stepdaughter, Freya Jones, on our Summer School programme, starting 10th August. This will be a wonderful opportunity for Freya to make friends before the start of the autumn term.

I look forward to welcoming her next week.

Kind regards,
Dr Agatha Evans, Head Teacher
Brendon Hall School for Girls

No.

This has to be a joke. They're not even waiting until term officially starts in September. They're sending me away *in less than a week*.

I sink to the floor.

Only a few hours ago, I thought I could stand up to

Bella and stop the wedding. I was so naive. She's way too powerful, and she's totally in control of Dad.

"He'll be helping me on a project – something very special."

Whatever this project is – whatever she wants from him – she must want it badly. So badly, she won't risk anyone messing it up.

But what makes her think that person is me?

My phone pings with a message.

> *Snowdrop, please call me.*
> *We're worried. Dad x*

We're worried. Is that right? I'm sure Bella couldn't care less.

My phone pings again.

> *You have a message request from JDS.*

That's odd. It's come through my private social account. Only Sam contacts me that way. I press accept to release the text.

> *Hi Freya, this is Jas de Souza.*
> *We met in Camden.*
> *You're a difficult person to track down!*
> *I have a question for you.*

The girl in the market with the Afro. The one who gave me her card.

I push the hair out of my eyes.

> Hi. I remember. What do you want to know?

> *So … I'm working on a shoot for Seen*
> *magazine – a feature on Fashion Week.*
> *A model has pulled out and we need*
> *a replacement. Can you help?*

I stiffen.

A model, me?

Yet again, I suspect it's a wind-up, although why Jas would do something like that, I don't know.

> *It's only one portrait, next week.*
> *Unpaid, I'm afraid. And you'd need parental consent.*
> *I'd love you to do it. You'd be perfect!*

Perfect. She has to be joking.

Then I reread the text. *Next week.*

I stare at the brochure for Brendon Hall, my mind suddenly racing. Sure, I could refuse to go to this summer school – but who am I kidding? Bella will simply overrule me. Dad will cave under her gaze like he always does.

But what if I had a *proper* reason not to go? Taking part in this shoot would buy me some time. If I could stay here in London – at least a little longer – I could figure out what Bella's up to and keep a closer eye on Dad.

And find out what he's hiding from me.

Freya, are you still there?

I swallow. Bella can't object to one shoot, surely? She's a model herself.

Hello?
Freya?

A shoot means a lens in my face. My faults magnified, for everyone to see.

My palms are slick. I can't decide.

Throwing some clothes into a bag, I grab my camera and scrawl a note to Dad. I'll go to Sam's, talk this through with him.

I text Jas.

Let me think about it.

I press send.

I'm on the ninth–floor balcony of Sam's tower block, standing outside his front door. The sky is orange above the rooftops, Hampstead Heath a purple smudge in the distance. I blink back tears behind my viewfinder. London is my home, my backdrop.

I can't leave.

"Freya?" Sam's face forms a question as he opens the door. Seeing my bag, he pulls me into a hug.

"Come in. There's no one here. Mind your feet, though. Lil's been busy."

I follow him down the hall, carefully stepping over the half-naked bodies of a dozen Barbie dolls. I scowl at their spindly legs, thrusting chests and tiny waists. Mini prototype Bellas.

"So." Sam slides the biscuit jar towards me and makes tea. "I take it the wedding went well?"

It all comes out. The ceremony and my pathetic attempt to interrupt it. My choking fit. Bella and the paparazzo. The disastrous lunch at Kagami. Sam's eyes grow wider until I reach the news about school, then crumbs spray the counter.

"They're making you leave London? But you can't! Your life is here. What about your exam results? College?"

"Bella doesn't care about that. She wants me out of the way so she can work on some project with Dad."

"What kind of project?"

"I don't know." I shrug. "Dad's not even trying to stop her. He goes along with everything she says. This school they've chosen – there isn't even a photography department. That's how I know it's her idea!"

"You can't let her do this! Tell your dad how you feel, he'll understand."

"It's not that easy!" I say. "You don't know Bella. She's got this *hold* on him – on everyone."

Sam rubs his forehead. "Freya, you *can't* go. This is your home, your life. And – and I need you."

The way he says it makes me pause. "Is something wrong?" I search his face.

"Oh, forget it." He sighs and looks away. "You're not the only one whose dad is on another planet, that's all."

There's a clatter as the front door opens and a whirlwind hurtles down the hall. "Freya!"

"Hey, Lily." I hug Sam's six-year-old sister as his mum, Carla, appears.

"Mum, can Freya stay over?" Sam asks.

"Sure." Carla smiles. If she notices my red eyes, she's tactful enough not to comment. Sam would definitely have told her about the wedding. He and his mum are close.

"Get the airbed from Lil's room. Tom's at the pub, watching the match, and there's not much in the fridge. How do fish and chips sound?"

My stomach growls.

"OK, I'll run out!" Carla laughs. "Sam, set the table. Keep an eye on Lil."

As soon as Carla's gone, Sam rounds on me again. "Freya, seriously. You can't just accept this, like it's fate!"

"Well…" I pass him my phone. "I might not have to."

When Sam reads Jas's messages, his jaw hits the floor. "Wait a minute. Are you saying you've been scouted?"

"*Scouted?*"

"Talent-spotted! Loads of models are discovered that way. Kate Moss was at an airport. Lily Cole was shopping.

Gisele Bündchen was in McDonald's…" His eyebrows are cartoon-level, leaping off his head. "Look at what happened to them!"

"Shh! It's not anything like that," I hiss. "It's one portrait, that's all."

"It's still amazing!" he whispers. "*Seen* magazine is all over London. It's totally legit. And the shoot is next week; it couldn't be more perfect. You are gonna do it, right?"

"I don't know," I say truthfully. "You know how I feel about pictures." I ignore Sam's sigh. "Plus, I need Dad's permission…"

"Freya?" Lily's pulling on my leg. "Freya, will you play with me?"

I take advantage of the interruption. "Sure. What do you want to play?"

"Makeovers!" Lily grins, revealing two missing front teeth.

"Do we have to?" I pull a face.

"Good idea, Lil," Sam says slyly. "Freya *loves* makeovers. You can use my phone to take a picture when you're finished."

I shoot him an evil look.

"Please, Freya!" Lily jumps up and down.

"Go on." Sam nudges me. "There's nothing to be *afraid* of."

I sigh. "OK."

As things go, it's not a bad distraction from my dilemma. I give into Lily's whims, trying not to flinch as she dabs lipgloss on my eyelids and paints my nails a lurid green. "Finished!" she finally announces, grabbing Sam's phone. "Wanna see?"

"No, thanks!" I duck out of the way, fear flitting through my mind again.

I'll have to face the camera at the shoot.

"Food's up, people." Carla's back, carrying two plastic bags. Lily bounces to the table, photoshoot forgotten.

"Hey, Mum," Sam says, dishing out chips. "What d'you think of Freya's new look?"

My cheeks grow warm as Carla surveys me. "Is this your work, Lil? Very creative! Mind you, Freya's gorgeous as she is." She winks.

"I know what you're trying to do," I whisper to Sam.

"Dunno what you mean." He silences me with a chip.

I'm lying on the airbed in Sam's room. The light is dim and my belly feels full, the edges of the day smoothed away.

Almost.

"There's honestly nothing to be afraid of," Sam says again, stretching on his bed. "It's just a shoot. How hard can it be?"

He really has no idea.

I gaze at the wall above me, entirely covered in photos. Fashion photos. Black-and-white and colour, close-up and full length – hundreds of pages torn from magazines. Sam moved into his older sister Jenna's room when she went off to study retail at uni. Luckily, she's away travelling this summer.

"Are you ever going to take those down?" I say, nodding at the pictures. The models make me nervous. They're so pretty and perfect, like Saskia and Bella. Nothing at all like me.

Sam shrugs. "One day, maybe. What's the rush?"

"I thought your dad offered to redecorate?"

"He did." Sam scowls. "And stop changing the subject. If you do this shoot, you won't have to go to summer school! It's the perfect excuse. You'd get to stay in London."

"Not necessarily. They could still send me away in September."

"It's better than nothing. What if this is the beginning?"

"The beginning of what?"

"Your international modelling career!"

I shudder. "No thanks."

"*Fine.*" Sam sighs dramatically. "But think about it, Freya. Wouldn't it be cool? You'd meet a real photographer, see them at work. Think how much you'd learn! Your dad is bound to give consent."

I grimace. "Maybe. But Bella's calling the shots. And she only cares about her project."

"That's another thing," Sam says, sitting up. "You reckon she's using your dad, but you don't know how. You need to find out more about this project. The fashion world is small, Jenna says. I bet people gossip. This shoot is like a golden ticket – it gets you into Bella's world! Someone is bound to know something. You can avoid summer school, keep an eye on your dad *and* solve the mystery of this project, all in one."

He cues some music on his phone, like everything's sorted. Meanwhile, thoughts are tumbling in my head.

I'm not imagining things. Bella's up to something, and I've got a chance to find out what. If I can prove she's bad news, I'll get my life back on track – my photography plans, college here in London, my relationship with Dad.

And maybe the truth about Mum.

Like Sam says, it's just a shoot.

I stare at the beautiful faces taped on Jenna's wall.

There's only one small problem. Somehow, I've got to pass as one of them.

The dark-haired girl responded to my call.
She looked into my glass,
powerless to resist.
But when her fingers touched
my frame, I realized something clearly:
this girl was different.
An artist. A creator.
With her, I could do much more.
So I reached further – deep inside
her head – unravelling old thoughts
and weaving new ones.
Her skill and my vision.
Her talent and my power.
Together we would make the perfect team.

13

"Good luck!" Sam says, as I leave his flat the next day. "Get your dad on his own. Be assertive. Let me know how you get on."

He's been drilling me all morning – how to persuade Dad to let me stay. He's so sure I can pull this off, so sure the photoshoot will be a breeze.

I wish I had half Sam's belief.

Dad and Bella are at the kitchen table, huddled over a newspaper. They don't look up as I come in. *So much for being worried.*

Then I spot the screwed-up tissues, the faint red tinge to Bella's eyes. Has she been *crying*? About me?

"Snowdrop, you're home!" I stiffen as Dad kisses me. He's not forgiven yet.

"What's wrong?" I ask, my eyes flicking to Bella. In fluffy cerise angora, she almost looks huggable, but I'm not fooled.

"Nothing," she snaps, getting up with a toss of the head.

"Bella, darling, forget it!" Dad grabs her hand. "You're beautiful. It was a wonderful day. People will always be jealous."

For a second she looks unsure. *What's going on?* I've never seen them this way – him strong, her vulnerable.

It doesn't last.

Bella's face hardens. She snatches up the newspaper, dropping it in the bin as she sweeps out of the room.

"What was that about?"

"Nothing." Dad shakes his head. "There are some nasty people in the world. The paparazzi are vermin, out for a quick buck. No, Freya, don't…"

It's too late. I've rescued the newspaper and spread it on the table. It doesn't take long to figure out what made Bella so upset.

A photograph dominates the third page. I recognize our wedding party on the town hall steps. Dad is there, flushed and sheepish, next to Victor, bronzed and slick. Raven's scowling at the back and even I'm in the frame, although my hair is covering my face.

But it's Bella who draws my attention.

Gone is the magnificent creature of yesterday, and in her place is someone … *ordinary*. Her posture is a little stooped, her face a little drawn, her lips a little thin. Even her hair looks different – less spun gold, more dull straw – and where it's twisted up, I make out a vein on her neck, the tiniest suggestion of a double chin.

I let out a breath. Bright sunlight can be unflattering in photos, I've noticed that before. But even so, the difference between this image and the woman who was sitting here, only a moment ago, is staggering.

The caption lands the biggest blow:

Ageing supermodel snags new younger husband!

"Wow."

"Disgusting," Dad says. "Shaming people to sell papers."

I nod. It's strange, feeling sorry for Bella, but I push away the thought. I can't waste this chance to talk to Dad alone. As he tosses the newspaper aside, I seize the opportunity.

"Dad—"

I follow Sam's script to the letter, telling him all about Jas's shoot. Dad listens, his face giving nothing away.

"*What did you say?*" Bella's standing in the doorway, like a cat about to pounce. "*You've* been asked to model?"

"Why not?" I hold my nerve, avoiding eye contact. Keeping my tone calm. "It's just a portrait for something next week. A feature on Fashion Week in *Seen* magazine."

97

"*Fashion Week*?" Bella echoes. I look up. She's curiously pale. She moves towards Dad. "This is not a good idea."

"No one asked you!"

She blinks. "Well, perhaps someone should! I know about these things. You'd hate every second, Freya, trust me. Fashion is a very tough business. It's no place for a young girl like you. Anyway, summer school is paid for, everything's confirmed." She grips Dad's shoulder, looks him in the eye. "Tell her, Nick."

"Dad, please? I need your consent—"

"No." He sounds so adamant even Bella looks surprised. "I don't want you mixed up in that world," he says firmly.

"But *Bella's* mixed up in it!" I splutter. "And now, so are you! Don't be a hypocrite, Dad!"

"I'm trying to protect you." He gestures at the newspaper. "You've seen the way it is. Superficial. Vicious." A fleck of spit lands on the floor. "Bella's right. Fashion is a tough business. If you're not careful it can destroy you."

"What? Dad, no—"

"Sorry, Freya. This conversation is closed."

They leave me standing, stunned.

It's obvious that Bella wants me as far from the fashion world as possible. But so does Dad. He's never shut me down like that before – and I'm certain that was *him* talking, not her.

Bleakly, I text Sam a single thumbs down.

There's no point pursuing this. It's over.

*

A few days later, I'm packing, eyes blurry with tears, barely aware of what I'm throwing into my case. I've had no more chances to speak to Dad. Either he's avoiding me, or Bella hasn't let him out of her sight. As for this morning, he hasn't even shown his face. He should be ashamed of himself, letting Bella send me away. I zip my suitcase closed, a rock wedged in my throat. I look for my camera bag hanging on the back of my door.

A horn blasts in the street – the driver Bella arranged has come early. I'm not ready.

I'll never be ready.

Bella barges in without knocking, red spiked heels denting the carpet. I wipe my eyes and lift my chin. I won't let her think she's won.

"Freya, darling, it's time. Your car is downstairs."

"Already? My friend Sam was going to come and say goodbye."

"I'm afraid so. Don't keep the driver waiting!" She flounces out, leaving my door flung wide.

Numb, I take a last look around my room. *My photo of Mum!* It's still sitting on the shelf. I wrap it in a T-shirt and squeeze it into my case.

Voices rise up from below. "Dad?" I call, dragging my case on to the landing.

"Shh!" Bella hisses up the stairs. "Don't wake him! He's asleep!"

Asleep?

I drop my case.

Their bedroom is dark, the curtains closed. Bella's mirror is a shadowy shape, shrouded by her scarf like before. I rush to Dad. He's lying in bed, absolutely still with his eyes shut and his copper hair glued to the pillow with sweat. The room has the stale smell of sickness, and another scent, strange and bitter, like tomatoes past their best.

"Dad?"

"Tess?" His eyelids flutter. His breath hits me, sharp and foul.

"Dad, it's Freya. What's the matter? Are you ill?"

Fear flaps like a bird in my chest.

"I told you not to wake him!" Bella is there. She grabs hold of my elbow and steers me into the hall. "It's just a touch of flu. I've given him some medicine and it's wiped him out. I'll make a doctor's appointment later."

"But—"

"It's nothing to worry about. He'll be fine once he's slept it off." Shoving my case at me, she marches me down the stairs.

A breeze whips up from the open front door, where a teenage boy is standing on the step. Despite my fears about Dad, I can't help doing a double take. Tall and angular, with floppy dark hair falling in his eyes, he looks like he's just stepped off the set of some indie movie. His hands are jammed into the pockets of his jeans. I'm immediately conscious of my uncool clothes and unbrushed hair.

"Hunter, wasn't it?" Bella purrs, dropping my wrist. "Do you have the address?"

The boy nods, eyes fixed on her. "I'll need money for petrol," he says.

I frown. *He's my driver?* He can't be much older than me.

Bella hands over some notes and the boy – Hunter – pockets them. Then he reaches for my case, at the exact same time I do. Our fingers brush.

I snatch back my hand. "I can manage!" It comes out snappier than I intended. My face is burning up.

"Suit yourself." Hunter shrugs.

He unlocks the boot of a battered metallic-blue car.

"Drive straight to the school without stopping," Bella tells him. "I want her taken right to the door. And let me know when it's done." Then she adds more sweetly, "Or I'll worry, won't I, darling?"

"But Dad—" I look back at the house, an acid taste in my mouth.

"I told you, I'll ring the doctor in a moment," Bella coos. "Now, off you go."

Hunter's already in the driver's seat. Bella throws my case into the boot and opens the rear passenger door.

"*No,*" I say, squaring up to her. Her eyes lock with mine. Suddenly I feel numb, like I'm under anaesthetic. My limbs liquefy. Determination dissolves.

I crumple into the back seat.

"There's a good girl." Bella smiles. "Have a lovely trip!"

Hunter crunches into gear.

I turn in my seat, watching my house shrink into the

distance. The house I've lived in since I was a baby. The house where, right now, Dad is suddenly strangely sick.

I belong *there*.

But instead, I'm stuck in a car, on my way to some middle-of-nowhere school, leaving everything I love far behind.

14

I slump in the back seat, taking deep breaths.

Tears fog my eyes. The invisible thread tying me to home is stretching thinner and thinner, like chewing gum. Soon it will snap for good.

I text Sam.

> She made me leave early. I'm in the car.
> Dad doesn't know. He's sick in bed.

> *What??? Can't you do something?*

> I'm thinking!

We cross London in silence, my mind calculating desperately. It's useless. I'm all out of ideas. In what feels like no time at all, we've reached the slip road for the motorway. Hunter drums the steering wheel impatiently as we join the long snake of traffic. His fingers are quite elegant, I notice, although his nails are chewed like mine. For a second, our eyes meet in the rear-view mirror and my treacherous face flames.

I pretend to dig in my bag. That's when I remember. *My camera*. It's still hanging on my bedroom door.

"We have to go back!"

Hunter doesn't reply. We merge on to the motorway.

"Please! We need to turn around!"

The car sways as a lorry zooms past. I feel like I've been flipped upside down. "I left something important. I need it!"

"Get someone to send it." Hunter scowls at the traffic ahead. "I need to be back in town by seven tonight, not stuck on a road trip to Devon. I don't have time to turn around now."

Rude. I clench my fists. "Believe me, I don't want to be doing this any more than you."

"Oh, really?" He glances in the mirror. "And why's that?"

I hesitate. *He's working for Bella.* I can't tell him the truth.

Hunter frowns and pulls into the fast lane, overtaking a Volvo with a red-haired guy at the wheel. The back of the car is crammed with camping gear and a little girl is strapped into her car seat, squeezed between the bedding rolls. A lump fills my throat. That was me and Dad. We used to camp every year when I was small.

It feels like a lifetime ago.

"Hey, I'm sorry." Hunter's voice is softer as I scrub the tear from my cheek. "I didn't mean to be rude. Family problems?"

I nod.

"They're the worst." He tosses me a packet of tissues. "I'll put some music on."

I blow my nose while he fiddles with the ancient radio dial. I'm surprised when he stops on a station playing soft acoustic folk songs. The melancholy music fits my mood.

We travel without talking for a while. As the green fields zip by, Hunter weaves through the traffic, changing lanes. I risk another peek in the mirror. Concentration coats his face. It can't be that long since he passed his driving test. I look closer, noticing how the sun picks out dark flecks in his hazel eyes. There's a chickenpox scar in his left eyebrow, and a dent at the bridge of his nose. I zoom in with an imaginary camera. I like these tiny details; they break up his beauty and make him seem more human. He probably hates that.

"What's your name?"

I jump. "Uh … Freya."

"I'm Jake."

"Oh. I thought—"

"Hunter's my last name."

"Right." Silence.

"You don't look like her," he says, after a while.

"Who? *Bella*?" I almost laugh. *He's noticed I'm not model material, then.* "She's my dad's wife. My real mum died."

"I'm sorry," Jake says, softly.

I shrug. "I was a baby when it happened."

We're both quiet.

"Now that I think about it, Bella doesn't seem the maternal type."

"That's an understatement," I say. We share a smile.

A signpost flashes past, too fast to read. I wonder how far away I am from home.

"Is she the one sending you to this school?"

I look up. "How did you guess?"

Jake pulls a face. "I've seen her around the agency. She seems to … get her own way."

"You work at Façade?"

He makes a non-committal noise. "Only for the summer. I'm like an intern. Victor gives me all the crap jobs to do."

"Like this one, you mean?"

He has the good grace to look embarrassed.

"I'd have thought you'd like working there. Hanging out with all those models."

I'm only joking, but Jake's face darkens. "Why would I like it? The fashion industry is fake."

"Why do it, then?" I ask, intrigued.

"Because I need the money. I'm saving for…" He stops.

"For what?"

The guarded look is back. "You really want to know?"

I nod.

"I'm into movies," he says. "Making them, I mean. I've been working on a show reel. It's mostly digital, but I've been shooting on film too – Super Eight. It's grainy and rough, not so perfect..." He catches himself and flushes. "I'm boring you."

"You're not." I shake my head. "My dad had a Super Eight camera once." The memory makes me smile. "I remember, we made a film one weekend. Dad had to send it off to be processed before we could watch it back. It was beautiful. All silent and flickery."

"Magical," Jake agrees. Our eyes meet and he grins.

"I like movies too," I tell him. "But I prefer taking pictures."

"You're a photographer?"

"Yes. I mean, no. Err … I guess."

Well done, Freya. I slide down, cringing in my seat. What's got into me? I'm meant to be figuring out a way back to London, not bonding over cameras with some boy I've just met. Plus, reality check. Boys like Jake aren't interested in girls like me.

The conversation dies and I assume Jake's relieved. So I'm surprised when, at the next service station, he pulls over.

"It'll be easier for us to talk if you sit up front with me."

*

107

Back on the motorway, the landscape is changing. Cute farmhouses, shimmering lakes and clusters of horses pepper the view. It's pretty, but I can't appreciate it. I'm still heading in the wrong direction, further and further from Dad.

I send him a message.

> How are you feeling? Text me
> when you wake up x

No answer.

Jake is driving one-handed, using the other to cram a service station sandwich into his mouth. He offers me the other half.

"No, thanks. I'm not hungry."

He raises an eyebrow. "If you say so."

In the well beneath the handbrake, his phone beeps. As it lights up, I can't help noticing that the lock screen image shows Jake, with his arm around a pretty brunette. A message pops up underneath:

> *Amy:*
> *Still OK to pick me up tonight?*
> *7pm Primrose Hill? Xxxx*

Jake flips the phone face down. I chew my lip. So that's why he needs to get back to London. He has a date tonight, with *Amy*.

I pull myself together: I've got bigger things to worry about. I stare out of the window. In the distance, far across the fields, a train is running parallel with the motorway. As we hit a dense patch of traffic and slow, the train starts to pull ahead.

An idea takes root.

"Going on this trip must have messed up your day."

Jake sighs. "Yeah, but it's not your fault."

"You said you need to be back in London by seven?"

He pulls a face. "There's no chance. Devon's still miles away."

With almost perfect timing, a traffic announcement suddenly interrupts the radio. *"Severe tailbacks are forming on the western M3, after Junction 7. Travellers are advised to find alternative routes."*

Jake tuts. My heart is beating hard. I'm pretty sure we've just passed Junction 5. I open up the map on my phone. "Wouldn't the journey be quicker by train?"

"Of course," Jake says. "But you heard Bella. She wants you delivered to the door like a bunch of flowers."

"Only to keep Dad happy," I say, lightly. "He's protective. Bella couldn't care less. As long as I get to school in one piece, no one needs to know how." I zoom in on my map. "Junction 6 is Basingstoke. There's a railway station not far from the motorway." I google at lightning speed. "Trains run from there to Devon!" *And back to London,* I notice, but I keep that to myself. "You could drop me off and turn back before the traffic gets worse."

Jake falls silent, thinking. "I can't lose this job," he murmurs.

"I won't say a thing," I tell him. "And I'll text when I get there, so you can let Bella know."

The exit sign for Junction 6 is looming. "Promise you'll keep quiet?" Jake's hazel eyes search mine. *He must be keen to make this date.*

"Yes," I say. "I promise."

We swerve into Basingstoke station. Jake pops the boot, and I grab my suitcase, ready to run. He reaches for my arm.

"I'll come and buy your ticket."

"You don't have to."

"No, you're doing me a favour. I want to."

The parking app won't work on Jake's phone and the machine is out of order, so Jake has to risk it. We find the ticket office, where I watch him buy a single to Exeter, eyebrows shooting skywards at the cost. I feel bad about wasting his money, but there's nothing I can do.

"Here." He hands me the ticket, and keys his number into my phone. "Thanks for this, Freya. I mean it."

I stare at the departure board, feeling guilty again. There's a train to London in fifteen minutes. If Jake leaves now, I could make it.

"It's platform two for Exeter," he says, shoving what's left of Bella's money into my hand. "For a taxi at the other end. And something to eat?"

"Thanks." His kindness makes me feel worse. I think about Amy instead. "So, I guess this is goodbye."

He doesn't move.

Please, Jake, go!

"Look!" I point out of the ticket office window, sending a heartfelt prayer of thanks to the parking attendant zeroing in on Jake's car.

It does the trick. Jake swears under his breath. "Don't forget to text!" he says.

Then he's gone.

I collapse on to a bench and pull out my phone, heart hammering. Thank god Dad never changes his email password. It's literally been "Snowdrop123" for years.

My sweaty fingers slide over the keys.

Dear Professor Evans,

I regret to inform you that my daughter Freya Jones
will not be taking up her place at summer school,
due to a family situation. Please don't contact me at
this time.

Kind regards,
Nick Jones

I delete the email from Dad's sent folder. Now for the hard part.

I've had enough of being scared. It's time to take control.

I open my messages and find the one from Jas.

I can do the shoot if you still want me to.

Her reply pings straight back.

Girl, it's tomorrow!! Does that work for you?
I had someone else lined up but I'll cancel...

Guilt twists again. I'm taking an opportunity from someone, for something I've no desire to do. I can't help it, though. I don't have a choice.

Tomorrow works.

Great! Give me your email, I'll send
the call sheet and consent forms.
Don't forget to bring them with you!

Deep breath. Deep breath.
I can do Dad's signature. What's one more forged note?

Thanks. I will!

Time to buy a ticket back to London.

15

Before I'm even halfway back to London, Jas emails with all the information.

> Hey Freya,
>
> Here's all the paperwork. So excited you're doing this! You'll be great. Can't wait to work with you!
>
> Jas 😊

Butterflies dance in my belly. This is real.

The rest of the journey passes in a blur. I text Sam to fill him in and when I get to Paddington, he's waiting at the barriers with a grin so wide it almost splits his face in two.

"Sorry, who are you, and what have you done with Freya Jones?"

"Very funny."

My head is spinning. I've lied to Jake and the head teacher at this school. I'm defying Bella, and I'm about to fake my dad's signature on a consent form so I can do a fashion shoot. Sam's right, this is so not me.

I'm doing it for Dad.

"Can I stay at yours? What will we tell your parents?"

"We can say your dad and Bella need time alone. Like a honeymoon."

"Eww. Gross."

As we wait for the bus to Camden, I show Sam the itinerary Jas has sent through.

"It's *tomorrow*?" His forehead furrows briefly, then he sniggers. "Never mind. Get this: '*Call time for Talent: 10:30.*' Talent! That means you."

"Stop it." I punch his arm. "How are models talented? They're nothing but an accident of genetics." I'm joking around to stop the panic setting in, but Sam gives me a stern look.

"There's more to it than that, Freya."

My stomach swoops.

He reads on. "It says here, if you're under eighteen, you need an adult chaperone."

"You're kidding." I look at him. "What am I going to do?"

"Well, it's obvious, isn't it?" The bus pulls up and Sam swings himself on board. "You'll just have to bring your tall, charismatic, extremely good-looking older *cousin* with you."

"But I don't…" Facepalm. "*You?*"

He winks. "I'll let you know if I'm free."

Carla doesn't question our story. Summer school cancelled due to staff shortages. Dad and Bella wanting privacy. Just saying it makes me feel sick. Sam's dad, Tom, is quiet, scrubbing paint off his hands at the sink.

"Stay as long as you like," Carla tells me. Tom shoots her a look.

"Cheers, Mum." Sam heads to his room. As I go after him, his parents' whispers follow me down the hall.

"Relax, Tom, they're only friends."

"Are you sure? I know what I was like at that age."

"Well, Sam's not you. And you should trust your own son."

"I do. Which reminds me. *Sam, mate…*" Tom's shout startles me. "Remember your promise!"

"What promise?" I ask, pulling the bedroom door closed.

"Nothing," Sam grunts. "Forget it." He drops on to his bed.

"Does your dad think we're dating?" The idea is so funny, I giggle.

"Dunno." Sam's face is stony. "Who cares what he thinks?"

I frown. Sure, Sam's never had a boyfriend, but I'm pretty sure that Carla's guessed he's gay. Wouldn't Tom have worked it out? Before I can say anything, my phone alarm kicks in, reminding me to text Jake.

I still feel bad about tricking him, so I keep my tone light.

> Made it safely to Hogwarts!
> You can report back to You-Know-Who.
> I hope you have fun tonight. Freya.

> *I will, thanks to you x*

I stare at that kiss, confused.

My phone pings again and my heart leaps. It's Dad.

> *Feeling much better now, darling.*
> *Hope you're settling in at school.*
> *Speak soon. Love Dad x*

I show the message to Sam.

"See? He sounds fine."

"Hmm." I run my fingers through my hair.

"What are you thinking?"

"I wish I could be sure."

"Well, you can't go home."

"No, obviously. Although I left my camera there—"

"Chill," Sam soothes. "We'll get it tomorrow. We'll

sneak over, after the shoot — if your dad is better, they'll both be at work, right? Don't dwell on it now." He grins. "Let's talk about your big fashion moment instead!"

"Are you trying to make me feel worse?"

"Come on." He gets up. "You think models aren't talented? They just stand there, doing nothing? Let's see, shall we?" He beckons me over to the photo wall. "Revision time for your big test."

"What are you on about?"

"Look. And learn."

Reluctantly, I join him and together we stare at the photos. I busy my brain, analysing camera angles and lighting tricks. I can't look at the models themselves. They're too intimidating, with their dewy skin and spider lashes, their glossy mouths and luscious limbs.

"Getting inspiration?" Sam says.

"Not really."

"Come on, Freya! Other girls would kill to be in your shoes."

I think of Saskia and feel guilty. I study the images more closely. One model is getting out of a cab, all sultry in sequins and stilettoes. Another poses in a red phone box, wearing a Union Jack hat. A group of models are cosied around a campfire, laughing like they've heard the world's greatest joke. I know the pictures are staged, that the girls are only acting — but they look so confident, so convincing. How do they do it?

"See her?" Sam points at a close-up shot, the model's lips puckered in a pout. "She's saying *Thursday*."

117

I snort. "Stop."

"Honestly! I heard it somewhere. It's an old trick models do. Try it. *Thurrrsday.*"

"When did you become an expert?"

"Only trying to help."

I sigh. "I know." *These are the rules I need to learn.* "OK, then. What other tips do you have?"

Sam considers. "Well, which is your good side?"

"Is that a real question?"

"Never mind." He tuts and demonstrates. "Chin down, eyes up, three-quarters profile. That's the most flattering angle. Weight on your back leg. How come you don't know this stuff?"

"How come you *do*?"

He holds up his hands. "A little-known invention called the internet? Oh, and Jenna left these." He drags a pile of magazines out from under the bed and throws the top one at me. It weighs a ton. "Stop stressing. The photographer will tell you what to do. And there's always Photoshop." He nods at the model on the cover. "I bet she's nothing like that in real life."

I stare at the cover model's smooth symmetrical face. Sam's probably right. The trouble is, it's easy to forget. Sure, they tell you to "be yourself" because "it's what's inside that counts" – but they still print images like this without bothering to mention the important stuff: *this photo has been digitally enhanced.*

"It's fake," I say, echoing Jake.

Sam shrugs. "It's nothing new. Fake has been going on for centuries. You know, there was this plant – *atropic, atropa* something? I forget. They used to put the oil into eyedrops to make your pupils dilate. It was totally poisonous – the wrong dose could kill you – but they used it in medicines and beauty products anyway. I guess they thought it was worth the risk, if it made you look good."

"That makes no sense." I throw the magazine down.

"Right. So relax. You're doing one photoshoot, not risking your life."

Even so, I lie awake for hours that night.

If "beauty sleep" is real, no wonder I'm an insomniac.

She took me to her studio, where
I kept vigil as she worked.
When she picked up her pencil, I
whispered in her ear – and perfect
forms appeared upon the page.
As she cut her patterns, I
guided her hand – transferring
my magic to those gowns.
Scarlet, crimson, ruby, carmine: the
colours of seduction and desire.
I could feel my perfect vision
beginning to unfold, like the rippling
silks and satins all around.

16

Next morning, we take the tube to Old Street.

Sam is bouncing with energy. Meanwhile, I'm treading water. *Will they believe he's my older cousin? Will we get away with this?* I pat my pocket again, my forged consent form folded safely inside.

We leave the station and join the steady stream of hipsters heading to Hoxton.

The area is unfamiliar. Across the street, a huge mirrored office block looms next to a building covered in punky art. Young guys in tight shirts sip coffee through froth-flecked beards, while surly girls ride by on retro bikes. They blank me, in my no-name sweatshirt and jeans. I'm not on their radar, as out of place here as I am at school.

I wish I had my camera: my shield, protecting me.

Because this is a whole new world.

"It's here."

We've reached a warehouse building with a gated entrance.

BLAZE STUDIOS

Sam jabs the buzzer.

"Yes?" A voice drifts through the speaker.

Sam pushes me forwards.

"Um… It's Freya Jones… I'm here for *Seen*—"

"Studio Five." The intercom disconnects. The gate clicks open.

Studio Five is on the top floor. As we climb the winding stairs, the thud of bass-heavy music gets louder. At the top is a door. Sam knocks, but it's pointless. Nobody can hear.

"Now what do we do?"

"I guess we let ourselves in."

He pushes open the door. The sound inside is deafening. I want to jam my fingers in my ears.

"My internal organs are vibrating," Sam yells, and I nod. It's impossible to distinguish between the noise and the pounding of my heart.

We take in the scene. The space is large and open

plan, but four young guys are moving massive sheets of polystyrene to create a room within a room. Another is on a ladder, rigging up a large roll of paper. His mate pulls the paper down to fix it to the floor.

"That's the backdrop!" I shout to Sam. "They're building the set!" I've seen Dad do it in his workshop.

An older guy with a silver goatee is adjusting a tripod, and on top is the most amazing camera I've ever seen. A nearby table is filled with lenses of every shape and size. Excitement flickers through me, pushing my nerves away.

Almost.

An assistant stands in front of Goatee's camera, holding something up to his face. There's a sudden flash, and a high-pitched beep pierces the music for a second. Both Sam and I jump, though no one else reacts at all.

Goatee turns to a monitor just outside the set, where an image of his assistant uploads on to the screen. A computer operator zooms in on the assistant's face.

"Oh!" I breathe. "I get it. They're checking the light and the focus."

"Awesome!" Sam shouts back.

But he's not looking at the screen.

On the other side of the studio, a dressing table area is installed. Naked light bulbs frame a huge mirror, and on the table in front of it, a vast array of make-up and hair-styling products are arranged. A beautiful girl is sitting on a stool, while a punky guy with an armful of tattoos twists up her white-blonde hair. An earnest-looking younger guy with curly hair and cool chunky glasses hovers nearby, passing hairpins. I stare at the girl. She reminds me of something from a fairy tale. An arrogant ice queen. She catches me looking and I flush.

Next to the make-up station, a rail full of clothes is crammed with hundreds of garments. There's a table nearby, laden with accessories and dozens of pairs of shoes. A strange contraption sits beside the table, emitting puffs of steam.

"Wow," Sam murmurs. "Welcome to Bella's world."

I swallow. *What am I doing here?*

"Freya! You made it!"

A familiar face emerges from behind the clothes rail. Jas comes over to give me a hug. "Turn the music down!" she yells. The volume drops.

"I'm so glad you came! I wasn't sure if you'd show." She turns to Sam. "I'm Jas. And you're…?"

"Sam. Freya's my … younger cousin." He pulls back his shoulders, making the most of his height.

"My dad had to work," I add quickly, pulling out the consent form. "But he's given permission." Jas looks unsure, so I gamble. "You can ring him if you like."

Luckily, Punky Guy interrupts us.

"Hey, Jas! We're ready over here."

"OK, Freya." Jas smiles. "Let's introduce you to the team."

She leads us to the make-up station.

"So you're Freya." Punky Guy looks me up and down. "Nice to meet you. I'm Karim. This is Liam, my assistant."

Liam pushes his glasses up his nose and grins at Sam and me. "And this gorgeous creature is Māra."

Now Ice Queen's staring too. I fight the urge to run.

"Come on, Māra, let's get you dressed." Jas leads Ice Queen to the clothes rail like a zookeeper herding a glamorous giraffe.

Karim turns to me. "Take a seat."

"Do you mind if I watch?" Sam asks.

"Yes," Karim says. Sam's face falls. Then Karim winks. "You can help instead. Liam, go with Māra to the set, and be ready for any touch-ups. Sam, was it? You take over here. Pass me things when I say."

"I can do that!" Sam's cheeks are pink.

Before I can object, Karim plonks me down and deftly clips back my hair. My safety curtain has gone. I stare at my face in the mirror, grim and exposed. My jaw aches from clenching.

"Don't look so worried!" Karim laughs.

Behind me, I hear activity on the set. Flashes, bangs and yelps of enthusiasm that sound like they're coming from Goatee. Ice Queen must be out there, doing whatever it is you're supposed to do. The roller coaster in my tummy loops the loop.

Jas is back. "So what do you think?" she asks Karim. They both look at me.

This is when they realize their mistake.

"Interesting." Karim lifts my chin. "Although we'll have to please Clarissa, of course."

"Of course." Jas sighs.

"Who's Clarissa?" I ask.

"Clarissa Seaton-Payne. She's been the senior fashion editor at *Seen* for ever," Jas explains. "I'm her assistant. She stepped out to make an urgent call to Milan, but don't you worry…" She grimaces. "You'll be acquainted soon."

Karim starts on my face. He sifts through tubes and pots and sticks of cream, mixing colours on his hand to find a match for my dodgy complexion. My shoulders tense as he sponges on the base.

"Relax, your forehead's creasing. Is this your first shoot?"

I nod, zooming in on his face to distract myself. A gold tooth, a scar on his chin, a daisy tattooed behind his ear. I wonder how he came to have them. Mentally, I take a photo: *Frame. Focus. Click.*

"Close your eyes." Karim dabs my eyelids with a brush, minty breath tickling my face. I shiver at the cold sweep of eyeliner, and blink as he coats my lashes in mascara.

So many new sensations.

Karim's concentration is calming, though — and as my tummy starts to uncoil, I remember my mission: find out about Bella. I open my mouth.

"Sorry! No talking," Karim says, starting on my lips.

Silenced, I try to catch Sam's eye, but he's too engrossed, watching Karim work.

"What do you think?" Karim finishes my lips and steps back. Suddenly all the questions I've prepared fly out of my mind.

126

The girl in the mirror is a stranger. There isn't a trace of me left. Every blemish is covered; every flaw is disguised. Even my freckles have gone. And while my eyes are still the same old grey, they've been outlined – elongated – into a slick, feline shape, while my lips are fuller, stained a glistening sheen.

I stare.

The problem items on my checklist. They've been corrected. Erased.

Just like I've always wanted.

"So?" Karim waits for my verdict.

"Wow…" I'm lost for words. "I look—"

"*Perfect*," he finishes for me. "Clarissa will approve. Time for hair!"

The work begins again. This time Karim is behind me, yanking my hair with his brush and searing it with the dryer. Sam passes hairpins when he's called.

My head feels woozy. I can't stop staring at Not-Freya, emerging before my eyes. I think of Bella, drinking in her reflection in the mirror. Now I understand.

Imagine looking like this all the time.

"Read, if you want." Karim tosses a fashion magazine into my lap. I flick through it half-heartedly. The whole thing is mainly ads. But one advert makes me stop.

The image is dark and moody, with creeping plants like a forest, covering the page. A flash of colour catches my eye. I look closer. Behind the vines is a woman in a red dress. Her face is almost entirely obscured by leaves;

I can't make out her features. Only one eye, glinting in the light.

The slogan at the bottom reads:

ALL EYES ON HER
01/09

I stare, fascinated. *What is the image advertising*? A perfume, maybe? Or a film?

"Check out the editorial on page 206," Karim breaks my trance. "That's one of mine."

I find the page. It's a fashion story, shot on location. A girl in a sumptuous evening gown is walking down a dirt track in a village. Her dress is covered in crystals, but it's trailing through the mud. Little children, wearing dirty clothes, have come out to stare. Technically, the photo is stunning – the backlit sun creating a starburst of gold around the girl's body. But something about it makes me uncomfortable. To see this model, carelessly destroying her designer frock in this place of poverty – it feels wrong. Offensive, even. *Are all fashion shoots like this?*

"Is that Seren Larsson?" Sam interrupts my thoughts.

"Well spotted." Karim switches off the dryer. "She's going to be huge."

"You must have worked with *loads* of famous models," Sam gushes. I give him a look – *loser* – then I realize what he's doing.

"A few," Karim agrees.

"What about Belladonna Wilde?"

"*Belladonna Wilde.*" Karim lays down his comb. "Now, there's a good question."

"So you have worked with her?" I ask.

Karim nods. "Twice."

"What was she like?"

He takes his time to answer. "Let's just say both times were … memorable."

Sam and I exchange glances.

"Go on," Sam says. "We're intrigued."

Karim lowers his voice. "The first time was in Paris, about twenty years ago. It was show season. We were both just starting out. She'd been in Tokyo briefly, but this was her first time doing runway."

"She'd been in Tokyo?"

Karim waves a comb. "Lots of models go there at the beginning of their careers, to build up their portfolios."

I shift on my seat.

"Anyway," Karim continues, "I was assisting a famous make-up artist, so I got to see Belladonna Wilde up close. Nobody could take their eyes off her. She was so beautiful, I've never seen anything like it. Almost … *otherworldly.*"

I shiver.

"Beautiful inside and out?" Sam asks.

Karim snorts. "Not at all. Behind that gorgeous face was a witch, to put it mildly. She treated everyone like dirt. I was a newbie, just like her, but she clearly felt she was above us all."

Rings a bell.

"Her runway pictures were *incredible*." Karim twists my hair into a knot. "The photos were everywhere the next day. Some models work for months, years even, before they get a break, but Bella Wilde's career went stratospheric overnight." He snaps his fingers. "Like magic."

Sam passes Karim a pin. "So what about the next time you worked together? Was she the same?"

"Yes and no." Karim gives a dark laugh. "It was only last year. A minor shoot, nothing special. Not the kind of job I would have expected Bella Wilde to do. Although she's dropped off the radar, I guess. Anyway, when she walked into the studio, it blew my mind. She hadn't aged a day. But here's the strange thing." His voice dips. "Although she looked great in the flesh, she'd totally lost it on camera. The pictures were terrible, the client couldn't use them. The retouching bill would have cost a fortune."

I take this in. "Did Bella know?"

"Of course she knew." Karim shakes his head. "It was obvious on the shoot. She started screaming and yelling, blaming the photographer, blaming me. She called my work *shoddy and amateur.*" His eyes are flints. "That client never booked me again."

"That's terrible," Sam says. "She could have ruined your career."

Karim nods. "It was tough, but I've rebuilt my reputation. I can't say the same for her. I haven't seen her since."

"You don't know what she's doing now?"

"No idea." Karim grows thoughtful. "I heard a rumour she got married — probably to a rich guy who can keep her in diamonds, so she never has to work." I bite my lip. Karim goes on. "You know, the fashion world is changing, becoming more diverse. And that's a good thing. But older models are still in the minority. Past a certain age, no one wants to know. Plus, there's always fresh young blood waiting in the wings, ready to knock you off your perch."

He winks at me. I squirm.

"Hey now. Belladonna Wilde does *not* deserve your pity. Fashion is fickle. Looks don't last for ever. That's just the way it is. It's not your fault she fell for her own hype." He fixes a final strand of my hair in place. "Bella Wilde's career is well and truly over. Wherever she is now, I bet she'd do anything to get it back."

17

I'm dying to confer with Sam, but there isn't time.

Karim takes me to Jas, who's standing with a woman I don't know. She's dressed head to toe in black, sipping coffee from a tiny cup.

"Freya, meet Clarissa, our senior fashion editor."

Clarissa ignores my outstretched hand. "*This* is the girl you meant?" She blinks.

"Yes, I scouted Freya in Camden." Jas smiles, but Clarissa steers her aside. Terse whispers start to fly.

A moment later, they return. Jas seems to be fighting back tears.

"I'll give you a chance this time," Clarissa announces,

and I'm not quite sure who she means. "We're horribly late with this feature and we only need one little shot. Let's get on with it."

She pulls me to the clothes rail. Jas moves away. Karim has his arm around her.

Is Jas in trouble because of me?

"Street casting," Clarissa mutters to herself, sliding hangers along the rail. "What nonsense." She snaps her fingers at me. "OK, pay attention. I expect you don't know a thing. This shoot is very important. Each year, we run a Fashion Week issue, to showcase the new designers. We call in samples and make a selection. One portrait per label. *Seen* magazine is very influential." She smooths her immaculate fringe. "People look to us for direction on which collections to watch."

"So Fashion Week is a big deal?" I ask, to be polite. "When is it?"

Clarissa looks horrified. "In three weeks' time, of course! And yes, it is a 'big deal', as you so charmingly put it. If a designer is a hit at Fashion Week, their success is guaranteed. And being featured in *Seen* is wonderful exposure."

Exposure.

Even the word makes me shiver. It suddenly hits me. *What if Bella sees this shoot?* I cast the thought from my mind. It's only one shot. The feature won't be out for ages. It's Future Freya's problem, not mine.

"Put this on." Clarissa waves a scrap of fabric in my face.

I gape. "Is that a *dress*? It's very … um … revealing…"

Clarissa stares openly at my chest. "Darling, you have nothing to reveal."

My face grows hot. "What about that one?"

I point at another dress on the rail. It's short, but it's better than Clarissa's choice. The sleeves are long at least, and there's a little chiffon cape.

Clarissa screws up her face. "No, darling. Red's not your colour at all. We don't have much background on that garment, anyway. *Nightshade* is the label, but they've only sent one sample. I'm not convinced they're serious. They don't even have an atelier."

"Atelier?"

Clarissa's eyes roll. "A design studio. No, this is the one for you."

She presses the flimsy silk scrap into my hands. "Get dressed quickly and I'll be back to pin you. Chop, chop!"

She strides off. I look around. Sam is standing by the set, chatting away to Liam. Goatee's assistants are milling around. Am I expected to undress *here*?

Jas comes to my rescue. "Take this," she says, handing me a robe. Her eyes are still red-rimmed. "You can change in the loo."

By the time I emerge from the toilet, I'm pretty sure my face is glowing, despite the layers of foundation Karim has plastered on. The silk dress is so transparent, I may as well be wearing cling film. I clutch the robe around

134

me, but Clarissa has other ideas. She whips it away, assessing me like a cow at market, and barks instructions at Jas.

"The snake belt! The net tights! The patent slingbacks… No, the sandals!"

She yanks the dress tight around my waist. Then she fixes it with big silver clips – the kind we have at school – totally transforming its shape.

"Isn't that … false advertising?" I mutter.

"We won't see the clips on camera," Clarissa says, like that makes it all right.

Jas selects accessories, then Clarissa decorates me like a Christmas tree. A pendant is hung round my neck. Hoops are forced through the ancient holes in my ears. My feet are shoved into shoes two sizes too big. Clarissa jams tissue in the toes. I've never worn heels and I wobble on the spikes. My dress is hitched up, pulled down, hitched up. Finally, Clarissa is satisfied.

"Go. Before I change my mind."

Go.

I gulp like a dying fish. "You look great," Jas tries to reassure me. She guides me to the set, helping when I stumble. I hear Clarissa sigh.

Māra the Ice Queen is finishing up. I watch her posing effortlessly, her body forming fluid shapes. Her expression changes every few frames, with the ease of an Oscar-winning actor.

Sweat breaks out on my nose.

"And ... that's a wrap!" Goatee emerges from behind his camera.

Māra sidesteps his embrace. She winks at me – sarcastic or friendly, I can't tell. "Your turn, Freya. Good luck."

"Frey-ah! Let's see you." Goatee looks me up and down, his eyes wandering all over my body. My cheeks are on fire. "I am Jean-Luc." My hand gets a limp shake. "Shall we start?"

He pushes me on to the set. My heart is pounding so badly, I half expect it to burst through the fabric of my dress. Lights blast me, turning the room into a black hole. Jean-Luc is a shadow behind his camera, the cold glass lens a Cyclops eye.

"Music!" someone shouts, and the speakers crank up. Jean-Luc's voice strains over the bass.

"OK, Frey-ah! Give me everything you have!"

I have literally no idea what to do.

My body is rigid. My feet are glued to the floor. Someone turns on a wind machine and a sheet of air slams into me, chilling me to the core. From behind his camera, Jean-Luc blasts commands.

"Look left! Too far. Chin up! More! Look into the lens... Oh, *merde*! Why do you look so scared?"

I think of Saskia, posing for selfies, all Sam's good advice. But every time the flash explodes, I jump.

What's the matter with me? Why can't I do this stuff?

Jean-Luc appears, sweat dripping from his brow. "Let's take a break."

The wind machine dies down and the studio lights

come on. Jean-Luc and Clarissa hover by the monitor with their team. As my image appears on screen, the operator zooms in and Clarissa throws up her hands.

A sob hitches in my throat.

"You OK?" Jas appears on the set.

"They hate me." I sniff.

"No, they don't," she says, kindly. "You're inexperienced. That's not your fault."

"Clarissa blames you, doesn't she? For picking some random off the street."

"She'll get over it." Jas pulls a face and whispers, "Clarissa's *old school*. So out of touch. She only casts models like Māra. *Seen* magazine needs to change. When the other model dropped out, Clarissa asked me to find a replacement. I wasn't going to waste that chance! Street casting is the future. Real women, real beauty. You're not random, you're refreshing! To be honest, I'd go further, but that will have to wait until I've got Clarissa's job." She grins. "It's time to shake things up and break the mould!" Her curls bounce, emphasizing her point. "I believe in you, Freya. Believe in yourself."

The studio lights fade. We start again.

Even with Jas's pep talk, minutes become hours. Clarissa pulls me back to the clothes rail to try a different scrap of fabric, then I'm pushed under the lights again, where Jean-Luc's instructions confuse me and turn me to stone. Each shot is enlarged and analysed on screen. At one point, Clarissa makes Karim pin back my ears with eyelash glue.

Later still, she slides a hand inside my dress, pressing a pad on to my shoulder. When I turn for the other one, her lip curls. "Only one. You're lop-sided, darling. Didn't you know?"

I'm back on Karim's stool. It's after two and we still haven't stopped for lunch. My stomach growls and Clarissa looks disgusted. I can't miss the frosty vibes rolling off her, or the way she's taking her temper out on Jas.

Jean-Luc sidles up.

"Frey-ah, we have a problem. This is not working. You are too…" He does an impression: *Bambi on the motorway.* "Let's stop."

I hang my head.

It doesn't matter, I tell myself, through the burning shame. *I found out some things about Bella. That's what I came for.*

I step off the stool.

"Wait!" Jas comes forward. "I have an idea." She rests a hand on my shoulder. "Freya's not confident in *front* of the camera, but she's a natural *behind* it. What if she took her own picture?"

"You mean a *selfie*?" Clarissa drips disdain.

"A self-portrait," Jas corrects. "Do it for me?" she whispers in my ear.

Jean-Luc sneers. Clarissa's face is granite.

"We'd meet our deadline," Jas reminds her.

Finally, Clarissa nods. "It's worth a try."

*

138

I'm at the clothes rail with Sam and Liam, Karim and Jas. Jean-Luc and Clarissa have disappeared to make calls.

"This is the fun part," Jas tries to convince me.

"There's a fun part?"

"Definitely! Play around with different pieces. Experiment. Express yourself!" The tension in her voice betrays her nerves. I just want to leave, but Jas is nice, and this is important to her. I can't let her down.

My eyes fall once more on the Nightshade dress. Something about it feels familiar, like I've seen it before. I slip it on, surprised when it fits. For the first time all day, I feel calm. The dress has a different vibe from everything else on the rail. Wearing it is like looking into the past, or listening to a story from long ago.

One of Jean-Luc's assistants shows me how to operate the camera with a remote control. I place Karim's stool in the middle of the set. At my request, he's let down my hair, but he persuaded me to keep my make-up for the lights. Somehow, I feel safer behind the mask.

Sam gives me a thumbs-up. Everybody leaves.

I look into the lens, my pulse racing.

It's only a self-portrait, Freya.

Except … I've barely taken one before.

I clutch the remote control, my fingers trembling.

Then I take a deep breath and press the button.

18

My face is scrubbed clean and my hair feels like straw.

As we take the Northern line home, I loll on Sam's shoulder, grunting as he chatters on: *Karim this, Liam that.* I'm too tired to tease him. Anyway, I need to think.

Was it worth it, today?

Shame scorches me, remembering how it felt to stand on the set wearing next to nothing, Jean-Luc and Clarissa's faces full of contempt. I want to lock up the memory and throw away the key.

I did it for Dad.

But what did I learn?

That Bella's a nightmare to work with. Ambitious and

ruthless – no surprise there. But Karim's story of her recent, disastrous shoot – that was interesting.

"Karim said Bella's 'lost it' on camera," I say to Sam. "What do you think he meant?"

"Well, I suppose he meant she's ageing…" he says. "Which is natural; nothing wrong with that. The industry prefers younger models, that's all."

"She *isn't* ageing, though," I argue. "At least, not in real life. Karim thought that too. Bella still looks youthful, radiant. Sickeningly so."

I think of the unflattering paparazzi shot in the newspaper, the strange picture I took of Bella in the kitchen. Those images were surprising, but I'd put them down to harsh lighting, dodgy camera settings. They were exceptions – weren't they?

"It doesn't make sense," I say. "How can someone look flawless in the flesh – but different in photographs?"

"Mmm." Sam muses. "Usually these days, it's the other way round."

"Well, whatever the reason, I guess one mystery is solved," I say. "Dad is a Photoshop wizard. Bella would have learned that when they met. I suppose with him on her team, as her own private retoucher, her photos can be fixed. She can maintain her perfect image."

"Yeah, but how long can that go on?" Sam frowns. "If nobody wants to work with Bella, won't your dad run out of pictures to retouch? Nah. I don't think that's her 'project'." He says something else, but I'm not listening. Karim's voice echoes in my head.

"Bella Wilde's career is well and truly over. I bet she'd do anything to get it back."

Sam's right. There has to be more to this. One thing I know for sure: Bella's not been honest. She told Dad she'd never been to Japan, but Karim said she'd spent time in Tokyo. Why on earth would she lie?

Sam pokes me in the ribs. "You're not listening."

"I am."

"What did I just say?"

"Um … Karim has sacked Liam and asked you to be his new assistant?"

"Funny." He punches my arm. "And for your information, Liam only assists Karim in the holidays. He's studying film make-up at college – you know, special effects, prosthetics and stuff? He gave me his number. We're gonna meet for coffee so he can show me some of his pictures." He blushes and changes the subject. "What I actually said was – d'you reckon *Seen* will use your shot? Wouldn't it be amazing to have your own photo published in a magazine!"

"I suppose."

The truth is, I'm not holding my breath. I only took a handful of frames and we didn't hang around to see them upload. Jean-Luc and Clarissa's verdict on my modelling was bad enough, I couldn't take it if they slammed my photography as well. I hope the shot looked OK – for Jas's sake, more than mine.

The train pulls into Camden. Sam nudges me. "Still on for our stake-out?"

"Stake-out?"

"Your dad and Bella, remember? If they're out, we can go and get your camera. You do still want to, don't you?"

"Of course!"

"Come on, then."

He tugs my arm and we dash up the escalator. Best case scenario: the house is empty. If Dad is well, he'll be at work. I need my camera back; I can't think clearly without it. Once I've got it back, everything is bound to make more sense.

But it's not that easy. At street level, Sam's phone starts blowing up with missed calls. He listens to his voicemail and sighs.

"Sorry, Freya, I've gotta get home. My dad is—"

"What?"

He waves me away. "We'll go for your camera tomorrow."

"*Tomorrow*?" My heart falls. I can't wait another day. I check the time; it's not that late. I could be in and out in seconds.

"Don't risk it on your own," Sam says, reading my mind.

"I'll be careful."

He purses his lips. "Well … OK. But hurry. In case I need backup."

He's gone before I can ask him what he means.

Head down and hood up, I turn into my street. At rush hour, this route is a rat run, but for now at least, it's quiet.

Keeping my distance on the opposite side of the street, I peer at number five.

My house.

No signs of life. So far so good.

I cut down the side street to see round the back. The curtains are open in Dad and Bella's room. Another good sign.

I dig out my key. I'm pretty sure it's safe. I'll run in, grab my camera and go.

My heart stops.

At the end of the road by the railway arch, a car is turning into the street. Its paintwork catches the light. *Metallic blue.*

I dive behind a hedge.

The car stops outside my house. I see the driver's sharp profile. His shock of dark hair.

Jake. What's he doing here?

The engine dies and the door to number five opens. My hand flies to my mouth. Bella is standing on the threshold. As Jake gets out of the car, she glances down the street. They disappear inside the house, closing the door behind them.

I move closer. There's a van parked opposite Jake's car. I duck behind it.

A few minutes later, the front door opens again. My senses switch to high alert. I peek through the van's windows, my legs stiff from crouching.

Jake is carrying a large, sealed box, staggering under its weight. Something is written on the box, but I can't quite see what it is.

"Put it in the car," Bella calls from the hall. "Then come back for the rest."

Jake places the box on the kerb and unlocks the boot. Now I can read the writing. A single letter T.

My mind screams with questions.

Jake goes back inside. A few minutes later he's back with another box, identical to the first. A third box follows, then the boot is full.

Bella locks the house behind her. "Let's go."

Suddenly, my phone pings. The sound is only small but in the still afternoon, it carries as clear as a bell.

Bella's head whips round, Komodo-dragon fast. I duck behind the van's wheel. My heart is elastic, snapping in my chest.

After an age, a door slams. An engine splutters into life. As Jake's car disappears around the corner, I read Sam's message.

Where R U? Everything OK?

I pause.

In my head, I'm compiling a list of Bella's possessions. Swanky designer clothes? *Check*. Creepy antique mirror? *Check*.

But no boxes. She doesn't have any boxes.

I text Sam back.

Things just got even more weird.

*Her teachers showered praise
upon the dark-haired girl, just
like I knew they would.
My vision was infectious. The
seeds were taking root.
Any creature or creation guided by my
influence acquires my powers to control.
With this chain reaction to my
perfect collection, I was poised
to transform the world.*

*It would have happened —
if not for the child.*

19

My fingers slip as I grapple with the lock.

Get a grip, Freya. I'm not breaking in. This is my home.

Somehow, it doesn't feel like it.

I tiptoe into the hall. Dad's favourite trainers are missing from the rack. I breathe a sigh of relief. He must be better after all.

The only sound is the hum of the fridge. As Kodak winds round my ankles, I glance about. It's not just my camera I need. It's answers. What has Bella taken? What do we have that she could possibly want?

I head upstairs.

First, I run to my room. My camera bag is still hanging

where I left it. I tuck it into my rucksack, feeling calmer. Then I try the door to Dad and Bella's room. I expect it to be locked, but it's not.

Because she thinks I'm "out of the way".

I push the door wide.

The bed is neatly made; the sheets pristine. You'd never guess that only two days ago, Dad was lying here, sick. I shiver.

Out of the corner of my eye, there's a flicker of light.

Then I feel it: an invisible force lifting my head. A whisper in my ear, like a caress.

Come.

My mind goes blank. My feet move by themselves.

I'm standing in front of Bella's mirror.

What? No, Freya. There isn't time...

Look.

I don't know who's speaking – or if it's me, inside my head. All I know is that I'm staring into the glass, transfixed by my own reflection.

Poor Freya. So flawed. But I can help.

Like a wave rolling over the sand, the glass seems to ripple.

I blink. Another girl is looking back. She looks like

me, but she isn't me. Freya-but-not-Freya, flawless and immaculate, just like at the shoot.

A strange lightheaded feeling washes over me. I sway on my feet, shut my eyes to stem the dizziness. Grip the chest of drawers with both hands. Eventually, the waters calm and I open my eyes.

The perfect girl has gone.

I'm tired, that's all. It's been a stressful day.

I pick up Bella's red scarf, lying on the chest of drawers. Tossing it over the glass, I feel better, more awake. There's no time to waste. I need to do some digging while I'm here.

The boxes. Where did they come from?

My gaze rises to the ceiling, to a white square board. The hatch for the attic. I've never been up there – Dad's forbidden it. He says the joists are rotten – you could go through the floor. But Bella went up with him on the day he found my lens, and…

In the carpet by my feet are two indents: neat rectangles pressed into the pile.

Someone's been in the attic today.

My focus is back, super sharp.

I shift Dad's bedside table, using it to reach the handle on the hatch. The door swings open and I pull down the ladder. Its feet slot neatly into the carpet dents.

Then I climb.

My head pokes into a cool, dark space, pungent with the smell of dust and damp. I feel for a light switch. No luck. A few shreds of daylight are fighting their way

149

through a grimy central skylight, but the edges of the attic are dark.

I wait for my eyes to adjust. Soon, objects take shape: camping gear, old electrical goods, boxes marked "WINTER COATS" and "XMAS DECS". I spy our artificial Christmas tree, complete with paper-plate angel fixed to the top, along with loads of other random items I'd forgotten all about. My roller skates. A swing-ball set. Hand weights from Dad's short-lived fitness phase. Even a sewing machine, its needle bent, dust furring up the bobbin winder.

Another of Dad's fads, I guess.

One corner of the attic is empty, the dust-covered floor broken by three clean squares.

That's where the boxes were.

But what was inside?

I pivot, using the torch on my phone to penetrate the shadows. There are no more boxes like the ones Bella took, nothing even similar. Then I notice something else.

Squeezed under the eaves is a small, dark chest, and on the side is a letter T.

I crawl towards it, adrenaline racing, weaving through the junk like a cat.

The chest is wedged firmly in place. I summon all my strength to yank it free. Then, propping my phone on a filing cabinet to angle the light, I ease off the lid.

I stop breathing.

The chest is full of impossible things.

A teddy: moth-eaten, button-eyed. A little jacket,

printed with a pattern of a rabbit and a moon. A miniature pair of scuffed red shoes.

My baby things. They've got to be.

My hands start to shake.

Dad said he couldn't keep anything. Mum's parents took most of it, he said. Everything else, he left in Japan. It cost too much to bring it back to England. It was better to start from scratch.

I believed him. Why would he lie?

I rummage in the chest and pull out more things – picture books with cutesy characters, some in English, some Japanese. At the bottom of the chest are two large books, different from the rest. One is brown, the other black. Both have woven bindings, like expensive scrapbooks. I pull out the brown one and open it.

On the first page is a photograph.

The world falls away as I stare.

I'm looking at a woman in jeans and a T-shirt, her dark hair cropped short. She's standing on a city street with neon billboards all around. Behind is a busy crossroads with people rushing past. But the woman isn't looking at them. She's not even looking at the camera. Her gaze is glued on the baby in her arms, who's oblivious to the chaos, fast asleep.

It's Tess. *My mum.*

And me.

My shoulders shake and the image goes blurry. I wipe my eyes before I spoil the page. I stare at my crazy mop of hair. At Mum's expression, half shattered, half serene.

It's the first picture I've seen of us, together.

I drink in every detail. Force myself to turn the page.

There's more. Page after page of photographs.

Here she is again – *Mum!* – pushing the baby – *me!* – on a swing, my chubby face squealing in the wind. And here I'm lying in the grass, legs kicking, while Mum sprinkles me with blossom. Sometimes it's Dad in the pictures: a younger, happier version, tossing me in the air, or wiping juice from my chin.

It hits me full force, the life I once had.

Might still have, if Mum hadn't died.

The letter T. *It stands for Tokyo. Or … Tess.*

I let out a breath. Whatever Bella's taken, it came from the past. Mine. Dad's. *Mum's*. But what is it, and why does she want it? For me, this is treasure. Surely it's only trash to her?

A key scrapes in a lock. My blood runs cold. *Someone's coming.*

Quickly, I shove everything back into the chest and scramble over to the hatch. I can't pull up the ladder! Fear makes my hair stand on end.

Sharp heels clatter on wooden floorboards. A voice echoes up from the hall. "Check one more time. I want nothing missed."

Bella.

Muffled footsteps on the stairs.

She's coming. There's nothing I can do.

I squeeze behind the Christmas tree, as the bedroom door clicks. Feet clatter on the ladder's metal rungs.

I'm trapped.

20

I peer through plastic pine needles. Jake's tousled head surfaces through the hatch.

My heart rate doubles.

"Is someone there?" he asks the darkness.

"What's that?" Bella calls from downstairs. "Hunter?"

I have no choice. I crawl out from my hiding place, a finger pressed to my lips.

Jake's eyes grow huge. "Freya?"

"She can't know I'm here!" I whisper.

"Why *are* you here?" Jake's voice is low, confused. "You took the train."

"I can explain! Don't give me away!"

153

"Hunter!" Bella's voice makes us jump. She's on the landing now. "Are you doing what I asked?"

"Yes, I'm checking," Jake calls back. "There's a lot of *surprising* stuff up here." He looks at me.

"I want any more boxes like the others," Bella snaps. "It's hardly rocket science. Hurry!"

I breathe out as her footsteps retreat.

"Thank you," I mouth.

Jake doesn't reply. He scans the attic, prodding items and pushing them aside. Sparks ignite in my stomach.

"Stop!" I hiss. "What are you doing? This is *our* stuff. It belongs to my family. It's got nothing to do with her!"

Jake crawls in further on hands and knees. "That's not what she said."

"She's lying!" My hands form fists. I'm trying to be quiet, but the sparks in my stomach are flickering flames.

Jake's eyes continue to roam. I watch in horror as they land on the chest. He spots the letter *T*. "What's that?"

"Nothing."

We move at the same time.

"No! You can't let her have it!" My voice cracks as Jake gets there first and pulls the chest towards him. Tears prick my eyes. "Jake, please!"

Finally, he looks at me properly, then he lets go of the chest. I fall on it, crying silently with relief.

"There's nothing else up here!" Jake calls down to Bella.

"Are you sure?" She sounds sceptical.

"I'm sure," he says, still focused on me.

I wipe my eyes, my face suddenly hot. I wish it were the mirror girl that Jake could see right now, not my hideous, tear-stained face.

"Come down, then." Bella breaks the moment. "We've wasted enough time. I need to get back to the agency."

She's leaving. Relief floods through me. "Thank you," I say to Jake again.

"I don't know what's going on," he whispers, "but that's twice I've risked my job for you. You owe me an explanation, Freya."

"You're the one sneaking around in my house!" I whisper back. "I reckon you owe *me*."

His mouth quirks.

"Hunter!" Bella summons from the hall.

"Better go." Jake disappears down the hatch. A moment later, the front door slams.

I turn to the chest once again. It's way too bulky to carry and I don't have room for everything in my bag. I slide the two albums into my rucksack, and push the chest back under the eaves. Then I climb down the ladder, carefully closing the hatch.

I head to Sam's, my precious cargo on my back.

Even before the lift opens, I hear arguing. As I walk along the balcony to Sam's front door, the voices get louder.

"Embarrassing … let down…" It's Tom, Sam's dad, but I can hear Sam's defensive tone, and Carla trying to keep the peace. In the background, Lily wails.

My hand hovers over the doorbell, guilt clawing at me. Something's wrong in Sam's world, but I've been so focused on Dad and Bella, I've ignored the signs.

The front door opens. Tom comes out, red-faced and flustered. "Your girlfriend's here!" he shouts, stomping off down the stairwell.

I stare after him, open-mouthed.

"Don't mind him, Freya love." Carla appears in the hallway, Lily clinging to her leg. "He's stressed with work."

I find Sam lying on his bed, staring at the ceiling.

"Sam?"

No answer.

"What's going on? Why is your dad upset? Is it something to do with me?"

"Not everything is about you, Freya."

I sink on to the bed and push the past two hours from my mind. Now is not the time for my problems. "OK, so talk to me."

Sam rolls over to face the wall. "I said I'd do something for Dad today. But I … forgot."

"What was it?" I think of Tom's warning. *"Sam, mate. Remember your promise!"*

"Nothing. Just an errand at the paint yard."

I swallow, guilt rising again. Sam came to the shoot with me instead of helping out his dad. "Why didn't you say? I would have gone on my own…"

"No, you wouldn't," Sam huffs. "And you needed a chaperone, remember? But that's not the point. I didn't just do it for you, Freya." He hoists himself up on to his elbows. "Why would I waste my time at the paint yard, when I could do what we did today?" His eyes glisten. "It was amazing!"

"I'm glad one of us had fun." I say, gently. "So what did Tom say when he found out where you were?"

"You're joking," Sam sniffs. "I didn't tell him! It's obvious what he'd say." He puts on a deep macho voice: *"You blew me out for some girly fashion shoot?"*

"Are you sure?"

He gives a bitter laugh. "Of course I'm sure. Why d'you think he doesn't want me working at the salon? He thinks it's 'inappropriate' for his son."

"He actually said that?"

"Not in so many words." Sam sighs. "But he may as well have. I made up an excuse. Said I lost track of time, taking pictures with you. It's near enough the truth." He swivels round to face me. "Dad thinks he's doing me a favour, giving me jobs to do, errands to run. He's got this idea in his head that I should do an apprenticeship, in September, just like he did all those years ago. And he's angry because I said no."

"You did?" I'm silent. It doesn't seem like the worst idea in the world.

"I didn't mean to offend him," Sam goes on. "But it's not me. It's not *who I am*. He never asks what I want, what I like. He honestly believes you're my girlfriend. Or maybe that's what he wants to believe…" He chokes up. "My own dad doesn't know the first thing about me."

157

I reach for his hand. Sam wipes his eyes with his sleeve.

"Today was the best day of my life. I realized something huge, Freya!' He pauses. "I wanna be a hair and make-up artist, like Karim."

I nod. It totally fits. Sam's artistic talent and his beauty knowledge; the model pictures on his wall; the YouTube videos, the fashion shoot hints and tips.

"So why didn't you tell him that?"

"Because he wouldn't get it."

"You don't know for sure," I say, trying to prise Sam's fingers from his face. "Give him a chance. If this is your dream, there's no point pretending. Tell Tom the truth – the whole truth. How bad could it be?"

"*How bad could it be?*" Sam shakes me off. "You have no idea. Your dad loves you, no matter what." He laughs bitterly. "Don't lecture me about pretending, Freya. You're just the same. You're always hiding, afraid to be you. And it's worse, because *you* don't even have a good reason!"

My mouth falls open.

"I'm going to bed." He turns off the light without waiting for my reply, plunging the room into darkness. Exhaustion hits me like a wave. I crash on to the airbed, not caring about my clothes, or my hair, still crispy with hairspray.

I lie there, thinking about what Sam said.

He's wrong. I *do* have a good reason to hide.

Life is … *safer* that way.

21

Sam's not in bed when I wake up, but an Ariana Grande tribute act is performing in the shower down the hall. I guess the weekend has improved his mood.

I'm feeling better too. Calmer, more clear-headed. In the cool light of day, my encounter with Bella's mirror seems like nothing more than a dream — the wild imaginings of a tired mind. And the shoot is done. I managed to survive. My brush with Bella's world is over.

Or is it?

Misgivings gather like storm clouds. Perhaps Bella *does* want Dad for his retouching skills, but after yesterday evening, I'm starting to agree with Sam. There must be more to her project than that. Is it something to do with my family? She's stolen our stuff – why?

Foreboding flickers like a faulty light bulb. I push it away and reach for my bag instead.

The photo albums.

My fingers tingle. Yesterday I was interrupted. Today I can take my time.

I pull out the brown book, breathing in the scent of leather and musty paper. Now that it's daylight, I can see that some of the photographs have captions. The neat, precise print makes my heart skip a beat. This isn't Dad's scrawl.

It's *her* handwriting. Mum's.

> *Freya at six months, Tokyo Zoo.*
> *Nick and Freya in Hakone, July.*
> *Tess's research trip to Kobe.*

I linger on the last image. In it, Mum is standing on the steps of a strange building. It looks a bit like a spaceship. She's smiling from ear to ear. I'm wondering what "research" she could have been doing when Sam comes in, hair spiky-wet.

"I come in peace." He slides a plate of toast on to the bedside table. "Sorry I was mean last night – I was upset."

"Apology accepted. For what it's worth, I'm sorry too. I've been so distracted by Dad and Bella, I haven't been paying attention."

Sam nods and his eyes land on the album. "What are you looking at?"

I turn it around. "I found it in the attic, when I went back for my camera."

"No way!" He whistles, turning the pages. "So that's why you took so long. Oh my God, is this you? Look at your hair!" He sniggers, then his eyes grow wide. "Wait. Is that—"

"My mum." I nod. "Dad had pictures all along."

Sam frowns. "He never said?"

I shake my head.

"Your mum was cool." Sam points at one picture. In it, she's wearing a striking green coat with batwing sleeves and looking off camera, thoughtful and aloof. "And your dad was pretty hot then too."

"Eww. Stop!"

"Sorry." He touches my arm. "This must be hard for you."

"I don't understand why he kept this from me," I say. "He saved other things from Tokyo too."

I tell Sam about the boxes, about Bella making Jake put them in his car.

"She *took* them?" Sam's eyebrows fly up. "Where? Why? What use are your family snaps to her?"

I shrug, and stroke the brown album. "I'm glad she missed this, anyway. There's another one too."

I reach into my bag for the black album, but the moment I take it out, I realize – it's not another photo album at all.

The cover isn't leather but soft black canvas, and there are no photographs inside.

Only drawings.

"Oooh! A sketchbook!" Sam pounces on it. "You think it's one of your dad's from art school?"

"I guess," I say. "It must have fallen in with the Tokyo things."

We sit side by side, flipping through the first few pages. Dozens of portraits in pencil and ink and charcoal and pastel and chalk. Each drawing has a lightness of touch – the essence of the subject captured in just a few strokes.

"Wow," Sam murmurs. "These are really good. I didn't know your dad could draw. I thought he was just a photographer."

"What do you mean *just*?" I thump his arm, though he does have a point. I've never seen Dad so much as doodle on an envelope.

I turn the page, and catch my breath. The next portraits are nudes. Mostly women, the occasional male figure here or there. I wait for Sam to make a wisecrack, but he's just as entranced as me.

"Life drawings," he breathes.

Together, we marvel at the subtle shading; the way the light falls on every curve. These drawings have been done with such respect, such detail – every single body is presented as beautiful, regardless of shape or age or size.

"These are seriously amazing," Sam says. "Your dad's talented."

162

"Mmm." Confusion clouds my head.

Then we fall silent.

Because the figures on the next page are different yet again. These women – and they're all women this time – are dynamic, stylized, and fully clothed.

"Whoa." Sam grips my arm. "You know what these are, don't you?"

I frown. "They look like—"

"Fashion designs," he finishes.

We stare.

A vibrant army of women parades before us, dressed in a mind-blowing array of garments. And they're not your usual pale-skinned stick figures either. Women of every age, size, shape and colour dance defiantly across the page.

I spy skirts and trousers, dresses and jackets, all the usual things. But nothing is straightforward. Every piece has some kind of twist or unexpected detail that makes it unique – whether it's an outrageous ruffle, an exaggerated pleat or an asymmetric hem.

A strange feeling fizzes through me.

I turn the page, and the designer gets more daring. These women are in a state of metamorphosis – part-human, part-animal – with sleeves like wings and shoes like claws. And here they have curves and angles in totally unexpected places, as though the designer were trying to create a brand-new silhouette.

"Look," Sam giggles, pointing to a dress with bumpy padding all over. "Imagine wearing that to go shopping!"

I laugh, but my skin is tingling. These women aren't simple fashion dummies. They're witches and warriors, goddesses and queens. They're not trying to be pretty, or blend in with the crowd. They've got presence and power. They jump right off the page.

"I love it," I say, surprised to find I mean it. All my life, I've felt locked out of fashion, like it's some impossible exam that I can never ever pass. But these clothes are different – eccentric and individual. They're about freedom and fun, not following trends. These women are showing the world how they feel and who they are.

All too soon, we reach the end.

"Is that it?" Sam's as disappointed as me.

A stamp on the back cover catches my eye.

PROPERTY OF KAWAKUBO COLLEGE

I blink.

"Your dad had some pretty out-there ideas." Sam flicks back through the sketchbook again. "And what's with the little house thing?"

"House?"

I follow his finger. Incorporated into each design is a tiny drawing, cleverly hidden. It does look a bit like a house on stilts, with two floors and an open skylight.

Suddenly I feel dizzy. Like I'm standing on the edge of a volcano that's about to explode. "I don't think that's a house," I say. "I think it's a signature."

"Are you sure?"

"I think it's Japanese." I think of the picture books from the attic, the menus in Kagami. "What if this isn't my dad's sketchbook?" I say. "What if it belonged to someone else?"

"So let's translate it," Sam says.

"How?"

"With my app." He grins and pulls out his phone. "It's rubbish they wouldn't let me use it in my French exam."

He switches to camera mode in the language app. Then, holding it over the sketchbook, he zooms in on one of the little symbols. The cursor swirls and I tense, waiting for the translation to appear.

"Oh." Sam tuts. "It's a colour, not a name. *Shiro*. It means … *white*."

White.

I let out a breath. *I knew it.*

The symbol means White. For *Tess White*.

This sketchbook belonged to my mum.

My fingers feel rubbery; I keep making typos. We've looked up Kawakubo College and it's an actual art and design college in Tokyo, with all sorts of different fashion and design courses. Sam checks the email before I send it.

From: freyayukijones@icloud.com
To: info@kawakubocollege.ac.jp
Subject: Tess White

Hello,

My name is Freya Jones. I'm seeking information
about my mother, Tess White. I think she studied at
Kawakubo College in the mid 2000s. If you can help
at all, please contact me.
    Thank you.

    Freya Jones

I include my contact details – my phone number, even my address, just in case. With a *whoosh*, the email's gone.

"Wow. Your mum was an actual fashion designer!" Sam says. "Well, studying to be."

I leaf back through the pages of the sketchbook. After so long wondering about my mum, it's like finally getting a glimpse inside her head.

"You think she could speak Japanese?" Sam muses. "She must have done, I guess."

Talented. Creative. Bilingual. Why didn't Dad tell me? It doesn't make sense.

"I wonder where the rest of her work is," Sam goes on. "I mean, she'd be bound to have more than one sketchbook, right?"

"I don't know!" I snap. "I told you, I don't know anything!"

He looks hurt, and I sigh. None of this is Sam's fault.

"Sorry," I mutter. "You're right. Those boxes Bella took – what if more of Mum's work was inside?" I look at him. "I should speak to Dad."

"Is that a good idea?"

I shrug.

When Sam heads off to the kitchen for more toast, I dial Dad's number. I don't know what I'm going to say, I just know I need answers, and…

Abruptly, it cuts to voicemail.

He declined my call.

A message pings. Dad's name pops up on the screen.

> *I can't talk now, Freya. I'm working.*
> *I'll be in contact soon.*

He's at work? On a Saturday? He'll "be in contact" soon?

"What's the matter?" Sam asks, coming back in.

I stare at the text. Each word is a punch to the gut.

I stab my reply.

> Dad, I need to talk to you urgently.
> It's about Mum.
> Please. It's important!

Silence. He's gone.

I show Sam the message, feeling sick. "It's not him," I say, realizing the truth as I speak. "It doesn't sound like him. It's too formal. Also, he's addicted to emojis – it's embarrassing. He hasn't even signed off with a kiss! I need to see him, face to face. Find out what's going on."

Sam's eyebrows shoot up. "He thinks you're in Devon."

"It doesn't matter any more." I start to pull my trainers on.

"Wait. Slow down, Freya! Where are you going? Not to Bella's agency?" Sam runs his fingers through his hair. "Think about this for a second. Say your dad is there – and he's with Bella – will you really find out the truth if she's around? She's the one who convinced him to send you to boarding school. She'll just send you away again – only this time she'll make sure you get there. And then you'll be finished. No photography. No future. Game over. There has to be something else you can do."

I close my eyes and a face floats into my mind. Hazel-flecked eyes and tousled hair.

Jake.

Jake works at Façade. He could get a message to Dad. He helped Bella with the boxes, he'll know where they are now. He might even know what was inside.

Can I trust him, though?

I feel like I can, but is that misguided? After all, he works for Bella.

Then again, he did help me, up in the attic. And I can't quite shake the idea that there's a … *connection* between us.

168

Though that's misguided too, because of Amy.

"Any ideas?" Sam asks.

"One." I go with my gut. I don't have another choice.

> Hi Jake, it's Freya.
> We need to talk. Name a time and place.
> I'll buy you coffee 😊

I don't expect the reply to be so quick.

> *How about 12 p.m. Oxford Circus*
> *station? Argyll Street exit* 😊

"He's keen." Sam peers over my shoulder.

A smile steals over my face.

Because I'm going to get some answers, that's all.

The child belonged to the dark-haired girl.
It shared her spirit, but not her doubts.
I should have paid it no heed — this
interloper in our midst. This rival for
the dark-haired girl's attention.
But I was strong, and growing stronger.
The challenge was impossible to resist.
To fill an empty vessel with my vision!
I called to the child, resolved
to make it come.

22

It takes ages to wash the hairspray and gunk out of my hair, even with Carla's posh salon shampoo. Yanking a brush through the knots, I finally get it looking almost decent.

"Want me to come with you?" Sam asks.

"I'll be OK."

I grab my grey hoodie, then change my mind and root through my case, wishing I'd put more effort into packing. My stripy top will do.

"So, he's cute then, this intern of Bella's?" Sam smirks.

I ignore him and check the time. Eleven thirty. Time to go.

"OK. Well, call me if anything feels weird."

"I told you. Everything is weird."

I give Sam a hug, then I grab my camera bag and go.

The bus drops me on the south side of Oxford Street.

Hundreds of out-of-towners are milling around, arms laden with bags. Cyclists weave through the traffic, ignoring the taxis blasting their horns. Buses are backed up in every direction, waiting to spill their loads.

I stand still, getting my bearings. Which one is Argyll Street?

A bus pulls in front of me, blocking my view. On the side of the bus is an advert. My eyes are pulled to a vibrant flash of red – a woman's mouth, her lips glossy, the colour of blood. The rest of the woman's face is obscured by dark, twisting vines. A slogan reads:

WHISPER HER NAME
01/09

I stand, entranced. It's like the strange advert in the magazine, just a different version. I still can't figure out what it's for. The bus pulls away and I snap out of my reverie. Argyll Street is up ahead. I push my way through the throng.

Jake's not there.

He isn't coming. My cheeks grow warm. His reply was too quick. He's paying me back for tricking him. I wish the ground would swallow me up.

Then I see him.

He's standing at a crossing on the other side of Oxford Street, and he's not alone. A girl is with him, tall and slim in a teeny-tiny sundress – red with white polka dots. Dark hair falls to her waist. As she laughs at something Jake says, I catch sight of her face. *Amy*. With her wide eyes and high cheekbones, she's even prettier than I thought – out-of-this-world gorgeous, like some heroine from a Disney cartoon.

I thought he wasn't into models?

The lights change. Amy pecks Jake on the cheek and skips towards H&M. I stare at the ground.

"Freya! Sorry I'm late." Jake's eyes sparkle in the sun.

"It's fine." I shuffle on the spot.

He clears his throat. "Any preference where we go?"

"Not really, I—"

"Good." He grabs my hand, taking me aback. As we weave through the crowd, I clutch my camera bag, my right hand tingling in his. His skin feels warm and rough. I worry that my palms are sweating, then I have a stern word with myself.

He's got a girlfriend, remember? And you can't compete with her.

"This way."

We turn into an alley where steep steps drop to a dead-end road. The hubbub of Oxford Street dies as we arrive at a big glass building.

LONDON CENTRE FOR PHOTOGRAPHY

Jake grins. "You know it?"

I force a smile. Dad said we'd visit this summer – it's not far from his old workshop, he said. Another broken promise since Bella came along.

"The cafe's usually quiet." Jake looks down and realizes he's still holding my hand. He drops it quickly, his face turning red. "We can go somewhere else…"

My hand feels cold now that he's let go. "No," I say. "This is good."

Apart from a woman on her laptop, we're the only people in the cafe. Jake tries to buy the coffees, but I insist. We take them to a bench, and for a moment, neither of us speaks.

"So, attic mouse." Jake breaks the silence. "You go first."

I take a deep breath. "I'm sorry I tricked you at the train station. I needed to come back."

Jake nods. "You left something here in London?"

Instinctively I touch my camera bag, but really I'm thinking of Dad. "My dad was ill. I couldn't leave him. I'm worried about him." Another breath. "Does Bella know I'm in London?"

"Of course not!" Jake looks surprised. "I told you, I need this job. I sent her a text to say you made it to school. She believed it, as far as I know."

"That's good." I relax.

"You gave me a shock yesterday."

"You surprised me too!"

"Sorry," Jake says gently. "I was only doing my job.

174

Bella said she had something heavy she needed me to transport. I couldn't refuse."

I bite my lip.

"Are you angry?"

"Yes!" I say, then I pull myself together. "But not with you. Bella's *persuasive*, I know that. But those boxes weren't hers to take. I think they belonged to my mum!"

Jake frowns. "She said it was paperwork. Important documents."

"Anything else?"

He shakes his head. "They looked like archival boxes, the kind you use for storing artwork."

Artwork. *Patterns? Designs?*

"Did you look inside?"

"No."

"Where did you take them?"

"To the agency. It's just around the corner from here. Bella and Victor are there now. They're working all weekend in Victor's office. Something about a tight deadline. Whatever they're doing, they're putting in long hours. They called me in at seven and told me to be on standby in case they need anything, but then they shut the door and said they weren't to be disturbed. That's why I could sneak out to meet you."

My legs jiggle.

Bella could be rummaging through Mum's things right this minute. I have to get them back.

"Victor keeps the office locked," Jake says, reading my mind. "Bella's got other stuff there too. Lately, she's been getting deliveries from all over – China, India, Bangladesh. Long brown rolls and parcels. I've had to sign for them. But she's moving everything soon. Victor's rented her an ... atelier, or something."

I rub my eyes. *Locked offices. Rolls. Parcels. Ateliers.* Something brushes the corners of my mind, too faint to pin down. There's something else I need to know.

"Is my dad with them at the agency? He just started working there."

"What does he look like?"

"Tall. Ginger. Freckles like mine."

Jake considers. "I don't think so. I haven't seen him. But it's a big place. There are lots of offices. He might work on a different floor?"

"I need to get a message to him." My voice is shaky. "He won't return my calls."

Jake touches my arm and a bolt of electricity shoots through me. "Hey, I know you're worried, but it's been ridiculous at the agency lately. Fashion Week is coming up."

I plead with my eyes.

"All right. If I see him, what should I say?"

"Tell him to contact me. Urgently. When he's alone."

Jake nods.

I've done all I can. Grabbing my bag, I stand up.

"You're going?" Jake frowns. "Don't you want to see the gallery?"

I hesitate. *What about Amy?*

"I thought it might be fun." He fiddles with his cup.

Fun. No big deal. Just two people looking at photos.

"OK then," I say, and Jake's eyes light up. "Maybe I could stay a little longer."

The gallery is spread over three levels. We decide to start at the top. As I stand next to Jake in the lift, I'm super aware of his body next to mine. I can even smell the clean laundry scent of his shirt.

"I've heard this exhibition is good."

"Oh. Right."

Well done, Freya. My lips feel useless, like I've forgotten how to talk. What if I say the wrong thing? I'm clearly not Jake's type, but I don't want him thinking I'm an airhead as well.

The lift doors open and we head towards the exhibition entrance.

I needn't have worried.

For one thing, Jake gives me space. He doesn't hover or lead me around. We wander at our own pace. Every so often, I glance at him. His face is screwed up, sweetly unselfconscious, deep in concentration. I start to relax.

And then there are the photographs.

Hundreds of prints, covering the walls. They capture my attention, pulling me in, until soon I've forgotten everything.

On my left is a series of black and white images – portraits of women in a city. They remind me of stills from a movie. Each woman is caught in a moment of drama: one runs along the street, her headscarf blowing in the wind. Another reads a letter, her eyes filled with concern. One leans against a door in a corridor, like she's meeting someone for a secret tryst. Each image sucks me into a story, leaving me desperate to know more.

"It's cool, isn't it? All the characters she plays."

Jake's whisper makes me shiver. He's right behind me, and my skin tingles where his arm brushes mine.

"It's the same person in every shot?"

He nods. "She's the artist too."

I look again. It *is* the same person. Just different clothes, make-up, props and locations.

"They're self-portraits," I murmur. Inside me, a tiny spark ignites.

I walk into the next room. There are more self-portraits here – but colour this time, and the characters are different. For a start, they're not attractive, at least not conventionally so. Many seem deliberately strange. In one shot, the artist is a clown. In another, she's an old man. And in one, she's posing like a king from a painting, complete with bushy eyebrows and gold chain.

I wander from image to image, losing track of time, the spark inside me now a dancing flame.

Jake is waiting by the window. "So did you like it?" His face is open, interested. It doesn't feel like a test.

I take a moment, searching for the words. "She's brave," I say, finally.

"Brave?"

"Yeah. To play with her image like that. To be

vulnerable, or ugly, or … *raw*." I cringe at my bad choice of words, but Jake doesn't laugh.

"What do you mean?" he asks.

"Well, no one takes photos like that," I say. "Not of themselves, anyway." I think of Saskia's selfies, carefully filtered and curated. "People only want to show their good sides."

Or if they're like me, they hide.

"But this artist doesn't care about that," I go on, ideas seeding in my head. "It's like she's not scared of being judged. And in the end, it makes the photos stronger…" I trail away.

Jake is looking at me strangely. I wonder if I've bored him, then he smiles. "Yeah, you're right. Real is powerful, but we airbrush it away."

My cheeks grow warm. *How does he do that?* – make me reveal the things inside my head? And how come he listens, and takes me seriously, and doesn't laugh?

Jake's gaze is intense. I look away and my hair falls into my eyes.

He tucks a strand behind my ear.

Now what's he doing? He's got a girlfriend.

I move over to the window, my head spinning. "I should probably go."

"OK…" Jake looks confused. "Um, Freya…?" He fiddles with a button on his shirt. "I'm glad you texted. This was … fun. I like the way you see things. I feel like we could be … friends."

179

Friends.

Now I understand.

My face burns again, this time with shame. *Message received loud and clear.* I'm firmly in the friend zone. That connection I've imagined? It's all in my head.

I blink rapidly, staring down at the street below.

Then I see them. The couple on the steps.

Her golden hair burns against her vivid crimson dress. He's scruffy – unkempt, even. With a pallor to his face and a stubbly copper beard.

Is it?

It is.

Bella strides along the pavement, one slender arm raised. Dad is her shadow, following unsteadily behind. A taxi pulls up and they both get inside.

"Freya, are you OK? Did I … offend you in some way?"

I push past Jake and stumble to the door. Then I'm flying down the stairwell, swerving arty curators and students on their phones. Finally, I reach ground level and barge my way outside, just in time to see the taxi turn the corner, heading towards Soho.

"Dad!"

I sprint to the end of the road, but a swarm of tourists blocks my route.

No.

Dad was here just now, but I've lost him.

And when I get back to the gallery, Jake's gone too.

23

I stagger up the steps to Oxford Street, smacking straight into a woman with a toddler. Instead of giving me an earful, her face creases with concern. "You OK, love?"

No. I turn away. Nothing is OK.

Dad was there, but then he was gone. And he didn't look any better. If anything he seemed more zombie-like than ever. Bella can't have called a doctor. Does she care about him at all?

I slide down a wall.

And Jake.

My face flames.

He's guessed I like him. He was letting me down gently,

saying he wanted to be friends. Now he thinks I flipped out. No wonder he made his escape.

I bury the thought. *Focus on facts, Freya. Remember why you came.*

Bella's got the boxes at her agency. They must be precious, or they wouldn't be under lock and key. But my chances of getting them back are next to zero, and once she moves them to this atelier, there'll be no hope at all.

My brain flickers like a moth around a lantern.

Atelier.

That word again. I barely knew it before; now I've heard it twice in as many days. At the shoot, Clarissa said one label was so new, it didn't have a design studio – an *atelier* – yet.

Nightshade. The label that made the scarlet dress.

That dress felt so familiar…

Mentally, I slip it over my body one more time. I think of the details, the bell-shaped sleeves, the little chiffon cape…

I'm on my feet.

I know where I've seen that dress.

When I reach the bus stop, the traffic is at a standstill. No one's going anywhere.

"No!" I stamp in frustration. Then I look up. The shelter is lit by an advert. Yet again, it's the glimmer of red that pulls me in. I stare at the image, dazed. The twisted vines seem almost three-dimensional, thrusting towards me. Just as before, the woman behind is totally concealed – except

182

for one milky-white ear. The red punch in this image is her earring: a ruby. It looks like a drop of blood.

HAVE YOU HEARD?
01/09

In the heat of the sun, my blood chills. I recognize that earring.

And I recognize something else.

The vines aren't climbing randomly like I thought. They've been digitally manipulated, expertly Photoshopped, to form an initial, a logo, over and over again.

The letter *N*.

N for Nightshade?

And now I'm running again: hurtling north, past the big embassies, over the Marylebone Road, skirting Regent's Park and crossing the bridge into Camden, and then I'm slamming through the tourists and the street performers and the drug dealers, until finally I'm at Sam's flat, hammering on the door, and I crash into his room, dragging everything out of my case, until I find it.

"Look!" I thrust the silver frame into Sam's hands. "See what she's wearing?"

Sam peers at the picture of Mum. "It's cute."

"It's the dress I wore at the shoot!" I say. "OK, not the exact same one. This one is silver, and it's longer too – but the sleeves are the same, and so is the cape!"

Sam squints. "I thought that red dress was by a new

designer? The dress in this picture must be … sixteen years old." He shrugs. "It's similar, sure – but fashion goes in circles. It's a coincidence, that's all."

"No." I prise the photo from the frame. "See this crease? This photo was damaged, but not by me. Someone took it out."

"What are you saying?"

"Think about it. If Mum was a fashion student, wouldn't she design her own wedding dress? You saw her sketchbook. She was talented, right?"

Sam frowns. "I didn't see a drawing of this dress."

"There was a sewing machine up in the attic!" I bang shut the lid of my case. "I bet it was Mum's. Dad can't sew! I think *she* designed the dress in this photograph, and someone borrowed the photo and copied it to make a sample. They changed the colour and the length, but it's still the same design!"

Sam's eyebrows knit. "Bella?"

"Who else?" Another realization hits me. "The night she was on the phone to Victor, she mentioned some image she'd sent. Then she said there'd be 'plenty more'. I think she meant designs! Sketchbooks, patterns, that sort of thing. Bella has been to Tokyo. Somehow she *knew* about Mum's work. Why else would she steal those boxes and lock them in the agency?"

Sam's eyes widen. "That's where they are?"

"For now. She's moving them. Victor's involved too." I'm running short of breath. "The wedding was a con. Bella needed Dad's trust to get access to my family's things! She's

184

setting up an atelier – a design studio – with a whole team of people helping!"

"Helping her with what?"

"Oh, come on, Sam!" I'm almost shouting now. "What's the biggest event in the fashion calendar?"

"Fashion Week." Sam looks grim.

"Right! It's make or break for new designers. And the next one is—"

"In September," he finishes. "It's early this year too."

I nod. "That red dress isn't a one-off. I reckon Bella's got everything planned. She's going to launch her own label at Fashion Week and pass Mum's student work off as her own. Karim said her modelling career is over, and I saw her diary – it was full of cancelled shoots. But being a designer solves the problem! Modelling doesn't last for ever, but with a fashion label of her own, she can be a player *behind the scenes* instead. She's reinventing herself." I shiver, echoing Bella's words. "It's more than a comeback. It's a *renaissance*."

"Hmm." Sam rubs his nose. "You might be right. But it's not a long-term solution. Your mum's not around any more," he says, gently. "What happens when Bella runs out of designs?" When I don't answer, he shakes his head. "I think you're drawing a lot of conclusions based on two dresses and a photo. We don't know for sure what was inside those other boxes, and there's nothing else to link Bella with … What was the label called again?"

"Nightshade. And you're wrong."

I pull out my phone and type *"Nightshade"* into the

185

search engine. It doesn't matter if Sam is sceptical. Dad's ads will change his mind. Because they can only be Dad's work. He was amazing at Photoshop, however much he claimed to hate it. This is his "talent" that Bella claimed was indispensible to her project. She made him make these creepy teaser ads to publicize her show.

The search results load.

I frown. "That's not right." I'm looking at a list of botanical websites – flowers, plants, herbs. The ads are nowhere to be seen. "I'll try again."

"Wait." Sam points at the first entry on the list. A tiny thumbnail image shows a plant with purple-black berries and a twisting stem. He reads the text underneath. "*Attractive, psychoactive, dangerous. Deadly Nightshade is an important member of the Solanaceae family…*"

"OK, but give me my phone. That's not what I want to show you."

"No, Freya," he interrupts. "Look at the Latin name."

I follow his finger. "*Atropa Belladonna.*"

Belladonna.

"Attractive, dangerous. Sound like anyone we know?"

It can't be a coincidence. Bella's ego is big enough. She's stolen Mum's designs and found a clever way to name the label after herself.

I rub my eyes after a night of broken sleep.

"You sure about this?" Sam sprawls in bed, while I pull on my hoodie. It's early Sunday morning, a little after eight.

"Totally sure." I reach for my trainers. "Jake said that Bella's working all hours at the agency this weekend. She's probably going through Mum's work this instant." My jaw clenches. "Dad wasn't with her. He'll be at home, alone, right now. I can talk to him properly – tell him what's going on."

Sam raises an eyebrow. "If he doesn't already know."

I tug at my laces, pretending not to hear. We've already been over this.

Last night, after a little more searching, I finally found what I'd been looking for. Proof of Nightshade, the label. There were brand-new social media accounts, and even an official website. The home page said it all.

NIGHTSHADE
S/S
PRÊT-À-PORTER
Launching 1 September
London Fashion Week

"The spring/summer ready-to-wear collection," Sam had translated. "Looks like the show is scheduled for 1st September. Wow, Bella's team will have to work fast. That's less than three weeks away!"

1st September.

My heart had squeezed, remembering the illustration in Bella's diary – the initial *N* that I mistook to mean "Nick".

Sam's next words had filled me with dread.

"You're assuming your dad is clueless, Freya. But what if he's helping Bella? He hid your mum's past, and he created these ads. What if he deliberately told her about your mum's work and where to find it?"

"No." I refused to believe it. "Look at the ads. They're ambiguous. They're designed to get your attention, to make you wonder. But they don't say 'Nightshade', and they don't show any clothes. Dad could have made them without knowing what they were for. He wasn't there when Bella took the boxes, and he wasn't in the office with her and Victor. I bet he doesn't know a thing."

I'm not sure Sam was convinced.

I pull up my hoodie and tiptoe out of the flat, leaving Sam and his dodgy conspiracy theory behind. But as I cut down the alley to my house, fear swirls in my belly.

Dad wouldn't betray Mum's memory. Would he?

I have to act quickly, while Dad is home alone.

It's the only way I'll get the truth.

Something feels off as soon as I open the door. The house is too quiet. There's a chill in the air.

"Dad?"

No reply.

Downstairs is dark, the blinds drawn. The cat flap clatters, making me jump. Kodak shoots in, hungry. No, starving.

"Poor kitty. Haven't you been fed?" Quickly, I put down food in the silent kitchen and rush upstairs, heart racing.

"Dad?" My voice bounces off the walls.

Their bedroom door is wide open and the first things I see are the suitcases. Two of them, sitting at the end of the bed. One is swanky and designer, the other old and battered. As different as the people who own them.

What's going on?

A bad feeling worms its way inside me. I fling open the wardrobe: bare shelves and empty hangers. I check the drawers; they're empty too.

My chest feels tight.

Bella and Dad are leaving. Leaving, without telling me. They're going somewhere, but where?

I sink on to the bed.

That's when I feel it. The sensation of being watched. A tug, like puppet strings, making me lift my head.

Come.

I look up. Bella's mirror is sitting on the chest of drawers. It's been carefully wrapped in bubble wrap, but the tape has come unstuck. The top edge of the frame and a portion of glass is peeping out.

Come.

The mirror pulls me to it. My brain goes foggy, my limbs numb. I can't resist or move away.

Look.

Wordlessly, I obey. My fingers move without my bidding, yanking off the rest of the bubble wrap and pulling the glass towards me. My questions about Dad and Bella seem like a distant dream.

Poor Freya. Still so flawed.
Remember, I can help.

The whisper is soothing, yet sly. Like an invisible frenemy, balancing sympathy with shame. I lean into the cloudy glass and stare at my reflection: murky eyes, wonky nose. Two limp curtains of hair. A brand-new pimple glows like a beacon on my chin.

I can make you perfect.

The glass seems to flash and the surface ripples. I don't flinch or look away. Suddenly, I know that if I keep on looking, I'll see that flawless girl again.

The need to see her is overwhelming.

Yes. Go on. Show me.

My face begins to change.

Like the sun emerging from behind a cloud, my skin softens and smooths and clears. My freckles fade. My nose straightens. My pimple disappears. My hair hangs glossy, richer, full. I stare at this Mirror Me, enraptured. My face is balanced, proportioned, symmetrical. My eyes are bigger, brighter, blue. Everything about me is vibrant, saturated…

Perfect.

Just like Bella. I almost swoon.

And now my head fills with another sound: a murmur, growing clear.

All shall be perfect.

All shall be perfect.

Do you believe it, Freya? Tell me.

"All shall be perfect," I say it slowly, savouring the taste.

Again.

"All shall be perfect," I repeat the words, growing more and more certain each time.

A noise breaks my concentration and I groan. In the side street, a vehicle is reversing. The beeping and the blaring radio are impossible to ignore. Brakes screech, doors slam, footsteps pound the pavement. Someone's speaking, making a call.

"Which house is it? Number five?"

I snap out of my trance. Tearing myself from the mirror, I lurch to the window.

A van is parked on the street below.

24

My brain wastes seconds trying to process. Downstairs, the front door clicks.

I throw myself under the bed, crawling as far as I can. My heart explodes like popcorn in my chest.

"What am I collecting?" a rough voice barks.

The tinny sound of a person on speakerphone: "She said it would all be upstairs, ready to go."

A pair of brown work boots enters the room, grinding flakes of mud into the carpet. I turn myself to stone.

"Just the two cases? Is that all?"

"Apparently there's a mirror too."

Brown Boots pauses by the chest of drawers. "This

thing? It looks antique. The wrapping's come off. I'm not taking responsibility if it gets smashed."

"Chuck something over it."

"Like what?"

"Dunno, a towel?"

"I'll look. Move, cat."

Kodak is in the doorway. She skitters sideways as Brown Boots disappears into the hall. Picking up my scent, she pokes her head under the bed.

"No, Kodak. Shoo!" My arm is throbbing with pins and needles. Something hard is wedged against my leg. I can't shift position, though; Brown Boots will be back soon.

Sure enough, he returns from the bathroom, trailing one of our towels. I hear muffled sounds, then Dad and Bella's suitcases are dragged into the hall.

"I'll stick the mirror up front. How far have I gotta go?"

"Central London first, then south east, near the river. I'll text you the addresses." The tinny voice is drowned out by the sound of suitcases bumping down the stairs.

The door slams and I unfreeze.

The first thing I do is reach down to remove whatever is imprinted in my thigh. My fingers close around hard plastic. I ease into the room on my elbows and look at the object in my hand.

It's an iPhone – an old one – in a faded black case. The screen is a spider's web of shattered glass. Despite that, I recognize it straight away.

It's Dad's.

I switch it on. The screen blazes with rainbow-coloured lines and scattered pixels, impossible to read. It flickers a moment, then dies.

I pull out my own phone, and text Sam.

U still at home?

Just on Parkway, why?

Can you meet me on Primrose Hill?
It's urgent!

I stumble on to the street. My brain feels mushy, slow to process. Just when I thought I'd figured things out, Bella manages to stay a step ahead. If it's not bad enough that she's stolen Mum's designs, now she's stolen Dad as well.

I turn over the phone in my hand. The glass splinters graze my skin.

Did Dad go willingly? Or was he forced?

After all, how useful is he to Bella now? She's got what she wanted – access to Mum's designs. He's done her dirty work and made her creepy ads.

I shiver in the heat.

And what about her mirror?

This time, I *know* I wasn't imagining things. My flaws – they had gone.

I cross the footbridge that leads to Primrose Hill.

Her mirror is magic.

It can't be true, but it's the only explanation. Is that how Bella manages to look so extraordinary – without beauty products or make-up? *Otherworldly*, Karim said. Is it the mirror's doing? Does it have *supernatural* powers? I shake my head. It's totally impossible, I—

"Hey!" A guy slams into me, sending Dad's phone flying. "Watch where you're going!" Our eyes meet and he double-takes. "Sorry, sorry. My bad. Let me get that for you." He scrabbles in the gutter for Dad's phone. "Oh man. It's smashed."

"It was broken already." I take the phone and go to walk on, but now the guy is blocking my way.

"Let me buy you coffee to apologize." He moves closer, flashing a grin. "You're stunning, sweetheart. Did anyone ever tell you that?"

I blink at him. "Let me past."

"Aww, at least tell me your name."

I dart around him and break into a run. Primrose Hill lies just ahead, beyond a parade of swanky shops. I head towards it, not stopping until I've left Creepy Guy far behind. I pause to catch my breath in front of a chic boutique selling designer outfits for dogs.

But as I gaze through the window, it's not the ridiculous prices that make my heart start beating triple-time.

Mirror Me is looking back.

The child touched my glass, and
I knew what I must do.
Before it would listen, I
had to make it doubt.
So I whispered. Broke its will.
Poured dark fears into its head.
I killed its confidence stone dead.
It happened so quickly.
The child screamed. The tide turned.
And all at once, I knew: I'd lost
my grip on the dark-haired girl.
She came at me with violence in her eyes.
I pleaded, but her mind was shut.
And then, an angel saved me.

25

The mirror's magic – the illusion – it's fixed.

All shall be perfect.

I spoke the words aloud. That's what did it.

I'm perfect.

I swear I feel a difference as soon as I reach the park. Someone holds the gate open for me. People step aside to let me pass. I throw back my shoulders and lift my chin, trying to suppress a smile.

So *this* is what it's like to be Bella.

I amble towards the summit of the hill. The urgency I felt when I texted Sam has started to slip away. The day is scorching, and dozens of people are here. Families with picnics, couples holding hands, and hordes of Camden teenagers lounging on the grass.

I sense them looking. Heads turning. Eyes tracking as I climb the hill. I let them stare, taking my time, revelling in the attention. It's exhilarating, satisfying. A shivery sort of thrill.

All too soon, I reach the summit. Sam's not there, so I pull out my camera instead. London is like me, a feast for the eyes, dazzling and gorgeous in my lens. In a daze, I take pictures – *zoom, frame, focus, click* – thoughts of Dad and Bella fading away.

"Oh. My. God. *Is that…?*"

Voices wake me from my weird, distracted state. Strutting towards me, tanned and taut in scarlet-splashed sundresses, are Saskia, Ruby and Lila.

"It *is*."

"*No way.*"

"What did she *do*?"

I glance about me, but no one else is near.

"What happened to you, Freya?"

They stare, open-mouthed.

"You actually look decent, for a change."

I glance at Saskia. She hasn't spoken yet. The three girls cluster around me.

"You changed your hair!" Lila reaches out to touch.

"Who did your make-up?" Ruby demands.

"No one." I smile.

"Don't lie." She frowns. "You couldn't do that on your

own. That's a professional job. Tell us who did it. I want their number."

"Did *Bella* help you?" Saskia says slowly. She turns to the other girls. "Freya's dad is married to Belladonna Wilde."

The girls start talking over each other at once.

Saskia moves closer, all smiles. "You can hang out with us, Freya. If you want."

"Maybe." I shrug. I'm busy admiring her dress. I wish I was wearing a cute red sundress, instead of my baggy shirt and jeans. I need to showcase myself, and that colour looks incredible – I must tell Sam. I don't know why I've never worn it before.

Hazily, I look around. There's still no sign of Sam, but nearby some boys our age are lying on the grass. They're watching us. Saskia's noticed too. She slips an arm around me.

"I didn't know you take pictures, Freya." She flicks her hair. "Will you take a shot of us?"

"Ooh, yes!" Lila chimes in. Ruby begins to preen.

"I suppose." I lift up my camera. But someone interrupts us.

"'Scuse me." One of the boys has swaggered up. Tall, with smooth skin and diamond studs in both ears, he's obviously the leader of the group.

"Why don't I take a picture of you ladies? Can't leave you out, gorgeous." He winks at me.

Saskia stiffens, but covers it with a laugh. "Oh, yeah, sure. Freya should be in it too." She nudges Ruby and Lila aside to make room.

"Give me your camera, then." The boy holds out his hand.

I hesitate.

"No! Use my phone!" Saskia giggles. "Then I can share it on my socials."

"Whatever." He takes the phone, ignoring her. His lazy smile is all for me.

The girls crowd around me, their bodies squished in tightly. Before I know it, we're posing and pouting as one. Behind the phone, Diamond Stud leers. When I catch his eye, he licks his lips. My head spins. *He likes me best. Of course he does!* The feeling is powerful – a proper rush. I start to relax. Sam says I shouldn't hide, and maybe I don't have to...

Not now that I'm perfect.

"Hot." Diamond Stud is by my side, handing back Saskia's phone. "I put my number in, so you can send that shot to me." His arm snakes around my shoulders.

Just then, a shape in the distance catches my eye. A boy with scruffy dark hair and a lean, angular body is climbing the path to the summit.

Jake. My heart flips. *What's he doing here?*

A girl catches up to Jake and flings an arm around his shoulders. She's slim and striking, with glossy, waist-length hair.

Amy. I scowl. *That's right. She lives in Primrose Hill.*

They're heading towards us.

Snapping out of my stupor, I stand up taller, willing Jake

to look my way. He only knows the old Freya – poor, sad, friend-zone Freya.

Flawless Freya is in a different league.

Metres from the summit, he finally looks up. Our eyes lock and I see a flash of recognition, feel time stand still as Jake absorbs the scene. Diamond Stud whispers in my ear. I smile, but I'm not really listening. I'm focused on Jake, waiting for his face to change.

And it does.

Surprise. Confusion. *Hurt?*

Pulling Amy's arm, he veers away.

I don't understand.

"I should go," I mumble, thrusting the phone at Saskia.

"What's the rush?" Diamond Stud strokes my arm.

"I'm … meeting a friend."

"A boyfriend?"

"Freya doesn't have a boyfriend," Lila offers, helpfully.

Diamond Stud nods. "Good to know." He pulls me closer. "Freya, is it? Come on, Freya. Stay and hang out with me."

"Uh…" My head feels woozy. My thoughts won't clear. I don't think I like this boy and I need to find Sam, but Jake's reaction has thrown me. Plus, it's kind of irresistible – the way Diamond Stud ignores Saskia. The way he prefers me.

"*Freya?*"

I swing round to find Sam, glaring at me.

Diamond Stud drops his arm. "I was just messin', man.

201

No offence, yeah?" He slaps Sam's shoulder, and saunters back to his crew. Saskia and the others follow.

Sam's face is stony.

"Freya, what's going on? I was meeting Liam when your text came through. You said it was urgent! I thought you were in trouble! Then I find you hanging out with shallow Saskia and the vacant twins. And why do you look like *that*?"

"Like what?" I scowl.

"What have you done to your face? Are you wearing make-up? Did *they* do that to you?"

"Of course not!" I snap.

"You look *bizarre*."

"That's rich, coming from you." The mean words fall out easily.

Sam looks hurt. "Well, fill me in, Freya, because you're weirding me out. I thought you went to find your dad."

The mention of Dad cracks my defences. My head starts to clear. "I can explain."

I drag Sam to a bench in a quiet corner of the park.

"Dad and Bella have gone. Disappeared. Their bags were packed. A guy came while I was at the house and took everything away in a van, even Bella's mirror. I don't think they're coming back. I found Dad's phone smashed up."

"Smashed?" Sam echoes.

I show him. "It won't switch on, so I can't check his messages, and I don't know Bella's number. I've got no way of contacting him or knowing where he is. He could be anywhere!"

"OK…" Sam frowns. "But that doesn't explain *this*." He gestures at my face.

I pause. "I know it sounds ridiculous, but it's the mirror."

"Bella's mirror?" Sam rolls his eyes. "Let me guess. It's magic?"

"Just listen! It was at the house," I go on. "I looked into it. I didn't have any choice; it made me." Sam snorts. "It did! And then it made me whisper something, like a spell. I've seen Bella do it too! This is what happens."

"Freya…"

"I'm telling the truth!" I'm getting angry now. "The mirror erases any flaws. And if you repeat the spell while you're looking into the glass, the illusion lasts! That's why Bella doesn't need beauty products or make-up. That's why she looks the way she does."

"What words do you say?" Sam's eyes are narrow.

I swallow. "*All shall be perfect.*"

He shakes his head.

"Sam, look!" I grab his arm. "Look at me! I'm proof!"

He studies me closely, lips pursed. Finally, he nods. "OK, I believe you, I guess. Not sure about *perfect,* but you do look flawless, if that's what you mean. It's eerie. But say this mirror *is* magic, why didn't it work on me? I looked into it, remember? I didn't see anything strange."

I shrug. "Maybe you … don't need it?"

Sam guffaws, but suddenly I wonder if I'm right. I hate mirrors, yet Bella's attracts me like a magnet. Does it pick up on my insecurities – feed off them, even? There are loads of things I'd change about myself, but Sam is different. He's happy with the way he looks.

"*You* don't need it, Freya!" He sighs. "There was nothing wrong with the old you. At least the old you was unique! Now you remind me of *them*." He glances at Ruby, Lila and Saskia, draped over Diamond Stud on the other side of the hill. "It's like you're wearing a mask. It gives me the creeps."

I clench my fists. "Don't be hypocritical! You're into make-up. Why do people use it, if not to cover their flaws? You're OK with that, right? Why not this?"

Sam gives me a pitying look. "You really don't get it, do you? Make-up isn't just for covering stuff up. It's about making a statement, expressing yourself. I'd never want to make everyone look the same. Kevyn Aucoin – he was this amazing make-up artist – he said, 'Perfection is boring. If a face doesn't have mistakes, it's nothing'. But I don't expect you to understand that. You're way too scared to stand out."

I glare at Sam. His criticism stings. Being perfect is not at all what I expected. So far it seems to have created more problems than it's solved.

"Whatever," I say, getting to my feet. "I need to find my dad." I lift up my camera and focus on the city again. "The van was going into central London, then south east, near the river. I bet one of those places is Bella's atelier, but I don't know where to start looking."

Sam tuts. "So contact that intern. He'll know."

"Jake?" My face grows warm behind my lens. "I'm not sure he'll help."

"I thought he was into you." Sam peers at me closely. "Or is it the other way around? Wait. Is *that* who you're trying to impress?"

I storm across the grass, fuming. Sam runs to catch up. His phone starts ringing, but he ignores it.

"Freya, stop. I was only teasing. Look, your dad is missing. I get why you're upset. Maybe you should go to the police – file a report? They'll help you find him. You can report Bella as well. If she *has* stolen your mum's work, the police can investigate. It's a crime – intellectual property theft – I looked it up. You can be sent to prison!"

Prison?

I go cold. What if Dad *has* been helping Bella? Could that happen to him too? He's the only family I've got.

"I can't involve the police," I say. "Not before I've spoken to Dad. I need to find him." I turn to Sam. "Promise me you'll help?"

Sam looks at his feet. "I'll try."

"What do you mean, you'll *try*?"

His phone beeps yet again. "Freya, there's something I need to tell you. Dad and I – we sorted stuff out."

"You mean you told him? Everything?"

"Not exactly." Sam won't meet my eye. He crushes a dandelion under his heel. "I agreed to do the apprenticeship. Said I might go into business with him properly one day. He's really chuffed. He's got more work lined up over summer, so I'm gonna be pretty busy—"

"You changed your mind? What about the other day? You said—"

"That was a silly idea. I wasn't serious." Sam's face is red. "Liam told me how competitive it is, doing hair and make-up. I probably wouldn't be any good…"

"How do you know?" I burst out. "You're giving up, just like that?"

"I wanna make my dad happy," Sam mutters.

"But *you* won't be happy. It's not '*who you are*'." I don't know where the nasty voice comes from.

"Well, neither is *that*." Sam gestures at my face. "So we're even."

I'm silent.

He rubs his forehead. "Look, Freya, I've made a decision and I'm good with it. So let's leave it, OK?" Checking his phone, he sighs. "I'd better get back. Guess I'll see you later."

He shuffles off down the hill.

I watch him go, my heart heavy – and not just because I think Sam's making a mistake. The weight of the task ahead of me is pressing on my chest.

Evidence. That's what I need.

I need to find the Nightshade atelier and collect evidence against Bella. I'll prove she stole Mum's designs without Dad's knowledge. I'll establish his innocence and expose her lies.

Even if I have to do it alone.

26

When I get back to the flat, Sam and Tom are thick as thieves, watching some movie on Netflix. I make my excuses and head to Sam's room. Tom doesn't seem to notice my appearance, and Carla only calls out a greeting as I pass the kitchen door. For a second, I'm tempted to tell her everything, but what good would it do? Like Sam, she'll only suggest going to the police, and that's not an option. I've no real evidence of Bella's plans, no proof that Dad's in danger – and none that he's innocent either.

I take a shower and gaze at myself in the glass. Mirror Me is still there, looking back. I drink in my reflection, drowning out Jake's hurt, Sam's disapproval.

Perfect.

I can't get enough.

But how long will the magic last?

I find out the next day.

I wake up feeling groggy, body aching and head throbbing like I'm coming down with something. Sam is still fast asleep. I drag myself to the bathroom, then I see.

I'm me again.

Familiar, flawed Freya.

Dismay punches me in the gut. I limp back to bed, wallowing in self-pity. *I need it. I need the mirror.* The craving is alarming. In spite of the problems being perfect caused, I'm desperate to see Mirror Me again.

I reach for my phone.

Saskia's socials – I can check them. She's bound to have posted that picture. I scroll through her feed, searching.

There.

I shiver. The photo was shared yesterday afternoon, but the likes and comments are still coming in. Hundreds of people from school, from everywhere – all gushing and fawning over Saskia, Ruby, Lila…

And me.

> *isaac.baynes: Wow, Freya Jones – what a glow up!*
> *FlossieF: You guys look AMAZING!*
> *The_Real_SkyeG: OMG FREYA!* ♥ ♥ ♥

My skin tingles. Now I understand. This is what Bella loves – the thrill of other people's approval. She must have been devastated when it stopped.

Why has it stopped?

I put down my phone and think. Bella's mirror makes her perfect in real life, but her photos have started to tell a different story – hence her fear of the camera, her plan for a career behind the scenes.

And yet, the magic must have worked in pictures once. That would explain why her career took off like magic overnight, and why the illusion is so strong for me, in Saskia's photo, here.

Does the magic get weaker over time?

It could be that. But my strange sluggish feeling makes me wonder.

What if the mirror is addictive? What if it's like a drug, and Bella's used too much? Or what if it's simply no match for the natural ageing process?

Taking one last look at Saskia's feed, I force myself to face the truth. The reason doesn't really matter. In the end, what's happening to Bella would end up happening to me. These "likes" are bewitching, but they're based on lies. I haven't done anything to earn them.

They're for Mirror Me. Not the real me.

Do I want to be an addict, like Bella?

I try to talk my theories through with Sam, but things feel different between us – strained – like they've never been before. The next few days pass, and I barely see him at all. Tom's latest job is a revamp of some Highgate mansion and Sam leaves most days before I'm awake. He comes back in the evenings, overalls stinking, acting oafish and cracking jokes with Tom. I guess he really *is* good with his decision – although he never wants to talk about his day, and when I dare to ask if he's heard from Liam, he silences me with a death stare.

As for me, I've hit a wall. Alone in the flat for most of the day, I've got all the time in the world to obsess about Bella and her plans, but not the faintest idea of how to stop her. Meanwhile, my fears about Dad only grow. I'm sure that finding the Nightshade atelier is the key. But I need to act fast. It's mid–August, two weeks until 1st September, the day of the Nightshade show.

I stalk the internet, digging for information – any crumb or hint of a lead. At first, there isn't much – though Dad's eerie images seem to be everywhere, with their cryptic banners, and hypnotic pops of red. And I can see how this air of mystery is working to Bella's advantage. As I wade through myriad fashion blogs and websites, one thing is crystal clear.

People are talking about Nightshade.

Like a magic beanstalk, sprouting from the tiniest of seeds, the mentions seem to double by the day. It's a perfect word–of–mouth campaign, fuelled by hints and rumours: one blogger is suggesting that Nightshade is funded by the mafia. Another influencer is claiming that a huge

Hollywood celebrity will be opening the show. Someone else is speculating that the entire collection has been produced in Indian sweatshops. It doesn't seem to matter if the gossip is good or bad. The posts are shared over and over, and as people work themselves into a frenzy, the Nightshade hashtag starts to trend.

On Friday, I gape at my laptop, astonished.

In less than a week, Nightshade has gone from Complete Unknown to the Next Big Thing. It seems so fast – exactly like Bella's rapid rise to fame. Now I only have to type "Nightshade Fashion Show" and I'm bombarded – not only with Dad's mesmerizing images, but a long list of questions as well.

People also ask:

Where is the Nightshade show taking place?
Who is the designer behind Nightshade?
Where can I buy the Nightshade collection?
Is Nightshade the most important show at London Fashion Week?
Which models are walking in the Nightshade show?

So much speculation. Still no real answers.

I'm about to close my laptop, when I read the fifth question again. Two clicks later, and I'm on a daily fashion news site.

RED IS THE NEW BLACK

International models will descend on London next week when castings begin for September's hotly anticipated Fashion Week. And the show they all want to walk in? Mysterious newcomer *Nightshade*. The new label is rumoured to be the vision of a significant fashion player, and reports suggest this label has BIG plans for expansion. One thing's for sure, until the collection is revealed on 1st September, we're all OBSESSED with that signature red.

Red.

I've been seeing it everywhere. Not just on Bella, on other people too. Ever since Dad's ads first appeared.

But there's no time to think about it. A germ of an idea has rooted in my mind, so terrifying I can hardly face it.

Bella needs models for her show.

And to choose those models, there'll be a casting.

A casting.

A casting isn't a rumour, it's an actual event. An event where I could find things out, maybe even get access to the atelier. Then I could gather evidence against Bella. Evidence I can use to stop her.

And Dad might be there too.

I take a deep breath.

I thought I was finished with Bella's world. Perhaps it's not finished with me?

*

I text the one person I can think of who might help.

> Hi Jas, it's Freya. Can I ask
> you something, please?

Hey, Freya! Great to hear from you.
I've been meaning to get in touch.
Might have good news, I'll know more soon.
What's up?

Butterflies flutter.

> I heard about the Fashion Week castings.
> Can anybody try out?

Like you?
Models need to be 18.
And have an agency.
Sorry ☹

Deep breath. *Nobody said this would be easy.*
   I try a different tack. Fingers crossed Jas bites.

> Not for me. Project for college.
> 'Behind the scenes at Fashion Week'.

Oh, I see. No probs!
What do you want to know?

Where do the castings take place?

It depends. PR agencies or casting suites.

Not at the designer's atelier?

Not usually.

Hmm. That's disappointing. But it's not the end of the world.

What happens at a casting?

Models show up, try on clothes.
That's pretty much it!

Clothes from the collection?

Yes.

My heart skips a beat. *Clothes would definitely be evidence if I could show that they match Mum's designs.*

Who do the models see?

Whoever's head of casting.

I swallow.

Would that be the designer?

No. Usually a casting director or stylist.
Clarissa's casting loads of shows this season.

I breathe. This is good.

What do you know about the
Nightshade casting?
Any idea when or where it's happening?

LOL. Not you too!
Everyone is talking about that show.
I've never seen anything like it.
Why do you need to know?

Think, Freya.

I want to get an interview for my project.
Maybe from someone at the casting.

I wait.

Good luck with that.

A pause.

I can try and find out more if you want?

215

Could you?

No promises. Leave it with me x

I put down the phone, hands sweaty. Am I losing the plot? The Freya of a few weeks ago would never have done something like this. But that Freya would never have believed in malicious models and magic mirrors, either.

Things are different now. I'm desperate.

And if the next part of my plan works, I won't have to be Freya at all.

27

"You want to do the fashion-show castings?" Sam's jaw drops. "As a model?"

I nod. "Only one. The Nightshade show."

He whistles and shakes his head. His face is so speckled with paint, he gives my freckles a run for their money. Tossing his trainers across the room, he grabs a towel for his shower.

"Wait," I say, blocking his way. "Hear me out. In two weeks' time, Bella is going to get credit for work that isn't hers. I can't sit around and watch that happen! People are already going wild talking about it. She'll have money, power, a brand-new career – all at my family's expense.

217

She tricked Dad into helping her…" I give Sam a look, challenging him to disagree. "And now he's finished being useful, he's gone. I'm scared of what she's done." I swallow.

Sam narrows his eyes. "How does going to the casting help?"

"It gets me closer to the truth. I need to find the atelier and talk to Dad. If I can prove what Bella's doing, we can stop the Nightshade show from going ahead."

Sam looks sceptical. "You're forgetting something. Bella will recognize you. She'll throw you out."

"She won't be at the casting," I tell him. "Jas said that casting directors and stylists select models for the shows."

He raises an eyebrow. "It's still risky."

I nod. "That's why I was wondering…" I hug my knees to my chest and try to sound casual. "You said make-up isn't just covering stuff up. Could someone use it, not to *perfect* their face, but to *disguise* it?"

Sam pauses in the doorway. "I guess."

"How different could a person look?"

He considers. "Totally different," he says eventually. "You can do all kinds of stuff. There are loads of videos online."

"Could *you* do it?"

"*Me?*"

I nod. "Why not? You're an amazing artist."

He looks at me. "What exactly do you mean by *disguise?*"

"I can't go to this casting as myself," I explain. "I'm too young for a start, and it's too risky. But I *could* go as someone else." I think of the photos in the exhibition. "Like an actor, playing a part. But I need to look different – totally unrecognizable. Could you do it?" I hold my breath.

A smile flits across Sam's lips. "Probably." Then he scowls. "I know what you're up to, Freya. I'm not gonna mess things up with Dad."

I hold up my hands. "You'd be doing me a favour, that's all."

Suddenly he throws down his towel and sweeps up my hair. "The quickest way would be to use a wig."

"Could we get one?"

"There are some at the salon. The junior stylists practise on them. They're made of real hair, it's more convincing than synthetic." Excitement dances across his face.

"What about make-up? I don't have any of my own."

"No problem." He drops to his knees and drags a big black container out from under the bed. "Jenna left some stuff when she went travelling." I notice the expert way he pops the clasps. "We could contour your face a bit, change the shape slightly. But whatever we do, it would have to look natural. Models don't go to castings all made up."

"As long as I don't look like me."

Sam rifles through Jenna's stash. "When does this need to happen?"

"Soon." I drop down beside him. "Jas said she'd find out the details. Probably sometime next week."

"Next week?" Sam lays down the brush in his hand. "I'll be working with Dad."

"Every day?" My shoulders slump. "Can't you ask for time off?"

"And tell him what?"

"The truth?"

"Not this again." Sam slams the make-up box shut. Shoving it under the bed, he gets to his feet.

"Sam." I grab his hand. "Don't you want to know if you can do this? I can't manage by myself. I wouldn't know one end of a mascara stick from the other."

"Wand."

"What?"

He sighs. "It's called a mascara wand."

"See?"

He doesn't smile.

"I don't know what else to do," I say softly, scouring his face for a sign that he hasn't totally dismissed the idea. "Please, Sam. Will you help?"

He gives a tiny nod. "I suppose I'll think of something."

Jas's email arrives on Sunday night.

I blink at the screen. She's sent through the entire week's schedule of show castings. Many of the labels are household names. Saskia would give up her monthly manicure for this kind of fashion-world access. It feels wrong to waste it on me.

I scroll through the list, snakes squirming in my tummy.

"There." Sam points to the bottom of the page.

NIGHTSHADE
Casting 21st August.
2–4 p.m.
Requests only.
Warwick D'Angelo Productions
Redcross Way, SE1 1TA

"The twenty-first is tomorrow!" My heart is in my mouth. "What will you tell your dad?"

"Food poisoning," Sam shoots back. "He won't risk me puking on the client's rugs. They cost more than our flat." He reads the address again. "Redcross Way. That's south east, by the river. You think it's the atelier?"

"Warwick D'Angelo Productions…"

Sam shakes his head. "Right. Sounds like a casting studio to me."

"That's OK," I say. "I can still keep my eyes open, ask questions, find out stuff. And Bella won't be there."

"True." Sam snatches up some paper from his desk, his pencil flying as he starts to sketch. "So let's plan your disguise. You're gonna slay this, Freya."

"Um… You do know that's not the aim here? I don't want to get cast in the show, remember? I need to blend in, not stand out!"

"As usual." Sam sighs, flipping the paper around for me to see. The girl in his drawing oozes cool blonde, boho-hippy chic. "Doesn't mean you can't slay a teeny bit."

*

I relay the food-poisoning story at breakfast, while Sam groans dramatically in bed. Tom seems to buy it, but Carla raises an eyebrow.

"Your dad believed me, but I don't think your mum did," I say, back in the bedroom.

He shrugs. "If I'm going to borrow a wig from the salon, she'll need to know anyway."

On cue, Carla appears in the doorway and Sam launches his appeal.

"I don't know, love," she says when he's finished. "I understand that you want to help Freya, but I don't like you lying to your dad."

"Please, Mum!" Sam makes puppy eyes.

"Why can't Freya go to this casting as she is?"

We exchange glances. "It's ... complicated," I mutter.

Luckily, Carla doesn't press it. "OK. Come to the salon at eleven. I'll dig out what you need."

"You're the best!" Sam hugs her. "You won't tell Dad, will you?"

His mum frowns. "I won't. But, Sam—"

"What?"

"I wish *you* would."

It's midday, two hours before the Nightshade casting is due to start, and Sam has just come back from the salon.

I watch him lay out Jenna's products on his bed. Bullet-shaped lipsticks. Sharp kohl pencils. A proper beauty arsenal. For the first time ever, it makes me feel ... *excited*.

"You're sure you can do this?" I ask Sam.

"Oh, *now* you doubt my skills?" He tuts. "Don't worry. I know what I'm doing. I think."

He roots through the box, carefully selecting the products he wants to use, before turning his attention to some brushes. I smile as he inspects them. He starts his art projects exactly the same way.

Satisfied, he turns to the duffel bag on the floor, bulging since his trip to the salon. I watch him pull out an endless stream of items — high-tech hairdryer, hairbrushes, hair ties, hairspray — like Mary Poppins with her bottomless carpet bag.

If Mary Poppins wore hair gel and Adidas.

I lean over, trying to see what else is in there. At the bottom of the bag, wrapped in plastic, something soft and sandy is curled up like an animal.

"Is that…?"

"Yup." Sam lifts the wig out tenderly. Shoulder-length blonde with soft, wispy layers. It's the good hair day I've never had.

"It looks so real." I stroke a silky strand.

"That's because it is." Sam pulls out a chair and motions me to sit. He props up his phone in front of me. "You need to watch this. For inspiration."

He presses play on a video of a fashion show. The models glide, like they're walking on air. I shake my head. "How do they do that?"

"It's not that hard." Sam shrugs. "Shoulders back, walk

from the hips, one foot in front of the other." He sashays across the room.

"More rules." I laugh nervously. "I'm glad I've got an expert to help."

"That's me! An encyclopedia of fashion knowledge." Sam points at the video, coming to an end. He puts on a nerdy voice. "Did you know, the final look in a fashion show is traditionally the bride?"

"Is that true?"

He nods. "But never mind that. Turn round. We've got work to do."

He lifts my chin just like Karim did, and I pretend not to notice his trembling fingers. Falling silent as he works, I watch as he blends foundation on his hand, tongue poking out between his lips. Mentally, I frame a shot. There's no mirror, so I can't see his progress and I don't ask in case I put him off. When he's finished the base, he picks up a large brush and a slightly darker powder.

"Contour time," he announces, sweeping the sides of my cheeks and the edges of my nose. "It's just like shading, really."

His attention turns to my eyes and lips, fingers moving fluidly. He's moved into that weird state of flow I recognize from taking pictures – where time stands still and nothing else matters.

Finally, he's finished on my face. "Ready for your wig?" he asks, coiling my real hair tightly into a bun and pinning it flat. He fixes it with a quick spritz of hairspray.

Then he eases the wig on to my head. I'm expecting it to itch, but it's surprisingly comfortable, even snug. Long sandy strands graze my shoulders and fall into my eyes.

"Done." Sam passes me a hand mirror.

I gasp. Looking back is someone else. Not me. Not even Mirror Me. A different girl completely – a sun-kissed summer blonde, fresh from some cool music festival.

"How did you do that?"

"It wasn't hard." Sam smiles shyly.

I stare, mouth open. The only giveaway is a smattering of my freckles peeking through. Sam's struck the perfect balance: a dramatic transformation that still looks completely natural.

"You really *can* do this," I say.

His neck turns red. "It's just drawing and painting. Now what are you going to wear?"

"Um … jeans?"

"Let's see what Jenna left behind." Sam roots through a drawer and tosses me something. "This could work."

A tiny blue dress with a daisy print. It wouldn't be my choice, but this isn't about me. This is a costume. With its carefree summer vibe, I admit, the dress works for the character.

I check myself out in the hall mirror. My disguise is really good. I'm not Freya Jones, I'm some up-and-coming starlet with a backstage pass for Glastonbury. Is this the secret to confidence – playing someone else?

"Not those," I tell Sam, who's holding out a pair of

Jenna's strappy sandals. I reach for my trainers. "I won't fly under the radar if I fall on my face."

He shrugs. "It was worth a try."

I'm ready. It's time to go. Before we leave the flat, I pick up my camera and slip it into my bag.

"Final accessory. Just in case."

A golden-haired angel saved
me from destruction.
An ally, who shared my feelings of betrayal.
Rage simmered beneath my silver
surface. My work was wasted. My
vision dead before it could be born.
My angel understood.
As she looked into my glass, I
recognized ambition, and something
else: a hunger for revenge.
The dark-haired girl was dangerous,
now — a threat to be contained.
I whispered instructions in
my golden girl's ear.

28

We head to Chalk Farm station.

It's strange, being out on the street like *this*. A fancy-dress parade for one, the real me buried far beneath. I yank Jenna's dress over my thighs, my legs pale and ghostlike in the sun. I can't stop touching my new blonde tresses.

"Stop drawing attention to yourself!" Sam whispers.

"What if they style my hair?"

He waves a hand. "They won't have time. Stop stressing and start acting."

He's right. It's on me to make this work. What did our Year 9 drama teacher say? *"Inhabit your character."* Easier said than done. But if I don't figure it out before the casting, it'll be game over.

I force back my shoulders and lengthen my stride, trying to channel the attitude of a festival girl. Plenty of people pass without a second glance, but we haven't even reached the tube and the effort's almost killing me.

Being someone else is exhausting.

"Hello, Sam." Standing at the crossing is Ms Faulkner, our art and photography teacher from school. My heart turns somersaults, but her gaze skips over me, light as a feather. "Having a good summer?"

"Yeah, thanks," Sam mutters.

"Ready for your results on Thursday?"

Thursday. With everything going on, exam results have been the last thing on my mind.

Sam only grunts, and Ms Faulkner doesn't push. "Seen Freya lately?"

He bites back a smile. "A bit."

"Well, when you get the chance, say hi from me. Good luck with your results!"

The lights change, and Ms Faulkner waves goodbye. As soon as she's out of earshot, Sam whoops. "It's official, I am a *genius*! She didn't have a clue! Your cover's working, babe." He plants a kiss on my cheek.

We reach the tube station, and I let myself relax. I'm safe, disguised. Completely undercover.

This casting is going to be a breeze.

*

It all goes wrong at London Bridge. The station is heaving with travellers leaving for the coast.

"Wait." Sam hangs back, consulting his phone. "Which street do we want again?"

"Redcross Way." My jittery feeling is back. We've stopped next to a news stand. A big crowd of people is clustered round the magazines. I consider buying some chewing gum; I'm grinding my teeth to dust.

"Back in a second," I tell Sam, as the crowd at the news stand thins out. Then I see it.

My face. On the cover of a magazine.

The shock almost paralyses me, but it's the headline that drains the blood from my body.

THE UNSTOPPABLE RISE OF NIGHTSHADE

No.

"What's up?" Sam follows my gaze. "Oh. My. God!" He shoots towards the stand.

"Stop! What are you doing?"

He plucks the magazine from the rack.

"Hey! You gonna pay for that?"

Thrusting some cash at the guy behind the stand, Sam bounces back to me. "Oh my God, this is unreal! Freya, you're a cover star!"

"Shut up!" I hiss. "People will hear!"

I think I'm going to be sick. Snatching the magazine from Sam, I lean against a wall. *Breathe.* It's the fabled

Fashion Week edition of *Seen* magazine, and *my* face is on the front, staring out for all to see.

Jas's comment slides into my mind. *Might have good news.* This is what she meant.

"I can't believe it." Sam's dancing on the spot. "It's so surreal!"

"You're telling me."

The picture is weird on so many levels. First there's my expression – part-defiant, part-terrified. Then there's the bright-red background. *That* wasn't there at the shoot. Finally, the photo has a soft-focus quality that makes me certain it's been airbrushed, even after all Karim's work.

"I don't look real."

"It works with the caption." Sam points at the small print.

The Picture-Perfect Look Everyone Wants.

"Not funny." My palms are sweating. My wig feels tight and hot. "This isn't good. Bella will see this! There's no way she won't! I don't understand, it was meant to be one small picture! I thought it would come out in September!"

Sam prises the magazine from my hands. "They publish early. The designers need exposure *before* Fashion Week to help promote their shows."

"I didn't know that!" I wail. "Oh God, you're saying I've helped her?"

"Calm down." People are staring. Sam tries to lead me away.

I dig in my heels. "I can't do the casting now. What if Bella shows up? She'll be on the alert." I wave at the magazine. "This is like a fanfare!"

"Don't be silly," Sam soothes. "It's literally just come out. We don't know that Bella's seen it yet, but even if she has, you're in disguise."

I bury my face in my hands, suddenly thinking of Jake. If Bella sees this picture, she'll realize he didn't drive me to Devon. He might lose his job.

"It's your call," Sam says gently. "Just … try to remember why you're doing this."

For Mum. For Dad.

I nod.

"Hey, it's not all bad," Sam says, leading me through the arches on to Tooley Street. "You did get a credit, you know."

"A credit?"

He opens the magazine. I follow his finger to read the small print.

Cover photograph by Freya Jones.

A tiny thrill shoots through me.

A photograph, taken by me, published in a magazine!

If it wasn't so dangerous, I could almost be happy.

*

232

"This way."

I follow Sam under a railway bridge and down a narrow street. Old Victorian buildings line one side. We're near Borough Market, and the scent of chai spice and fried chicken blends with the traffic fumes, making me feel queasy. I grip my bag with sticky hands, taking comfort from the feel of my camera inside.

"Which building is it again?"

We don't have to check. At the far end of the street, a door opens and out steps a girl in a red dress. My heart stops. For a second, I think it's Bella. But it isn't, it's just a model, clutching an over-sized, expensive-looking bag. She stands there, sunlight bouncing off her cheekbones, a dazed expression on her face. A moment later she blinks and strides away.

"Come on." Sam drags me towards the door.

A silver plaque is mounted on it.

WARWICK D'ANGELO PRODUCTIONS

"Ready?" Sam inspects me. "Stand up straight. Shoulders back." He rolls his eyes. "Confidence, Freya! You know what they say? 'Fake it till you make it!'"

"I'm trying!"

Blood is pumping in my ears. I press the buzzer and the door clicks open.

"Good luck," Sam says, stepping back.

"You're not coming with me?" Panic floods my brain.

"Models don't bring friends to castings. You'll be fine."

I gulp. "Will you wait?"

He pulls a face. "Depends how long you take. I have to be back before Dad and fake being in agony, don't I? Stop stressing. Just go."

He pushes me over the threshold before I can change my mind.

I'm standing in a concrete lobby. A dingy stairwell curls off to the left. On the wall is a tatty sheet of paper with the word "CASTING" written in biro. There's an arrow pointing up.

I take a deep breath and climb.

I've just passed the first floor when I come across the girl. She's sitting on the stone steps, pale blonde head buried in a book. Her legs are goose-pimpled in tiny scarlet shorts.

"Is this the Nightshade casting?" My voice is a squeak. The girl doesn't answer, then I spot her earbuds. On the half-landing beyond, another girl is scrolling on her phone.

I push past them, head down.

"Hey!" The second girl comes to life. "Wait your turn!"

I look up. Around the corner, dozens more girls are jammed into the stairwell. An ominous black door looms at the top. I shrink. I've never seen so many beautiful girls in one place. They're like an alien species, totally intimidating. Lots of them are wearing red. *Did it say that on the casting form?* I gulp. My blue dress marks me out as an imposter.

I shuffle back downstairs. Safely at the end of the queue, I glance back. My pulse slows. Nobody is the least bit interested in me, and now that I look closer, I can see – these girls aren't aliens at all, just ordinary teenagers. Cold, tired and bored. One girl stifles a yawn, while another picks at her flaking nail polish. Suddenly, I itch to take a picture. There's a story here – another side of fashion – not glittering and glamorous, but real and raw.

Jake would get it, I think.

"It's very slow." The girl in the shorts looks up. Her voice betrays a hint of an accent. As she pulls out an earbud, a jolt of recognition hits me. It's Ice Queen from the *Seen* shoot. I tense, but she only sighs. "We'll be here for *hours.*"

She shifts over to make room for me. Hesitantly, I sit down.

Then we wait.

And wait.

Time passes slowly. My backside grows numb. One by one, the girls ahead disappear through the big black door. They stride in full of energy, but when they come out, they seem different. Distant and preoccupied. They all look strangely similar. I never noticed that before.

"What's your name?" Ice Queen makes me jump.

"Oh…" A name pops into my head and I seize it without thinking. "Tess."

"Māra." Ice Queen offers her hand. "Nice to meet you. Where are you from?"

"London. You?"

"Latvia."

"Wow. You're a long way from home." I'm keen to flip the focus far from me. "Do you miss it?"

"Of course." Māra's eyes light up as she tells me about her family, her girlfriend Liene, and her literature studies in Riga.

"You go to university?" I blink.

"Why? You didn't expect me to be smart?" Māra looks stern, but there's a twinkle underneath. "What do people say? '*Never judge a book by its cover!*'"

"Sorry." I flush.

"It's OK. I'm teasing. Actually, I had to quit." She bites her lip.

"Why?"

"My mother got sick. She couldn't work, so I had to get a job. People said I should try modelling. The money can be good. So I joined an agency in Riga. They sent me first to Paris, and now here."

"And do you work a lot?" I ask, interested. I'm surprised to find there's something warm about Māra.

"Not enough." Her face clouds over and she twists a strand of white-blonde hair. "I owe a lot of money to my agency."

"*You* have to pay *them*?"

She nods. "I rent a room in their models' apartment. And I pay for promotion." She opens her bag and pulls out a headshot card. I frown. *Should I have cards like these, too?*

"I hope things change soon," Māra goes on. "My agency

236

said that if I want to be a big model, I should post more on social media to build my following. I would prefer to be private." She frowns. "But I do it anyway. I'm in the thousands now." Suddenly her expression brightens. "Anyway, today I feel lucky. Everyone says that Nightshade will be the big success of Fashion Week. I never heard people so excited about a new label before."

Foreboding coils in my tummy. Jas said that too. She'd never seen anything like it. But no one had heard of Nightshade when I did my shoot.

"If I walk in the Nightshade show," Māra continues, "lots of clients will want to work with me. I'll be able to send money to my family. And one day, I'll go back to college."

She sounds so earnest, my heart clenches. I had made assumptions about Māra based only on the way she looks. She's no arrogant ice queen. Nothing could be further from the truth.

"Who's next?" someone calls. I look around. We've shuffled our way to the top. Dozens of girls are now queuing up behind.

"That's me!" Māra says. "Wish me luck."

Guilt grips me. Being cast in Bella's show could change Māra's life – but if I had my way, the show wouldn't be happening at all.

I plaster on a smile. "Good luck."

"Thank you, Tess." Māra winks. "You too."

29

With Māra gone, the butterflies in my stomach quiver again.

I pat my bag for the hundredth time, checking my camera's still inside. If anything behind this door amounts to evidence against Bella, I might need to use it.

Ten minutes later, Māra's back. "Tess, you're up." She's oddly subdued.

"How did it go?" I bite my tongue to stop the barrage of questions.

"Um…" She blinks. "I did a fitting. So … we'll see."

A fitting.

My pulse speeds up. There are definitely clothes in

there. *Are they Mum's designs?* There's only one way to find out.

I step through the door into an open-plan room – whitewashed, bare, anonymous. To my right is a lift shaft and on my left, a bamboo screen. At the far end of the room is a sofa and on it, two people are sitting, huddled over a coffee table. The man – Warwick D'Angelo, I presume – is wearing a suit with a thin scarlet tie. The woman is smaller, with a ruby-red bob.

No sign of Bella. I breathe.

Neither of the pair looks up, and as I move closer, I see why. Model cards, like the one Māra showed me, are spread out on the table. They're sorting them into piles: one large, one small.

The rejects and the chosen ones.

Warwick hesitates over one card and the woman snatches it.

"Not her. Remember the brief."

My body goes cold. I know this woman. It's Raven, the second witness at the wedding. She's dyed her hair. I tense. Will she recognize me?

I've reached the table. There's no going back.

"Name?" Warwick asks, bored.

"T-Tess," I stammer.

"From?"

"London."

"No." He sighs. "*Agency.*"

Panic pulses in my chest. I don't know the names of any

239

model agencies, only Bella's – Façade – and I can't say that with Raven here.

"There isn't a *Tess* on my list." Raven saves me from answering. She squints at her clipboard. "This is a *request* casting. *Invited* models only."

"I'm sorry. I didn't know." My legs tremble. "I'm … new."

Warwick frowns. "Can we see your book?"

"My book? You mean … portfolio?" I make a wild guess.

"Yes." He looks at me oddly. "On a tablet is fine too."

I hesitate.

"Is there a problem?"

"It's just … I don't have any pictures … yet."

Warwick sighs. "Well, what about a card?"

I shake my head.

Raven rolls her eyes. "This is a total waste of time."

"I'll get a headshot." Warwick picks up a Polaroid camera that's sitting in the middle of the table. "Push your hair out of your eyes." He thrusts the lens in my face.

I've no choice but to do as he says. I push back my hair, putting all my trust in Sam's skill. The camera spits out a shiny square. Warwick lays it aside.

"Can you walk?" Raven asks.

A giggle slips out. "Walk?"

"Of course." Her face darkens. "This is a casting for a fashion show. Walk to the door and back."

"Right. Yes. Sure." I turn, but she stops me.

"Wearing these."

240

The shoes she gives me look more like weapons, their spike heels spindly high. I pull off my trainers with shaking hands and squeeze the shoes over my socks, trying to summon up Sam's YouTube video and his helpful hints. He promised it was easy.

Turns out he was wrong.

First my legs wobble, then my knees knock. My ankles feel like they could snap. Somehow I stay upright long enough to stagger across the room. I glance at the bamboo screen. *It's a changing area.* If Mum's designs are behind it, I need to see. So far I've nothing to show for this ordeal.

I return to the sofa as Raven's phone buzzes. She gets up to take the call, and I bite the bullet. "Should I try something on?" I ask Warwick.

He frowns. "That depends."

"On what?"

"On your following."

"My following?" Then I get it. *He means on social media.*

"What are your numbers?"

"Oh. I don't…" I look at my feet. This is a non-starter. I try another tack. "Everyone's talking about Nightshade. Is the atelier near here?"

Warwick eyes me warily. "You're very curious."

"Just interested." I'm getting desperate. "I know someone who works for this label. Nick Jones. Have you ever met?"

The shutters are down. "I don't know who you mean."

Raven is back. She whispers in Warwick's ear.

241

"Now?" He looks annoyed. "But we haven't finished yet."

Raven shrugs. She turns to me. "You can go."

Go? I can't go yet. "But … what about a fitting?"

Raven glances at Warwick. "No followers," he confirms.

"A fitting won't be necessary." She gestures for me to take off the shoes. Snatching them, she turns to the cards on the table and briskly sweeps the larger pile into a bin.

I wince at the waste, thinking of Māra's debt to her agency.

"One last thing, Tess. Before you go…" Raven pauses, and my heart leaps. "Tell everyone outside that the casting is over."

What?

My fists curl. Across the room, the lift whirs, but I'm not paying attention. I'm thinking of the poor models in the stairwell, patiently waiting.

"But they've been out there for hours!"

Raven smirks. "Tough."

Something inside me bubbles up. Maybe it's sitting for hours in the cold, or being treated like a piece of meat. Maybe it's frustration because this whole thing has been pointless. I'm no nearer the atelier, I haven't found Dad, and I don't have the tiniest shred of evidence I can use to stop Bella from going ahead with her show.

"It's not fair!" The words burst from my mouth.

Behind me, the lift doors slide open. A sweet citrus scent fills the air.

242

"What's not fair?"

The voice sends shivers down my spine. I pull my wig close around my face, my heart flipping in my chest.

Bella's heels echo like gunshots. She's wearing sunglasses and a trench coat, with her collar pulled high and her hair scraped back. Something glossy and cylindrical is in her hand.

"What's going on here?"

Taking off her sunglasses, she stares pointedly at Raven. Raven's attitude dissolves.

"We've done everything the way you requested. These girls have been selected." She offers Bella the small pile of cards. "The choice was rather poor," she adds, glancing my way.

Bella's eyes burn into me. "And who is this?"

"This is Tess. But she's leaving." Warwick tosses my Polaroid into the bin. "I'll dismiss the others."

I grab my trainers, taking it as my cue.

"*Wait.*"

In one swift movement, Bella blocks my route. "*Tess,* did you say?" She grabs my chin and lifts it up. "Don't you have an interesting look?" My confidence crumbles as her eyes meet mine.

"She can't walk." Raven offers.

"No." Bella laughs. "I don't suppose she can. Nevertheless, there's something about this girl. Something very *curious.*"

She releases my chin roughly, and throws down the

243

thing she's been holding. It lands on the coffee table with a slap.

The new edition of *Seen* magazine, with my face on the cover.

Sweat pricks my temples.

"We've had some wonderful publicity, *Tess*," Bella continues. "Nightshade has been getting a lot of attention, and soon we'll be getting even more. We're destined for very big things." She turns to Raven. "I think Tess should do a fitting."

"Are you sure?" Raven looks confused. "Aren't we going to Creekside? I thought the taxi was waiting. This girl is nothing special, and she has no followers at all."

"I'm sure." Bella's voice is like silk. "I think it's time to see if Tess can *fit*. Or perhaps I should say, *conform*."

Raven nods, docile. She turns to me. "Put on the garment behind the screen. There's a mirror to help you."

A mirror?

A smile creeps across Bella's face and I swallow. *What's she playing at?* I wanted to get behind the bamboo screen – but not like this. I can't even take my camera with me. My bag's on the floor by Bella's feet.

"What are you waiting for, *Tess*?"

I walk to the screen, my insides like jelly. The first thing I see behind it is Bella's mirror, sitting on a table.

What's it doing here?

There's no time to wonder. The mirror tugs like a riptide, dragging me closer. I want to give in, but I know

I have to resist. I turn my back, trying to focus, and see a single garment hanging on a rail. *Is this one of Mum's designs?* It looks more like underwear; a nude slip dress with an old-fashioned corset at the top.

"Are you *changing,* Tess?"

Bella's question feels loaded. I slide the dress off the hanger. It's tiny! I'll never get it on.

Poor Freya. Still so flawed.
Why don't you let me help?

The words appear like sky-writing in my cloudy mind. With a massive effort, I push them away. I have to keep a clear head. I yank off Jenna's sundress and throw it over the glass.

That's better.

Somehow I manage to drag the slip dress over my hips and chest, but there's no way I can do it up.

"Need some assistance?" a voice breathes in my ear. I stifle a cry. Bella is behind the screen. I try to back away, but there's nowhere to go. Picking up the corset laces, she pulls.

"That's too tight!"

She laughs. "Well, you did choose the hard way." She glances at the mirror. "I hoped you would be more compliant. Sometimes we have to suffer for fashion, Freya. Your darling mother could have told you that."

I can't compute what she's saying. The bones of the corset are scraping my ribs. Every time I gasp for breath, Bella yanks tighter, like a boa constrictor.

"Stop! Please!"

"You're the one who needs to stop," she hisses. "You deceived me. You were meant to be at boarding school, not here in London, interfering in things you know nothing about."

"But … Mum…" The corset is crushing me. I'm too dizzy to form the words.

"This has nothing to do with her," Bella spits. "And nothing to do with you. This is about me. My status and respect. My renaissance is long overdue."

"Where … is … Dad?" The room is spinning. My knees begin to buckle.

"Where is he?" Bella repeats, as spots appear before my eyes. "He's exactly where he wants to be! He's my right-hand man." She laughs. "But no one is indispensable, so if you really do care about Daddy, you'll back off. *Now.* Do you understand?"

I nod. Stars pierce my vision.

"I'm glad I've made myself clear."

She drops the ties. My legs give way.

"You were right," I hear Bella tell Raven, as darkness swallows me. "Tess wasn't so special, after all."

30

"Hello?"

The voice is a life buoy, pulling me to shore. Slowly, I open my eyes. Strip-lighting flickers. A bamboo screen towers over me. My head throbs, and my fingers brush something soft on the cold floor. *My wig.* Bella must have ripped it off.

"Is anyone here?" The voice is closer. "Tess?"

Pain shoots through my ribs as I sit up. I ease the corset loose. Bruises are already blossoming on my skin. *Bella did this. She warned me to back off.* I groan. Have I put Dad in danger? What did she mean, *"He's where he wants to be"*?

"Tess?" A face appears from around the screen. Māra

drops to her knees. "Wait. *Freya?* From the *Seen* shoot? *You're* Tess? I don't understand."

"The mirror. Where is it?" The dressing table is empty. "Where are they? Have they gone?"

"Warwick and the two women?" Māra nods. "They took a taxi. I was standing on the street. I wasn't feeling well. Then the other girls came out and I saw that you weren't there. What's going on?"

"It's a long story." I struggle to my feet. Māra helps me to dress. "You wouldn't believe it."

"No?" She raises an eyebrow. "Try me."

I settle into a window seat in the tiny market cafe. It's late afternoon, and the stalls are packing up. Sam went home hours ago; he sent a text. I sip the hot chocolate Māra bought me, feeling my energy start to return.

"Explain." Māra's tone is kind, but firm.

I curl my hands around my camera. Will she believe me? Should I trust her?

She came back for me, I remind myself.

I take a deep breath and begin.

The whole time I'm talking, Māra doesn't say a word. She stirs her coffee as she listens, the ripples on its surface matching the furrows of her brow. I know how farfetched my story sounds, but she doesn't laugh or question my judgement. And when I tell her about the mirror, she leans forward.

"The mirror at the casting? The one behind the screen?"

248

"You saw it?"

She nods. "I did a fitting too, remember?"

"Did you look into the glass?" I remember how confused Māra seemed when she came out of the casting studio.

She nods again. "Of course."

"Do you remember what happened next?"

Māra frowns, thinking back. "I remember feeling ... fuzzy. Sort of ... unsure. There was a voice in my head, saying they would never cast me. And then..." She shakes her head. "I saw another version of myself." She laughs, embarrassed. "It was me, but ... better. Then they called me to come out, and I thought I must have imagined it."

I grip my camera. "You didn't imagine it. That's what that mirror does. It stops you from thinking clearly, and it makes you feel bad about yourself. Then it makes you perfect. It erases all your flaws."

"Like a filter." Māra's eyes widen.

"Exactly." I nod. "A beauty filter that makes everyone fit the same ideal. It's addictive. Like falling in love, only with yourself."

"Like Narcissus," Māra muses. "He fell in love with his own reflection."

"Right," I agree. "You can't stop looking. And if you say the right words, you don't have to. The mirror makes you perfect for a day."

Māra is quiet.

"I know it sounds ridiculous!" I flush.

"I didn't say that." She frowns. "You know, there are

stories of magic mirrors in many cultures. Why shouldn't it be true?" She tilts her head to one side. "Is that why the mirror was at the casting? To erase the models' flaws?"

I consider this. "I'm not sure. The Nightshade show is still eleven days away; I don't think the magic lasts that long. Plus, not everyone was asked to do a fitting. Only girls with social media followings."

"True," Māra agrees.

"The mirror doesn't seem to work on everyone," I say, remembering Sam. "I think the more self-confident you are, the more immune. Maybe Bella was trying to figure out which models are susceptible? It's strange the mirror worked on you."

Māra raises an eyebrow. "You think I'm confident?"

I look at her shiny hair and piercing eyes. "Aren't you?"

She puts down her coffee. "It's hard, don't you think? There's so much pressure to look a certain way. So you diet or exercise, buy face creams or beauty treatments, maybe even pay for surgery. Who wouldn't want a magic mirror? When you don't feel good enough, you'll try anything."

I blink. "*You* don't feel good enough?"

"Sometimes," she admits. "The world is obsessed with perfection. It's easy to get sucked in."

Wow. I shake my head. If Māra feels insecure, the world really is messed up.

"That's just the way it is." She shrugs. "Nothing we can do." She takes a sip of coffee, oat-milk froth clinging like a moustache to her lip.

"We should fight back," I say, lifting up my camera to grab the shot.

Mãra laughs with delight at the photo. She poses again, pulling silly faces. It's funny, I think, as we scroll back through the images. She's even more beautiful this way. The milk moustache adds character, story, depth. It makes the photo more interesting, less bland.

"You're good," Mãra says, wiping her mouth and growing thoughtful again. "But there's one thing I don't understand. If Bella Wilde can control her image, she could model for ever. She doesn't need to be a designer or hold a fashion show."

"Right." I replace my lens cap. "But that's the problem. She's only perfect in real life. In photographs, the magic has stopped working. Perhaps because she's used it too much, or because she's simply getting older?"

I explain about the paparazzi photo and my selfie on Primrose Hill.

"It's like my book!" Mãra digs out the paperback I saw her reading. "It's about a guy who has his portrait painted. It's so perfect, he makes a pact to switch places, so the painting will age instead of him."

She shows me the cover.

The Picture of Dorian Gray.

"Bella hates being photographed," I go on. "She's hardly working any more. Her modelling career is in freefall. The fashion world prefers youth."

Māra nods. "It's sad."

"It is," I agree. *Strange feeling sorry for Bella.* "Dad said Bella has no family. The fashion world is all she's ever known. And now that world is rejecting her. But if she reinvents herself as a *designer*, everyone will love her again. She'll be safe *behind* the camera, with just as much power as before."

"No," Māra corrects. "She'll have more power, Freya. *Much* more. Think about it. Some brands survive for generations. They start with fashion, then expand. Before you know it, they influence everything – what we wear, how we smell, the way we live – even what we do."

I take this in. It all makes sense. Bella is ambitious. She's not content to be powerful *right now*. She wants to be powerful for ever. And she can be – if she's the one dictating trends.

"Like with the red," I say, a thought occurring to me.

Māra looks quizzical.

"Red is everywhere right now," I say. "Haven't you noticed?"

She looks at her shorts. "I bought these yesterday. You're right. Red was all over the shops."

"Is it normal for a colour to become popular so fast?"

She considers. "It happens. The colours from the really successful fashion collections trickle down to the high street eventually. But it takes time."

"Could it happen *before* a collection is launched?"

"I don't see how. Why?"

"Bella's favourite colour is red," I tell her. "She wears it all the time. She put it in these ads that she got my dad to make. You must have seen them – the woman, hidden behind the vines. The pop of red catches your eye."

"Of course I've seen them." Māra nods. "They're everywhere."

"I read an article that said Nightshade's signature colour is red. People are wearing it already, before they've even seen the clothes. Don't you think that's strange? The same thing is happening with the label. When we did the shoot for *Seen* magazine, nobody had heard of Nightshade. Now it's all anyone is talking about."

"True. It's happening so fast."

"*Too* fast," I say. "I don't know how Bella's doing it. There's something about Nightshade that's impossible to resist."

"What does your dad think?" Māra asks.

"Honestly?" My heart lurches. "I don't know. I'm scared that he's involved. He kept Mum's work a secret from me – and he created those ads. And now he's disappeared." I push back tears, Bella's words echoing in my head: "*He's my right-hand man.*"

"There's so much hype and secrecy surrounding Nightshade." I pull myself together. "I came to the casting to learn more. If I can find Bella's atelier, I can prove that Bella's stolen Mum's work. And I might find my dad." My voice breaks. "Only now Bella knows I'm on to her. I've made the situation ten times worse and I haven't learned a thing."

Unless…

I rub my tender scalp. "Does 'Creekside' mean anything to you? That's where Bella and the others were heading."

"Hmm." Māra pulls up Maps on her phone and types into the search bar. The pin drops on to the map.

A road in south-east London, near the river.

My heart begins to beat faster.

"Ah!" Māra seems to realize something. She drags the little person icon on to the road and the screen switches to Street View. Large industrial buildings flank the street. She taps the arrow, fast-forwarding to a red brick warehouse, halfway down.

"The atelier. I bet it's here."

"How do you know?"

Māra smiles. "I recognize this street. This building. Falkland House. I've been there before on castings. Many designers have ateliers there."

I scramble to my feet.

"What are you doing?" She grabs my arm. "You can't go now."

I sink back down. Māra's right. Bella could still be there. Less than an hour ago, she nearly suffocated me and left me unconscious on the floor. Who knows what she might do next?

"I need to get inside."

"And then?"

"I told you. I'll get evidence, find Dad—"

"If he's there," Māra says, interrupting. "If not, what then?"

"Then I'll keep looking!" Tears begin to rise. "When he finds out what Bella's doing, he'll help me. We'll stop the show from going ahead!"

Māra takes my hand. "Unless he's part of this."

I try to block her out.

"Your father is a grown man," she goes on. "He's made his own decisions – or someone made them for him. You can't change that. But you *could* stop the show, Freya. Even by yourself."

I swallow. "How?"

Her voice drops to whisper. "You can't have a fashion show without any clothes."

I could destroy them.

The words hang unspoken in the air.

Māra shrugs. "If you could get inside the atelier, you could sabotage the collection. The clothes, the designs – *especially* the designs. So nothing can be recreated."

I think of Mum's sketchbook; her creations made real.

Could I really do it?

"The show is in eleven days," Māra says, gently. "You don't have time for a police investigation. And from what you've said, Bella Wilde sounds very *influential*. You have to act now."

I lift my chin. "Show me the building again."

She hands over her phone. Falkland House is forbidding:

four storeys high, ground floor windows barred, CCTV cameras at the front.

"It looks like a prison."

Māra nods. "It would be easier with a key." Her phone buzzes. Mouthing an apology, she steps outside.

A key.

Victor arranged the atelier for Bella. He'd be bound to have a key. And Jake has access to Victor. But would he help me again?

I think of his reaction on Primrose Hill. *Surprised, hurt, confused.*

Why does it feel like I've messed up any chance of being friends?

Just then, my phone pings with a message. My tummy twists when I see the sender's name.

Jake. It's a sign!

But when I open the message, my hopes are dashed.

> Nice cover.
> Shame it's gonna blow my cover.

He's attached the picture from *Seen* magazine.

I text back.

> Jake, I'm so sorry.
> I didn't mean for this to happen.
> Please let me explain.

I've heard that before.
I think I'll pass.

I bury my head in my hands.

"Freya?" Māra is back. "My agent just called. I have to go. I have another casting. Will you be OK?"

"I'll be fine." I force a smile. Māra's family depend on her modelling career, and she's already helped me loads.

"Swap numbers." She thrusts her phone at me. "If I can do anything, just call."

I look at Māra. "You hardly know me. Why would you want to help?"

She looks me in the eye. "I get a bad feeling about Nightshade. This hype, it isn't normal. Perfect Bella Wilde doesn't need more power. You said yourself, *we should fight back.*"

Outside the cafe, she hugs me. "Do you have a plan?"

Go to Façade. Find Jake. Tell him everything. Hope he understands.

"Not much of one," I admit.

"Just remember you have a weapon." Māra points at the camera in my hands. "The truth about Nightshade isn't the only thing that Bella Wilde wants to keep secret."

I crossed the ocean with my golden girl.
From that moment, we
belonged to one another.
It's true, she lacked the talents of the
dark-haired girl. I knew my progress
would be slow, my journey long.
But here was a follower.
A disciple who believed.
And to spread my message,
it only starts with one.
I gave her what she craved — perfect beauty,
reinvention. Potent, magnetizing charm.
And the world fell in love
with my golden girl.
At least, it did for a while.

31

My hands feel damp as I near the glass building not far from Oxford Circus. Façade's offices are on the top two floors.

I know Bella isn't here, but that doesn't mean I'm not paranoid about running into Victor. My disguise has almost fallen apart – although I'm still made up and wearing Jenna's dress, the blonde wig is a write-off, squashed at the bottom of my bag.

I slip into a small park opposite the building and find a bench with a view of the lobby. My phone says it's five-thirty. It dawns on me that I have no idea when Jake finishes work, or if he still has a job. Has Bella made the connection between my cover and him helping me? Has she fired him since he sent his text?

I lift up my camera and zoom in on the lobby's revolving doors: an endless stream of office workers knocking off for the day. Blokes in pinstripes, girls in blouses, but no Jake.

My phone pings. Sam.

U still at the casting?

I have so much to tell him, but the clock is ticking, and I can't take my eyes off those doors.

Outside Façade.
Need to speak to Jake.

Dad knows I lied to him today.

That grabs my attention.

How?

Forgot something, came back.
Saw I wasn't there.
Mum says he's furious.
She wants us to have a "talk".

When?

Tonight.

I can see Sam's still typing. There's a long pause, then:

> *This is it, Freya.*
> *Time to tell him everything.*

> *Everything*, everything?

An even longer pause.

> *Yeah. Everything.*
> *Not just the hair and*
> *make-up stuff.*
> *About Liam too.*
> *Dad gets home at 7:30.*
> *Will you be there?*

Before I can reply, he texts again.

> *Please, Freya. I need you x*

> You can count on me x

He sends back a hundred rainbow heart emojis with the echo effect. Not that he needs to. I'll admit, Sam hasn't been my priority recently, but this is huge. He needs my support and I'll be there for him.

Two hours before I need to get back. My leg bounces up and down.

Hurry up, Jake!

A sudden flash of neon catches my eye. With his scruffy trainers and mussed-up hair, Jake stands out among the suits. Swerving the crowds, he exits through a fire door.

I'm on my feet.

Jake turns left, picking up speed. I jog across the park, keeping track.

Then I falter.

Walking towards Jake is Amy. Part of me shrivels up inside.

But something isn't right. As Jake hugs Amy's narrow frame, her arms hang limply by her side. And when Jake pulls back, I notice dark circles under her eyes.

They cross the road, heading north.

Now what do I do?

Amy wasn't part of the plan, but I have to speak to Jake. I turn to follow and crash into a woman walking her dog. By the time I've apologized, Jake and Amy's matching dark heads are almost out of sight. I fly after them, my camera bouncing on my back.

At the top of the park is a long road with smart, cream town houses lining each side. Jake and Amy are fifty metres up ahead. They stop outside a building with wrought-iron railings and steps leading to a glossy front door. I hang back, catching my breath.

Jake is on the steps. He pulls Amy's arm but she resists.

Raised voices catch the wind. I edge closer, slipping behind a nearby gatepost. My eyes fall on a gold plaque fixed to the stone.

GOLDWATER CONSULTATION ROOMS
THE SANCTUARY GROUP

"Why can't you mind your own business?" Amy's voice interrupts my thoughts.

"Because I care!" Jake's own voice cracks. "Just try this, please. For me."

Amy twists away, running down the street towards me, her wet cheeks glistening in the sun. I flatten myself against the gatepost as she stumbles past, oblivious to Jake's pleas. She hails a cab and jumps in, slamming the door in his face.

Jake stands there, staring after the taxi. Finally he turns – and sees me.

"Freya? What the—"

"Jake." Heat blazes a path across my cheeks. "I need to talk to you."

His face is blank. I summon my courage.

"I want to apologize – about the magazine cover. And explain."

"There's nothing to explain." He shrugs, eyes cold. "I understand everything. You spun me a story about your dad and Bella, but really you came back to London to be a model."

"That's not true!" I say. "Well, it is, *kind* of, but—"

"I'm just surprised, that's all." He coughs. "Well, not *surprised*, obviously. I mean, you're ... beautiful. Amazing. That's not what I'm trying to say..." He trails off, flustered.

I stare, too stunned to speak.

"It's just ... I didn't think you cared about fashion," Jake tries again. "Or looking like everyone else. I thought you believed in *real*. That's what I like about you, Freya. You're cool with being you." His face is red. He turns to walk away. "I dunno. Maybe I've got it wrong."

I grab his arm.

"Jake, stop! You *have* got it wrong."

He comes to a halt.

"I did come back to London for that shoot – but you're wrong about why. I needed a way into Bella's world, so I could figure out what she's up to – and it worked, because now I know." I pause. "She's stolen my mum's student fashion designs – that's what was in those boxes – and she's launching a new label at Fashion Week. It's called Nightshade, and people are weirdly obsessed with it already. You know how nobody can resist Bella? That's exactly what's happening. It's scary."

Jake turns to face me. He's listening.

"You're wrong about something else too," I continue. "I'm not 'cool with being me' – not at all." I stare at my feet. "That time you saw me on Primrose Hill, I ... I wasn't myself. That wasn't me." I look up at him. "I thought the real me wasn't good enough. I do want to believe in *real*, but it's hard."

Jake's face softens. "I know."

"I haven't been honest," I admit. "I've made mistakes. But all this time, I've only wanted to protect my family. Bella doesn't need any more power. And she doesn't deserve recognition for work that belongs to my mum." Jake nods, giving me the strength to go on. "It matters to me that you know the truth, not because I need your help – although I do – but because..." I take a deep breath. "I thought we had a connection. If you still want to be friends, I'd like that. If your girlfriend doesn't mind, I mean."

"My girlfriend?" Jake blinks.

I shuffle. "I saw you just now, arguing. Is everything OK?"

"Not really." Jake's voice wobbles. "Actually, everything's a mess. And Amy's not my girlfriend. She's my sister."

His sister.

It's obvious. The dark hair, the hazel eyes, the long limbs.

"We're twins," Jake murmurs. "Amy isn't well, but she won't admit it. That's why I'm here. I booked an appointment with a specialist. I should have told her, but I thought if I did, she wouldn't show up. I'm scared, Freya."

I look at the town house with the glossy door. "It's a clinic?"

Jake nods. "One of the best in London. If anyone can help Amy's condition, they can. But she has to *want* help, I guess."

Her condition. I don't have to ask. I picture Amy's pinched

265

face, her birdlike frame. There were lots of girls at school like Amy: counting calories, skipping meals.

"Walk with me?" Jake asks.

We head back in the direction we came. After a while, Jake begins to talk.

"When we were kids, we did some modelling, Amy and me. Our mum works in PR – she got me the job at Façade. She used to put us forward for things. Twins get lots of work. I wasn't into it, so by the time we were teenagers, I quit. But Amy carried on. She wanted to make it her career. Only she didn't get as much work by herself..." He swallows. "She got this idea that there was something wrong with her, that maybe she needed to lose weight. I couldn't convince her that she was wrong, and her fashion clients didn't even try! She's had an eating disorder for years now. She's lost her spark, her energy – and it's only getting worse."

I nod.

This casts a new light on everything – Jake's bitterness about the fashion world, his sympathy for my "family stuff". I can guess what went through his head when he saw me taking selfies with Saskia, and when I popped up on the cover of *Seen* magazine. Another clueless clone, perpetuating perfect without a second thought.

Part of the problem harming Amy.

We've reached the park opposite Façade. Jake looks so forlorn that before I've thought it through properly, I reach out and hug him. He doesn't pull away.

"What you said in the gallery – about having to be brave to be yourself – it struck a chord," Jake says when we finally break apart. "When people like Bella Wilde have a platform, it gets harder."

"That's why I want to stop her." We sit on a bench while I tell Jake my plan. "There can't be a show without a collection," I finish. "I have to destroy it. I can't see another way."

"There's a safe in Victor's office," he tells me. "If he does have a spare key for this atelier, that's where it'll be."

"Can we get it? Do you still have your job?" My stomach squirms.

Jake grimaces. "I think so. For now. But it won't be long until Bella puts two and two together. Better make the most of it while we can."

The lobby is quiet, the office workers gone. Cleaners push mops across the floor.

"What if Victor's still there?"

Jake shakes his head. "He already left. He has a site visit at some church-turned-gallery place. I'm meant to meet him there in an hour to discuss 'music and visuals' for something."

"*For the show*." I shiver. The gallery where Dad met Bella was a converted church in Camden. I bet she's chosen it for her venue.

We take the lift up to a slick, open-plan space. A long table filled with computer monitors takes centre stage.

"The booking table." Jake nods. "Wait here. Victor's office is out back."

"Isn't it locked? How will you get in?"

He winks. "You're not the only observant one. There's a code. I've seen him tap it in. The key to the safe is in his desk."

He disappears and I sink into one of the booking-table chairs. Looming above me is a bigger version of Sam's bedroom wall: racks and racks of model cards. Dozens of beautiful faces stare back at me.

I sit up tall.

None of it is real. None of these girls are perfect in real life. They're ordinary people, like Māra and Amy, full of doubts and insecurities, hopes and dreams. And these images could be so much more powerful if the photographer captured that, but they're all style over content – the same types of poses, the same type of beauty, over and over again.

I stroke my camera. *I could do a better job.*

A noise interrupts my thoughts. The whirring of the lift.

"Someone's coming!" I call, scrambling under the table as the lift doors roll back. A pointy pair of men's shoes steps out.

"I've had to come back to the agency," Victor speaks into his phone. "I forgot something. The headpiece arrived from the embroiderer today; I'll bring it with me to the gallery. If you've finished at Creekside, I'll see you there. The production team's waiting for us."

He pauses by the booking table, foot tapping.

"What do you mean, he's asking questions?" Victor swears sharply. "I told you to sever connection with the family! You insisted he was harmless. *Deal* with it, Bella. I don't care how. Take a detour. Do it now! You don't need him any more. And let's hope the girl takes the hint and *disappears* too. If she knows what's good for her."

I can't breathe.

"Security will be increased. Leave that with me. Now the collection is finished, we need to tidy up loose ends. Get rid of anything that leaves a trail."

Icy fingers clutch my throat. I spy the neon flash of Jake's trainers.

"Hunter?" Victor kills the call. "What are you doing here?"

"Forgot my phone." Jake manages to keep an even tone.

"Wait." Victor orders. "We'll go to the site together. I need to get something from my office first."

As soon as he's gone, I crawl out from under the table.

"Go, Freya! Quickly!" Jake shoves something into my hand. Sharp teeth bite into my palm. *Keys.* "Call me when you're done," Jake hisses. "I'll need the keys back tonight, before they're missed."

I don't have time to answer. Victor's footsteps are growing louder.

I dive into the lift.

32

I hesitate on the pavement.

If Bella's on her way to meet Victor at the show venue, I could go to the atelier now, break in, destroy the clothes. The Nightshade show is eleven days away. Tonight's my chance to sabotage the collection and prevent the show from going ahead.

But Dad *is* in danger.

There's no more doubt about that. Bella doesn't need him any more. He's a "loose end". And if he's not at the atelier, where is he?

I twist the keys in my hand. The atelier's my only lead – and thanks to Jake, I can get inside. I need to go there first, stick to the plan. And perhaps, if I'm lucky, I'll find a clue that will lead me to Dad.

By the time I get to Creekside, the sun is sliding down the sky, golden fingers of light slanting through the buildings. Falkland House is easy to find. Four floors of imposing brick on a corner plot, with toughened-glass windows on the ground floor, concealing the inside.

I lurk at a distance, watching for signs of life. The main entrance is hidden behind a graffiti-sprayed shutter. A CCTV camera peers ominously from above.

I study the keys on the ring Jake gave me. One is silver and heavy, one is small and gold, and one is rusty with a slender stem. A metal tag bears the number 44. I'm guessing the atelier is on the fourth floor, at the top, but I've still got no idea how to get in.

I feel exposed out on the road, so I duck down an alley running alongside Falkland House. That's when I see it: a small side door behind an ancient metal grille.

I look again at the rusty key. *That's it.*

My shoulders tense. The alley is dark and dingy. There are no cameras here, which means I won't be spotted – but it also means that anything could happen to me, and nobody would know.

The rusty key slots easily into the lock. Hinges groan as I pull back the grille. I try the silver key in the door behind.

Yes!

I'm in a windowless corridor, running the length of the

building, with a row of doors numbered one to four. I reach for the light switch then snatch back my hand. *Think, Freya!* I can't attract attention. I pull the grille shut and lock the door behind me, then pad along the corridor in the dark, fingers grazing the breeze-block walls.

I reach a stairwell and start to climb. Floorboards creak, making me wince. At the top of the building, another dark corridor greets me. I peer at the numbers on the doors: 41, 42, 43…

Number 44 is at the end.

This door is different from the others. Painted white, it almost seems to glow. My pulse quickens at the small gold sign fixed above the lock – a letter N, encircled by vines. I press my ear to the wood.

Silence.

I single out the golden key.

This is it. My heart is thumping. I'm seconds away from seeing Mum's work. The designs from her sketchbook, brought to life.

I push open the door and cry out.

At the far end of the room, a group of figures is standing in a semi-circle. I freeze, terror washing over me.

Nothing happens. I look again.

Honestly, Freya! They're only mannequins. I pull myself together. Sucking in a deep breath, I step inside.

The Nightshade atelier.

My eyes can't work out where to land. My senses overdose on texture, colour and light. The room is large and airy, with exposed brick walls to the right and big windows lining the left and far sides. The evening sun streams through, bathing everything in a fiery glow. In front of me are three benches, on which long rolls of scarlet fabric are unfurled. Dozens more rolls lean against the wall. There's a bank of sewing machines, each threaded in a different shade of red. Beside me, a lethal-looking pair of scissors shimmers on a bench.

I move further in.

To my right, the floor-to-ceiling shelves are crammed with spools of ribbon, cards of lace, boxes of velvet and felt. Mood boards fight for wall space, full of clippings from magazines. Fabric swatches flutter as I pass.

I head to the back of the room. There are twelve mannequins in total, their faces eerily blank. Backlit by the sun, the first thing that strikes me is their shape.

Each mannequin reminds me of Bella, with her impossible hourglass silhouette.

I move closer. Now I can see what they're wearing.

Strange.

It's not that the gowns aren't beautiful – they are. They're as glamorous as anything Bella would wear. But that's just it. They look like they've been plucked straight from her wardrobe. Each one is narrow, tight – restrictive even. Pushed up, controlled, sucked in. And every gown is a vivid shade of red.

Scarlet, garnet, crimson, carmine, vermilion, rust, blood.

I blink.

These are Mum's designs? There must be some mistake.

I think of the drawings in the sketchbook I found. The glorious colours. The warrior women. The reinvented silhouettes.

Where are they?

These gowns are beautifully made, exquisitely tailored – but there's nothing … *original* about them. Nothing unique. No quirky features, no wings for sleeves. And definitely no pockets. They're constrained and immaculate, not fun and free. A *one-size-fits-nobody* perfect uniform, for an army of Bella clones.

Beyond the mannequins, three rails are filled with dozens more blood-red outfits, plastic-wrapped and ready to go.

The Nightshade collection. Finished.

Doubt gnaws my stomach. I've got this wrong. There's no way Mum created this.

Or did she?

At the back of the room, there's a long row of plan chests: drawers open, patterns spilling out. And on top of the plan chests are sketchbooks. *Lots* of sketchbooks. Exactly like the one I found in the attic.

I rush over and snatch one up.

No.

Turning the pages, I see clearly. For every gown on a mannequin, every outfit on a rail, there's a matching drawing in one of these sketchbooks. This really *is* my mum's work. I recognize her loose ink style. And if I *still*

274

had doubts, there's even more proof. Hidden in each sketch is a flourish, like a little house on stilts.

Shiro. White. Mum's signature.

A hollow feeling eats my insides.

Is this what Mum considered beautiful? Bella's beauty? The very opposite of me?

I swallow my disappointment. It doesn't matter what I think. What matters is what I do next.

The scissors on the bench wink at me in the light. With just a few slashes, these clothes would be unwearable – the collection unsalvageable, the patterns gone.

The Nightshade show would be ruined.

I don't move.

I can't do it. I can't destroy these clothes. They came from Mum. It would be like destroying part of her.

But do I let Bella take the credit for herself?

I flick through the sketchbooks one more time. Bella's been clever, I'll give her that. She's done her best to cover her tracks. There's no sign of Mum's handwriting, not a single college stamp. Nothing to link the Nightshade collection to Mum.

Nothing except the secret signatures on every page.

In her attempt to erase the past, Bella's missed one crucial detail. And if I can't destroy the collection, perhaps I can do something else.

I can take photographs – collect evidence of Bella's theft. It's up to me to protect Mum's legacy.

I only wish I loved it more.

33

I need to document everything, quickly.

Mum's signature is proof that these designs are hers, no matter how cleverly Bella's tried to hide the fact.

I pull out my camera, the weight of it settling my mind. I need to be methodical, forensic. *A good photographer should tell the truth.*

That's what I'm going to do.

First, I photograph the clothes – framing, focusing, capturing – hems and cuffs, collars and sleeves. Then I move to the sketchbooks. For every outfit on a mannequin or a rail, I scour the pages until I've found its mirror image – the exact matching design. Each time, I zoom into the drawing carefully, making sure Mum's signature is visible in the frame.

The tiny details that tell a bigger story.

Finally, I've finished.

I check playback on my camera. I've documented at least sixty outfits, matched them up with sixty designs. It's got to be enough. Proof to take to the police.

Just as soon as I've found Dad.

Time to go. I need to get the keys back to Jake.

I scan the room, checking everything's in place. Then I bend down to pick up my camera bag. My elbow clips the corner of a large mood board, leaning against the window. It wavers, toppling forward. I lunge to catch it, then I see.

Behind the board, sitting on a shelf, is Bella's mirror.

I freeze.

A shimmer of silver. The mirror gleams. I can feel it calling; a tingle travelling through my body, tugging. Fainter than before, perhaps, but still there.

My mind goes cloudy. I stare blankly at my hands. *Why am I holding my camera?* I put it down and robot-like, move closer.

All shall be perfect.

The words dance like dust motes in my mind. If I want, I could see her again – Mirror Me. Speak the words and be that perfect girl.

Even as I think it, I'm not sure.

Then a whisper fills my head.

That's right, Freya. Come to me.

Don't you want to look like them?

Them?

I glance behind me at the mannequins in their semi-circle, with their teeny-tiny hourglass bodies and symmetrical blank faces.

*That's right. Perfect beauty
was your mother's muse.*

I blink, dazed. *How does the mirror know my mother?*

I can't think clearly. The glass begins to ripple...

Deep within the building, a door slams. I snap to attention. Everything comes rushing back: where I am and why I'm here. Clipped footsteps echo in the stairwell. They're getting closer.

I jerk away from the mirror, shoving the mood board back in front of it, and cast around frantically. *How do I get out?* The window's no good – I'm too high. There's nowhere to hide! Then my eyes snag on something half hidden behind a black garment bag hanging on a nail. A cupboard!

The footsteps reach the top corridor.

Grabbing my camera, I fly across the room and throw myself inside the cupboard, pulling the door shut. The garment bag falls with a muffled thump.

A jingle of keys. The click of a lock. In the inky darkness, my heart turns backflips. Someone has entered the atelier, but who?

Floorboards creak as the person moves around the space. Then a familiar voice chills my spine.

"I'm back at the atelier. There's one last thing I want to check."

Bella is outside the cupboard door. She's on the phone, I can tell that much. I can't breathe or even blink.

"Raven can deal with the guestlist. This is far more important. I've had an idea for the finale. Something to make a real impact. The final look has been ... *adjusted*. It's better than the sample we had made."

Her voice moves back into the room. "I want to see it with the headpiece. Just get on with your side of things, and leave this to me. I'll see you at your apartment, later on."

She ends the call. I hear a ripping sound.

What's she doing? I rest my forehead on the cupboard door, wishing I could see.

Something sharp pricks my skin. The end of the nail.

That's it.

Gently, I waggle the nail until it's loose. The next time I hear the ripping sound, I give the nail a soft tap. It drops out on the other side of the cupboard, leaving a hole.

Yes!

I peer through the tiny aperture. Now I have a clear view of Bella.

She's leaning over a bench, looking into a large box. Shiny wrapping tape is coiled around her ankles on the floor. The garment bag lies next to her, on the table.

I tense as her gaze briefly shifts in my direction, but her attention soon returns to the box. Peeling back a layer of tissue, she lifts up a long sweep of red embroidered mesh.

The headpiece.

Bella gives a satisfied sigh. Laying it down, she unzips the garment bag. When I see what's inside, my heart stops.

Wait. What?

It's the dress Mum wore for her wedding. But not a simple copy, like the sample at the shoot. This is a new version, taken to extremes. Cruella de Vil meets Jessica Rabbit meets old-school Disney Princess. All the subtlety, the humour of Mum's original design – it's gone.

Bella steps out of view. When she returns, she's wearing the gown. She reaches for the headpiece, and I realize what it is.

A veil.

It pops into my head – what Sam said, as we watched the runway video – "*You know the final look in a fashion show is the bride?*"

I should have guessed.

There's no way Bella will let another model close her fashion show. *She's* going to be the finale, all by herself. She could never hide behind the scenes. She's going to wear this dress to make her big reveal: designer and muse as one.

Except ... what will happen when she's photographed?

Bella pushes the veil off her face. Her lips are pursed.

Something isn't right. Then I notice she looks tired. Her eyes are shadowy and her shoulders are stooped. As she turns to one side, I see her dress doesn't quite fit; the seams are stretched, the waist unfastened. A soft belly protrudes.

I stare.

Not because I think she looks *bad*. Far from it.

Because she simply looks … real.

The magic's wearing off. She needs the mirror.

Bella realizes it too.

She strides across the room, lifting away the mood board and pulling the mirror towards her. The setting sun illuminates her face. As she murmurs into the glass, I see her skin smooth, her shoulders straighten and her lips plump. Her hair thickens and her eyes glow. But most mesmerizing of all is the way her body changes, shape-shifting to unbelievable proportions, until her cartoon wedding dress clings to every curve.

Bella smiles, but I feel empty.

Sad.

Then her perfect face contorts. Her eyes are fixed on something, under a bench.

My bag.

"Freya?"

Bella is on her feet. Swiftly she covers the mirror. "Freya, if you're in here, don't think for a second that I won't find you." Her eyes dart to and fro, then narrow, like a predator that's spotted its prey.

She strides across the studio towards the cupboard door.

The golden girl was greedy, selfish.
She drained my powers, kept me to herself.
My magic weakened, the more my
reach was limited. I tried to warn
her but she refused to listen:
I could not promise immortality.
My powers were no match for time.
The years left their mark on my golden girl.
Our illusion dimmed, her reputation waned.
As my influence declined, my
magic faded further.
Without a wider audience, my
message seemed doomed to die.

34

Bella yanks open the cupboard door.

My stiff limbs refuse to coordinate. I hit the floor, my body curled around my camera. Bella towers over me, her spike heel catching the hem of Jenna's dress, pinning me to the ground.

"I suppose you think you're clever, breaking into my atelier like a spy? You're not. You're as pathetic as your father."

Fury overrides my fear. How dare she stand there, wearing her ripped-off version of Mum's wedding dress, calling Dad pathetic?

I scramble to my feet, tearing Jenna's dress to get free.

"*You* made Dad change. He was fine before you came along." Spittle flies from my mouth. "I don't know what you've done to him, but I do know why. And I can prove it." My grip tightens on my camera.

"Oh, yes?" Bella's eyes gleam. "What exactly do you *think* you know?"

I gesture at the sketchbooks, the patterns, the collection surrounding us.

"Nightshade. None of it belongs to you. You stole these designs from my mum, Tess White. You're planning to claim it's yours." I gulp a breath. "It's part of some desperate attempt to resurrect your dying career. Well, you may think you can fool the fashion world, but you can't fool me. You're nothing but a liar and a thief!"

I rush at Bella, but she sidesteps and I strike a mannequin instead. It crashes to the ground, red beads pooling on the floor like drops of blood.

Bella blinks. When she speaks, her voice is soft.

"You think I *stole* this?" She gazes around the atelier, ablaze in the sunset.

"I know you did," I say. "These sketchbooks are my mum's. This is *her* work, from fashion college in Tokyo. She signed her drawings. She created them. You can't deny it!"

There's a faraway look in Bella's eyes. "Is that right?"

I'm thrown by her tone. "What do you mean?"

She wanders to the window. Backlit by the sun, her hair is a halo of flames.

"Oh, Freya." She sighs. "You want to believe that your

284

mother is the innocent victim here. Well, I'm sorry to disappoint you, but *she* was the traitor, not me."

I shake my head. "What do you mean?"

"There's something you should know." Bella gives a faint smile. "Once upon a time, I knew Tess White very well indeed."

I wait.

"We were friends." Bella's eyes drift over the rooftops. "At least, that's what I believed. But Tess destroyed that friendship when she betrayed me."

"*Betrayed* you?"

She gazes into the distance. "It was a long time ago. I was a young model in Tokyo, hoping for a break. Work was scarce. Then I met Tess."

"You *worked* for Mum?"

"Not for *her*." Bella scowls. "For her college. I was a fitting model. Do you know what that means?"

I shake my head but Bella doesn't notice. She's too lost in the memory.

"It's not a glamorous job, but it is important. The college hired professional models to work with the students as they prepared for their graduation shows. I was assigned to *Tess*."

Her bitter tone is chilling.

A street light flickers, reminding me it's late. The shadows in the studio are lengthening. Bella stands frozen at the window.

Don't listen! I tell myself. *She lies. You've got your evidence, now go!*

285

But I can't. I'm rooted to the spot. She's talking about Mum, and I'm hungry – no, famished – for information. I need to know more.

"You modelled Mum's work?" I say slowly. "She designed this collection on you?"

"Not just *on* me." Bella whirls around. "*With* me! I was her muse! Essential to the process. When we first met, your mother was nobody." She eyes me slyly. "A nobody, encumbered with a baby. So serious and awkward, with the most bizarre ideas about fashion. Her designs were *hideous*." She shakes her head. "That changed after I came along. I became her inspiration. Her work started getting attention. Suddenly, all the important fashion editors were clamouring to see her show." Bella pauses. "In return for my help, she made me a promise." Anger burns in her eyes. "Tess White was going to be a huge success. She promised to take me with her, all the way to the top."

I swallow. "What happened?"

Bella takes her time. "It was just before the graduation shows. I arrived at the college for my final fitting. Imagine my surprise to learn that my contract had been terminated." Her eyes are closed, as if the memory gives her pain. "My services were no longer required. Tess White's show had been cancelled. She had withdrawn from the college, betraying our agreement and denying me my big break."

"Her show was cancelled? She left?" I frown. "Something must have happened. Didn't she explain?"

Bella's face is stone cold. "I received no explanation.

286

Not that I needed one. I had a very good idea of what your mother had planned. She wanted me out of the picture, so she could take our collection elsewhere and claim all the credit for herself."

No.

This can't be right. This isn't how I've imagined Mum — ambitious, disloyal, unfair. But a seed of doubt has been planted in my mind. *What if I've been wrong?*

"And did she?" I whisper.

A smile flits across Bella's face. "As it happened, she didn't have the chance. Karma is a powerful thing. Within a matter of days, poor Tess White was dead."

"Mum had a brain aneurysm," I whisper. "She died when I was fourteen months old…"

My words die out. Bella is laughing, and the sound makes my skin prickle.

"An *aneurysm*? A bleed on the brain? Is that what you believe?" She composes herself. "Oh dear, no. Your mother was weak, Freya. Dreadfully insecure, with no real talent of her own. Do you honestly think she could have achieved *this,* all by herself?" She gestures at the Nightshade collection. "It wasn't an *aneurysm* that put an end to Tess's dreams. An *accident,* I believe they called it."

I stare at her. "An accident?"

"A tragic fall, from a bridge." Bella shakes her head. "That was the official verdict."

"Mum fell? From a bridge?" I echo. "I don't… How? What do you mean, 'official verdict'?" My head is spinning.

"Well, isn't it obvious what really happened?" Bella's voice brims with pity. "Clearly, Tess realized that, without me, she was no one. Destined to be a failure, with nothing worth living for..." Her gaze lingers on me, a moment too long. "I'm sorry to be the one to tell you, Freya, but the truth is, your darling mother took her own life."

35

No.

I grip the table, trying to stay upright.

"Sorry to spoil the illusion, but it's true. Tess White was not the perfect creature you may have thought."

I keep my face steady. *She's lying. She must be.*

Bella sighs. "Anyhow, I'm tired of talking about the past. It's the future I want to focus on. This collection was made *with* me, *for* me. It's as good as mine. Tess denied me success all those years ago, but I intend this work to see the light of day. In eleven days, the Nightshade show will go ahead, despite your pointless attempts to interfere. Your so-called 'proof' is worthless."

I look down at the camera in my hands.

"You think I haven't guessed what you've been up to?" She smirks. "Perhaps you were planning to show your pictures to your friends at *Seen* magazine, and tell them all about nasty Bella and her wicked plans? You don't think they'll care, do you? Not when Nightshade is exclusively launching its brand-new international advertising campaign in their very next issue! Your friend Jasmine de Souza would be out of a job if anything scuppered that deal."

Despair makes me reckless. I lift my chin. "Let's say you're right about Mum – that's still not the whole story. You've been deceiving people for years." My eyes flick to the mood board concealing the mirror. "What if your other little secret came out?"

Bella scowls. "What are you saying, Freya?"

"I know what your mirror does." I take a step closer to the window, dodging her gaze and trying to hold my nerve. "So tell me where Dad is, or I'll—"

"You'll what?"

We lunge at the same time. The mood board topples.

Bella slides her body in front of the mirror, like a lioness protecting her cub. "You can't have it," she snarls. "It's mine."

"I don't want it!" I say. But then I hear the whisper.

Freya.

I plant my feet and shut my ears.

"This mirror is mine," says Bella. She strokes it lovingly.

"It was my destiny to have it. Call it compensation — for your mother's betrayal. Tess White deprived me of the career I deserved, but this mirror gave it to me instead. You have *no* idea how powerful it is."

I close my eyes, trying to block out its call.

Freya, listen to me.

"It chose me," Bella goes on. "Don't pretend you haven't felt its strength. You'd give anything for a mirror like mine. Poor Freya: so flawed, so second-rate. If Tess could see you now, she'd be terribly disappointed. But I suppose she can't have cared much about you. She left you, after all."

The words are bullets, raining down on me.

Bella strikes, snatching the camera from my hands.

"Give it back!" I sob.

She turns to the window and flings it open. "I've tried to warn you before. This silly hobby of yours is getting tiresome. I won't take any more risks."

"No!"

Her fingers uncurl. My camera falls in slow motion, turning lens-down in the air. The sound it makes as it hits the ground shatters what's left of my heart.

Bella giggles. "How careless of me!"

My legs give way. I sink on to the floor. From somewhere comes a buzzing sound — my phone, ringing on silent.

"Expecting a call?" Bella pounces on my bag. "It won't be Daddy, I'm afraid. I know he's been a little out of touch.

291

His memory is appalling these days. It couldn't be helped. Collateral damage, you might say."

I hang my head. "What have you done?"

She doesn't reply. My bag, with my phone inside, follows my camera out of the window.

"Please!" I'm choking back tears. "You've got what you want. You can keep your mirror. You can have Nightshade. I won't interfere. Just tell me where Dad is!"

She crouches down, her perfect face uncomfortably close to mine. I stare into those hypnotic green eyes.

"There's no point, Freya. He doesn't remember who you are. His memories were problematic. They had to be controlled. He was grateful, actually, he wanted to forget. He's in his happy place now, doing what he loves."

She's talking in riddles. I curl into a ball. From far away, I hear her on the phone.

"We have an intruder in the Nightshade atelier. Please come up, immediately."

Moments later, footsteps pound down the hallway. Rough hands grab me and haul me to my feet.

"See this girl off the premises," Bella barks. "She is not welcome in this building, or in the vicinity of my fashion show. If she should be foolish enough to ignore this advice … I'll leave the consequences to you."

Bulky arms drag me into the corridor and force me down the stairs.

The last thing I hear is Bella laughing as I'm thrown into the alley.

36

It's over. Bella's won.

I slump against the wall of Falkland House. My knees sting with grit and my palms are dotted with blood. My arm is throbbing from where Bella's henchman gripped it.

But nothing compares to the pain in my heart.

Mum was weak and selfish. She left me. She took her own life. Is that why Dad kept silent all these years?

Sobs rock my body.

If Bella's destroyed Dad's memories, how will I ever know the truth?

Can he really have forgotten all about me?

With a stab of sorrow, I think of my camera – my

precious present from Dad – smashed to pieces on the street. I search the alley but it's too dark to see anything. I'm not safe here, but I don't know where to go.

Guilt crushes me. *Sam's talk with his dad*. I've missed it – I didn't even text him.

I sink my head into my knees and let out a moan.

"Freya?"

I don't know how much time has passed. Jake is crouching over me, eyes wide. He wraps his jacket around my shoulders and my body starts shaking again.

"Bella left the site visit early. I had a hunch she was coming here. I tried to call, but you didn't answer. What happened? Are you all right?"

He pulls me close and I relax into his warmth. Little by little, the tremors subside and my breathing calms enough to talk.

Jake listens, his mouth a hard line. "OK. Can you stand? Good. Come on."

He leads me down the alley, following the edge of the building. At the end, we veer right. We're standing in a small car park at the back of Falkland House. It's empty, save for a row of industrial-size bins. A few bags have spilled out on to the ground.

"Over there. Look!"

Dropping my hand, Jake rushes to where the remains of my camera are scattered over the concrete. I see my bag too, lying in the dirt. I snatch it up as Jake picks through the debris.

"Don't bother," I tell him. "It's pointless."

A dark shape catches my eye: the cylinder of my lens. It's next to a ripped bin bag, with scarlet scraps of fabric spewing out. I go to rescue it, then stop. In amongst the fabric scraps is a bottle.

I take it out.

The bottle is small and brown with a rubber stopper at the top, just like the one in Bella's drawer.

But this bottle has a label.

Tincture of Atropa Belladonna

A gallery of botanical images scrolls through my mind – purple-black berries and twisting stems. I unscrew the lid and inhale. The scent that hits my nostrils is like bitter tomatoes: sweet, cloying and horribly familiar.

Atropa Belladonna. Deadly Nightshade.

Attractive, psychoactive…

Dangerous.

Sweat breaks out on my skin. I scrabble for my phone, praying it still works. My fingers tremble as I type into the search engine.

The results come back.

"Symptoms of atropa belladonna poisoning include headaches, nausea, confusion and hallucinations, and in acute circumstances, may lead to…"

No.

Icy fingers grip me. *This* is the ancient lethal beauty drug Sam mentioned. If anyone could get it, Bella could. This is how she's tied up her "loose ends".

"What have you got there?" Jake squints at the bottle.

"It's poisonous," I whisper. "I think Bella's given it to Dad."

Jake's face darkens. "This is serious. We need to find him, now."

"But I don't know where he is!" My knees feel weak.

Bella's taunt echoes in my head. *"He's in his happy place, doing what he loves."*

Suddenly something crystallizes. A memory from the good times; me and Dad together...

In the murky gloom of the car park, a light goes on inside my head.

37

We run to the station, feet slamming the pavement.

Dad loves photography. That's what he cares about. And there's one place he loved to do it, where he could lose himself for hours in the process.

His old workshop. That's his happy place.

I can even guess why he's there. Bella said that Nightshade's new international campaign is being published in next month's *Seen* magazine. Now I've figured out her scene-stealing plans for the finale of her fashion show, I'll bet anything she's the star of these new pictures. Dad would be able to shoot them, *and* doctor them for her, just the way she likes. He never wanted to give up photography, not really. If Bella had asked him, he wouldn't have been able to resist.

"Where is this workshop?" Jake pants next to me.

"Somewhere near Soho." I sift through foggy memories. "There was a white tower block..."

"You mean Centre Point? That's at Tottenham Court Road. Think you'd remember the way from there?"

"I don't know. I can try." A train is pulling into the platform. Jake leaps on board, hauling me up behind him.

Our journey is agonizingly slow. As we snake our way into central London, I think of the drug in Dad's system – the deadly nightshade swimming through his veins, blotting out his memories ... perhaps even his life.

We *have* to get to him in time.

At Bank station, we head underground to the Tube platform. Jake nudges me to look up. The splash of red pulls my focus. Stretched across a hoarding on the opposite side of the track is a billboard. The twisting vines are all too familiar.

NIGHTSHADE
1 September
London Fashion Week

All around us, people are gazing at the billboard. No one can take their eyes off it. It's like they're in some kind of trance.

Something feels wrong, really wrong. But I don't have time to think about it. The train is pulling in. Pushing through the dazed crowd, we jump on board.

At Tottenham Court Road, we emerge into the night air. Jake points at the white tower looming over us. "Ring any bells?"

"Yes!" My heart leaps. I remember holding Dad's hand as we used to weave through these streets. "This way!"

We sprint down Charing Cross Road. When we pass the old entrance to Dad's art college, Central Saint Martins, I know we're on the right track. He would always point it out. Everything comes flooding back. At Cambridge Circus, instinct steers me left on to Shaftesbury Avenue, Jake matching me step for step.

"Down here!"

We dash across Endell Street and a hundred horns blare. I ignore them, my inner compass pulling me on. Finally, we reach an iron gate, squeezed between two buildings. A narrow alleyway lies just beyond.

"This is it." I bend over, sucking in air.

Jake rattles the gate. "It's locked."

"Wait." I point to a gap between the bars, wider than the rest. Slipping my wrist through, I feel for the buzzer on the inside wall. The gate releases with a clunk.

"Genius."

"Dad always forgot his keys."

I push into the alley. It's as dingy as I remember, piled with rubbish and abandoned crates. We veer left, arriving at a low building with a wooden door.

Dad's old workshop.

His sign is still there. The silly logo – a camera in a pointy hat.

NICK JONES
Darkroom Wizard

It catapults me into the past.

I never dreamt Dad would have kept the workshop all this time. I assumed he'd sold it years ago. I should have guessed from the way he talked about those days. He must have loved it too much to let it go.

"Mr Jones!" Jake bangs on the door. "Are you in there?"

"Dad!" I shout. "It's Freya. Let me in!"

"Look." Jake points to a window above the door, almost three metres up. He grabs some crates from the alley and stacks them for me to climb. I scrub at the filthy glass.

"Can you see anything?"

I squint into the darkness. As shapes emerge, I feel a pang. The workshop is just how I remember. The wonky furniture. The criss-crossed washing lines where Dad pegged up his prints. The curved slope of the infinity wall he built for shoots. The door leading to the darkroom at the back.

And something else.

The pulsing red light of a computer monitor on standby. In the darkest corner of the workshop is a desk. And slumped over the desk is a person.

"He's there!" I give a strangled cry. "Dad! Can you hear me?" I hammer on the glass.

"Get down," Jake says. "Stand back."

He swings a crate at the door. The wood is half rotten and the lock is old and weak. A few kicks finish it off.

"Dad!" I rush inside.

Dad's eyes are closed. The room smells strange and bitter. A pool of vomit glistens by his feet.

"Wake up!" I go to grab his shoulders.

"Don't move him," Jake warns. "I'll check his pulse."

I fall back, my heart in my mouth. *Please let him be alive. Don't let it be too late.*

"It's weak." Jake fumbles with his phone, his knuckles white. "He needs to get to hospital. Ambulance, please. Yes, it's an emergency."

I sink to my knees as Jake speaks to the operator, his voice reaching me in waves. "*Suspected poisoning ... atropa belladonna ... unconscious ... come quickly.*"

This is a dream.

A nightmare.

"Hold on," I whisper, tracing the veins on Dad's hand. His breathing is shallow, barely there.

"The ambulance is on its way," Jake says. "I'll wait outside and flag it down."

I stay with Dad.

Moonlight creeps through the door, casting a silvery light over the workshop. I start to notice things I didn't see before. Dad's suitcase, crammed with clothes. Blankets, pillows, cushions. A mini fridge. A folding camp-bed shoved against a wall.

Someone planned this well.

Some black-and-white prints are hanging on a washing line at the far end of the room. I stand up to take a closer look.

Just as I expected, every picture is of Bella. Some are full length, while others are close up, and in each one she's wearing a different gown – gowns I've seen tonight on the mannequins in her atelier. The key looks from the Nightshade collection.

But that's not why I stare.

I'm staring because every photograph shows Bella the way I've barely ever seen. Her face is lightly lined, her flesh is soft and yielding. She looks real, unretouched.

Beautiful.

I blink. *This* is her international campaign? No way. She'd never allow it.

I move back to Dad's desk. One tap of the keyboard and the monitor springs to life. Photoshop is open on the desktop. Quickly, I search for recent images. *I knew it.* Here they are – the washing-line portraits.

Except of course, they're not.

These images have been altered and distorted, slimmed and polished, totally beyond belief. And under each image, the Nightshade logo sears my brain with its vivid red text, impossible to ignore.

Rage burns in my stomach.

This is the campaign that will be shared around the world. Bella wants the whole world to idolize her, to want to be her. She's taken everything Dad loves – his truthful, authentic way of working – and made him corrupt it, to create this damaging illusion.

And when he'd finished, she tried to end his life.

I think of all the people who will see these images – impressionable young girls, like me, Saskia, Amy – and how this campaign will make them feel. Then I snatch up the mouse, pull the files into the trash and empty it.

It feels good. Like taking back control.

A siren wails. Jake is back, with three paramedics. They check Dad over, silent, serious, efficient. As two of them hoist Dad on to a stretcher, I hand the little bottle to the third. She frowns at the label and speaks into her radio.

As Dad is lifted into the ambulance, my eyes swim. He looks so small and fragile.

"Are you his daughter?" a paramedic asks. "Looks like you've had a bad night. Let's check you out too."

I'd forgotten my bruises, my torn clothes.

"Shall I come?" Jake asks.

"Sorry." The paramedic shakes her head. "There isn't room."

Jake looks unhappy but he nods. "Call me when you can," he says, pushing something small into my hand. *My memory card.* "I rescued it," he says, shyly. "Just in case."

We hug awkwardly, and I climb into the ambulance.

Right now, I can't think about my photos.

The only thing that matters is Dad.

My thoughts turned once more to the
dark-haired girl, from all those years ago.
She was clever, talented — long since
gone — but perhaps our work was not…
Might our work be recreated, if a plan
were put in place? A grieving widower
located? A lost legacy unearthed?
I breathed the scheme to my golden
girl, and harnessed our desires:
her beauty preserved. Her images restored.
My magic one thousand times as strong.

38

Dad is taken to Intensive Care.

Before they'll let me see him, the medical staff insist on checking me over and cleaning up my grazes. I fob off their questions, somehow managing to convince them that there's nothing I want to report.

Not until I've talked to Dad, at least.

The sight of him in a hospital gown, with a drip in one arm and a tube fastened to his mouth, chokes me up again.

"That's the ventilator, to help him breathe," a nurse tells me. The badge on his scrubs says *Toby*. "We had to pump his stomach as a precaution, because we don't know when he ingested the substance, or how much."

"Will he wake up?" I whisper.

Toby straightens the bed sheet. "Try not to worry."

A doctor comes in and sweeps up the notes at the end of Dad's bed. Her conversation with Toby is full of words I don't understand.

"*Atropine ... activated charcoal ... absorbs toxicity ... physostigmine ... effective...*"

I clutch the bed rail, knuckles white.

Toby leaves, and the doctor turns to me.

"Hello, Freya, I'm Dr Rahman. I'm sure you're worried about your dad, but do you mind if I ask you some questions?"

"OK."

"Thank you. As you know, your dad has ingested a very toxic substance. Do you know how he might have got hold of it?"

I look at the ground. "I'm not sure. I suppose ... someone might have given it to him."

"Any idea who?"

I shake my head. The last thing I want to do is protect Bella, but the idea of police getting involved feels terrifying. I'm still not sure of what Dad does and doesn't know.

"He will wake up, won't he?"

Dr Rahman smiles kindly. "He's been through a great deal. It's lucky he vomited, though, and it's extremely lucky you found him when you did. We've given him an antidote. Hopefully, he'll regain consciousness soon."

I blink back tears. "And will he ... will he be...?"

"His normal self? It's too soon to say. The long-term effects of this kind of poisoning are unpredictable. Until he wakes up, we won't know how his cognitive capacity has been affected."

"His…?"

"Sorry." She rests a hand on my arm. "I mean his brain. His ability to think, learn, remember. We'll have to wait and see. Stay and talk to him. It might help."

She slips out through the door.

I drop into a chair.

Dad's skin is like tissue paper, his veins visible beneath. He looks so … *old*. If Bella's erased his memories, what will happen to him? To us?

Will I ever know the truth about Mum?

I lean close and whisper in his ear.

"Please wake up, Dad. Wake up and remember."

"Freya?" Toby startles me awake. I peer at the clock through sleep-filled eyes. It's six in the morning. I've been with Dad all night.

He's still unconscious, fingers limp in my grasp.

"The cafe opens soon," Toby says. "Why don't you get breakfast while I do your dad's obs?"

I hesitate.

"I'll get you the moment there's any change."

I sleepwalk my way downstairs. The strip-lighting in the atrium flickers, making my head hurt. The only other person here is a cleaner, mopping to the music in his headphones. I buy a scalding black coffee, dump in two sugars, and sit on a red plastic chair. The caffeine and sugar wake my brain, churning up my fears again. I look for a distraction and think of my camera, smashed to smithereens.

My phone pings with a message from Jake.

Any news?

He's still unconscious.

He's in the best place.

A few moments later he adds:

I'm here if you need to talk x

The message brings me comfort, although I haven't got the headspace to analyse that kiss. I've just seen a chain of messages and missed calls from Sam from last night.

19:15
Freya where are you?

19:40
Dad just got in. He's in a foul mood.

20:15
Are you even coming?

22:29
Wow. Thanks for nothing.
Guess you're busy having fun with Jake.

I hang my head.

Sam's right to be angry – I'm a terrible friend, and I owe him more than he knows. If he'd never mentioned atropa belladonna, I wouldn't have realized the danger Dad was in. We might not have got help in time. It might have been too late.

Sam, I'm so sorry.
I know I let you down.
I don't expect you to forgive me.
I found Dad. He was in his old workshop.
Bella tried to poison him.
I'm at UCL Hospital.
I don't know if he's going to be OK.

It's too early for him to reply.

I don't even know if he will.

Force of habit kicks in next, guiding my fingers. Even though I know it's pointless, before I can stop myself, I'm on social media, checking for updates on Nightshade.

I nearly drop my phone.

This is getting ridiculous.

The articles and mentions have multiplied beyond all imagining. Now, famous celebrities are arguing in public about who is going to sit in the front row at the show. Models I recognize from the casting have posted on their accounts, raving about clothes they haven't even seen. People have shared their posts thousands of times.

This *has* to be more than clever marketing. The speed at which it's happening – it's *uncanny*.

I shiver.

Is something *supernatural* helping Nightshade's influence to spread?

Whatever the truth, my blood boils to think that Bella's got the world in the palm of her hand, while Dad's lying in hospital with his life in danger.

I have to let it go. I've lost and Bella has won.

I close my browser and stand up. I'm about to put my phone away when I see the red number one, hovering over my email icon.

Huh? It's probably spam, or something to do with college. I hardly ever use email. I'll quickly check and delete it before I go back up to Dad.

But when I open the email, I sink back into my seat.

The subject fires an arrow to my heart.

39

From: TAKAHASHI, Naoko
To: JONES, Freya
Subject: TESS WHITE

Dear Freya,

My name is Naoko. Your email was forwarded to me
by Kawakubo College. Many years ago, I worked in
the fashion department there. I understand you are
seeking information about your mother, Tess White.

Tess White was my friend. I miss her to this day.

You won't remember me, Freya, but I remember

you. I have often wondered what became of you
after you left Japan. It saddens me to think that
you have grown up knowing little of your mother.
She was a remarkable person. However, certain
memories have always troubled me. I will tell you
everything I remember. It is right that you should
know.

I stop reading for a moment. The text is jumping before
my eyes. This person – Naoko – knew my mum. She was
her friend. She calls Mum *remarkable*. How does that square
with Bella's version of events?

I work up the courage to scroll.

When Tess began her studies, I was working as a
seamstress – or sewing technician, as they say now.
I was aware of Tess, of course. It was not unknown
for international students to enrol at the college, but
it was still uncommon. I knew of her hard-working
attitude and impressive command of Japanese,
but it was not until her second year that I learned of
Tess's talent.
During that year, we became friends.

I pause. *Tess's talent.* I want to believe it, but according to
Bella, Mum was a nobody who needed her for inspiration.
Now I'm not sure what to think.

I'll never forget the first time Tess showed me her
designs. Her drawings were like nothing I'd ever
seen. Tess was inspired by ancient tales of powerful
women from all over the globe. Her work was
original and exciting. It said something new about
beauty and the female form.

But Tess did not share my belief in her. The
other students found Tess's ideas strange. It's true
that her designs were not "pretty". They were more
suited to an art gallery than a department store. But
I knew they had the potential to be important.

I told Tess I would help bring her vision to life.

I sip my coffee, thinking again about the sketchbook from
the attic. I'm sure this is the work Naoko is describing. It
must pre-date the designs at Bella's atelier. That would
explain why the sketchbook was in a different box. Bella
did say that Mum's work was "hideous" before she came
along, and it's true those drawings were outlandish – even
Sam giggled at them. I suppose they must have seemed even
more weird, all those years ago.

Not weird. I correct myself. *Just ... different.*

But Mum lost confidence. She doubted herself because
she didn't fit the mould. Is that why her work changed so
dramatically? Is that why she needed Bella's help?

I read on.

Tess and I met daily, creating samples from her

designs. Throughout this process, her ability was
clear. Tess had a natural feel for fabrics, an eye
for detail – and her pattern cutting was the best
I'd ever seen. This skill was especially impressive,
since she refused to use the tiny dressmaker's
mannequins in the studio, preferring to fit her
clothes on "real" bodies – her own and her friends'.
She rejected the narrow silhouette peddled by the
fashion magazines. Her clothes were for everyone,
she said.

Goosebumps pepper my arms. That's why Mum's
sketchbook resonated with me. Her clothes felt playful,
free. Not tied to rules and trends.

As Tess and I became close, she shared details of
her life. Her parents back in England disapproved
of the fashion world. They wanted Tess to find a
"proper" job. Tess was troubled by their rejection of
her dreams.

My eyes widen. I'd assumed Mum was confident, going to
Japan when she was young – but this sounds more like an
escape. How must it have felt to have parents who didn't
understand her?

Guilt sweeps over me again. This is what Sam's going
through. When he needed me, I let him down.

Then, in her second year, Tess discovered she was pregnant.

I shiver. That baby was me.

Tess worked hard throughout her pregnancy, and after you were born, Freya – on a snowy day in January, just before her third and final year – Tess returned to college quickly, determined to graduate as planned. Money was tight and your father worked long hours as a photographer's assistant, often away from home. Tess placed you in a crèche and ran to see you between lectures. She loved you, Freya, but life was difficult.

Very difficult indeed.

Around me, the hospital atrium is waking up, people arriving for appointments. I sip my coffee, barely tasting it, almost too nervous to read on.

The time came for Tess to start work on a final collection for the graduation shows. To help the students prepare, the college hired fitting models. The girl assigned to Tess was named Isabel – or Issy, as she liked to be known.

I suck in a breath.
Bella. It must be.

315

Tess was unhappy. The idea of fitting her
collection on a fashion model, instead of a real
woman, bothered her. In turn, Issy was rude and
opinionated, openly critical of Tess's work. It's safe
to say the two women did not get on.

But their relationship changed.

I can pinpoint the moment it happened. Tess
had decided to visit one of Tokyo's big antique
markets, looking for ideas. She loved anything
with a sense of history, a story to tell. When she
returned to college, she seemed different – distant,
preoccupied. In her arms was a mirror with a carved
wooden frame. She placed it in the corner of the
studio by her workspace, claiming it "inspired her".
She refused to let anyone near it. The mirror was
beautiful, but something about it made me wary.

It had a dark presence in the room.

The world around me fades away. Now there's nothing but
the words on my phone. I can't believe what I'm reading.

Bella's mirror. Mum found it.

It belonged to her first.

Tess worked hard on her graduation collection,
under the mirror's constant gaze. Day and night,
she sketched and cut and sewed, rejecting all my
offers of help.

I withdrew from the studio, uneasy. Tess

had always been so forward-thinking, but now
she seemed different – more anxious, more
conservative, more willing to conform. And her work
was different too. Gone was her vision of fashion for
everyone, and in its place was the very opposite.
When it finally came time to fit these new designs
of Tess's, my worst fears were confirmed. Her
collection was glamorous, but dull, conventional and
safe – compared to everything she'd done before.
And she'd designed it to fit one woman only – Issy –
who of course was delighted. The two women
became inseparable.

In my bones, I knew what had caused this
change in Tess.

It could only be the mirror.

My blood chills. My coffee is stone cold.

Naoko is describing the Nightshade collection, I'm sure
of it. But can she really be saying that the *mirror* was behind
it? That the mirror did something, not just to Mum herself,
but to her work?

I tried to express my worries, but Tess only laughed.
She was going to be a success! And the strange
thing was that everyone agreed. The other students
began to imitate her designs. Her tutors raved about
her to the department-store buyers. The fashion
editors wanted front-row seats at her graduation

317

show. As farfetched as it sounds, I knew it was the
mirror's doing. The hold it had on Tess infected
everyone around.

I pleaded, but Tess refused to listen.

Then something happened to make her see.

I take a deep breath, readying myself for whatever comes
next.

Shortly before the graduation shows, Tess arrived at
college, carrying you, Freya, in her arms. The crèche
was closed, your father was away. She begged me
to watch you so she could complete her fittings on
Issy. Seeing she was desperate, I agreed.

I settled you in the design studio, far from Tess's
mirror. You were a happy child, Freya. Curious,
confident, and just on the verge of walking.

Suddenly you pulled yourself to standing. When
Tess saw, she stopped and called your name. We
held our breath, waiting for you to take your first
steps.

And you did.

But not towards your mother.

You moved towards the mirror in a trance,
never once turning your head. When you touched
the glass, you let out a scream that chilled me to
the bone.

Tess leapt towards you and snatched you away.

It was as though she had woken from a very deep sleep. She believed me now, she said, trying to console you. The mirror must go. It was dangerous. She would have it destroyed.

It was Issy who offered to do it.

Solemnly, we made her promise. Tess could only think of comforting you, Freya, and I had no wish to touch that thing myself.

As soon as the mirror left the studio, the air seemed to clear, and Tess's true nature returned. As she held you, Freya, she looked at her work as if for the very first time. This collection did not reflect her beliefs, she said. She could not bring it into the world.

We destroyed it in the college incinerators, piece by piece.

In the end, it was you, Freya, who proved the greatest influence. You saved Tess from the mirror. Her love for you helped her to see.

I can't read any more. Tears are streaming down my cheeks. All my life I've wondered about my mum – what kind of person she was, what she believed in – and I built up a picture, which Bella ripped apart. Mum wasn't perfect, I know that now; but she was anything but weak. She broke free of the mirror's power and her convictions returned, stronger than ever before.

All because she loved me.

319

Mum had *everything* to live for. And if Bella was wrong about that, she has to be wrong about Mum's death.

I wipe my eyes.

> Of course, without a final collection, Tess was unable to graduate. She withdrew from her course and a few days later, the graduation shows took place without her.
>
> But that night brought terrible news.
>
> When I heard of your mother's untimely death, I felt a deep sense of loss – not only for you, and for myself, but for the world. Tess White was an artist, ahead of her time. It's a tragedy she never got the recognition she deserved.
>
> I resigned from the college soon afterwards. There would never be another student like Tess. I turned my back on the fashion world for good.
>
> I'm glad you made contact, Freya. When your father left Japan without a forwarding address, I had no way to reach you. I have some items belonging to your mother.
>
> I will return these to you now.
>
> Your friend, Naoko

40

The hospital foyer buzzes with activity, but I'm frozen. Caught in the eye of the storm.

Truth radiates from Naoko's words.

Mum found Bella's mirror – and it used its magic to twist her talent and promote its own ideas. *That's* why the Nightshade collection looked so different from the pictures in the attic sketchbook.

All shall be perfect.

The mirror's mantra, and the Nightshade collection in a nutshell.

Mum might have designed it, but it wasn't what she

believed. Mum loved diversity, not conformity. She thought fashion should be for everyone, that beauty lies in creativity, self-expression...

Being real.

The mirror made her change. It told her only one type of beauty was acceptable – Bella's beauty. One narrow definition. One totally unrealistic standard.

I shake my head. Naoko's right. Mum's death is bigger than my loss. It's a waste of talent. Her work – her *real* work – could have made a difference. She could have been an influence for good.

Influence.

The realization hits me, gripping me with fear.

The Nightshade collection doesn't belong to my mum *or* to Bella. It belongs to the mirror. And the mirror wants its message to be shared.

All this time, I've thought of Bella as the bad guy, stealing Mum's work to further her career. But what if she's not? What if she's just a puppet, performing the mirror's plans? Naoko described how the mirror started to infect everyone around it, like a chain reaction, a ripple effect.

The same thing is happening now.

Nightshade's incredible popularity has to be down to the mirror's magic. I don't know how exactly, and I don't know how to stop it, but it's the only thing that makes sense.

"Freya?"

Toby is standing in front of me. His shift must have

finished because he's not wearing scrubs. It takes me a second to place him, I'm so lost in my thoughts.

"You can go up." He smiles. "Your dad's awake."

Yasmin, the new duty nurse, lets me in.

Dad is lying propped up by pillows. A clear tube runs around his face and into his nose. His eyes are closed.

Relief becomes fear. *Will he know who I am?*

His eyelids flutter.

"Dad?"

Pinprick pupils search my face. I hold my breath, waiting for that spark of recognition. Nothing. I choke back a sob.

"Snowdrop." His eyes crinkle and he reaches out.

"Dad!" Sobs come juddering out. I want to wrap my arms around him, but I hang back, scared in case I hurt him.

"Be gentle," Yasmin warns. "He's very weak. I'll give the pair of you five minutes." She slips away, leaving us alone.

I move closer, taking Dad's hand and drinking in his face. He's like a wounded animal with his shadowy eyes and stubbled chin. "Dad, are you OK?"

"I am, thanks to you," he croaks. "The nurse told me you found me and brought me in. Freya, I've been so foolish."

My heart thumps.

"I should have listened to you." A tear snakes down his face. "Bella didn't love me. I was useful to her, that's all." His shoulders sag.

"Oh, Dad." My heart breaks for him. "Try not to get upset. You heard what the nurse said."

He pulls himself together. "I want to explain. I owe you that."

I nod.

"I was lonely," Dad whispers. "I fell for her flattery and her lies. She said she could get my photography career back on track. But first I had to prove myself, at the agency."

"Victor's trial?" I prompt gently. I can see how much effort speaking demands, but Dad needs to get this off his chest.

He nods. "Victor asked me to retouch some shots. Some close-up images of Bella. She wanted something dark, mysterious, like a fairy tale. A vivid shade of red." He takes a sip of water. "She stayed the whole time I did it. It was easy enough, and I liked making her happy. I assumed it was a one-off job. She mentioned some project in the pipeline, and said I'd be involved, taking pictures. But then Victor piled on more jobs: retouching for other models, work on a website. I was snowed under."

Keeping him busy, while Bella stole Mum's designs.

"Did she say what her project was?"

"Not really." Dad shrugs. "She was vague." He blinks, eyes watery. "I didn't ask questions, Freya. I don't know why. Whenever I was with her, they … flew out of my head. I wanted to please her, to do what she asked. I was in love…"

Or under a spell, I think. *The mirror's spell.* "She was

persuasive," I say instead. "Was it her idea to send me away?"

Dad reaches for my hand. "She said London schools were dreadful. That you were bored in Camden with me, faking an interest in photography for my sake. She said you'd deny it, but you wanted to get away."

I shake my head. "She lied."

"She was good at it." Dad looks away. "I meant to talk to you, but everything happened so fast. The day you left – I don't remember it. Bella said I had a virus. It's a blur."

"It wasn't your fault," I tell him. My heart aches to see Dad so ashamed and confused. I think of the bitter scent on his breath that day, like the smell in his workshop and the bottle I found. Was that the first time Bella gave Dad belladonna? To ensure he kept quiet until I was safely out of the way?

"After you left, things felt wrong," Dad goes on. "The most precious thing in my life was gone. I told Bella I was going to drive to the school and bring you back. That's when she asked to see the workshop."

"So she knew about it?"

"I told her when we met." Dad blushes. "I suppose I was trying to impress her. We took a taxi. She loved it. Said it was the perfect place to shoot her campaign."

I nod, my jaw clenched tightly.

"It felt so good to be back behind the camera." Dad smiles sadly. "When she looked into my lens, I'd forget everything else. We worked late into the evenings, losing track of time. Then during the day, I printed, scanned, retouched — whatever she asked. I couldn't refuse her — I didn't want to. We even slept there, on a camp bed. She brought things from home to make it feel more cosy. At the time it seemed romantic."

I bet she brought the mirror.

I think of the photos in Dad's workshop, the doctored campaign files ready for launch.

"What about the clothes she was wearing in the pictures?" I ask Dad. "Did you recognize them?"

He sips his water before answering. "Not at first." He pauses. "But one day, I was printing an image. Bella stepped out for a moment and I felt … different. *Lighter.* Like a fog had lifted. And something started nagging me."

I wait for him to go on.

"The dress she was wearing in the picture, I'd seen it — a version of it — before." He swallows. "It was like your mum's wedding dress. Which couldn't be right, because—"

"Because Mum designed that dress herself," I finish.

Dad stares. "You know?"

"Not everything," I whisper.

His face swirls with misery and regret.

"Then what happened?"

Dad draws a breath. "I remembered other things. How Bella had asked questions — about Tess, our time in Japan, what happened to Tess's things, after she died. Seeing that dress made me uneasy, so when Bella came back to the workshop, I confronted her."

"How did she react?"

"She called me crazy, said I was imagining things. I thought perhaps I was."

I shake my head. *Classic gaslighting. Classic Bella.*

"She said I was ungrateful, said she was doing me a favour, relaunching my career." He hangs his head. "Then she was sweet again, saying how beautiful I made her look, how talented I was, how much she loved me."

I link Dad's fingers in mine.

"She told me to finish the job and send the files to Victor. That if I did, we'd drive to your school and bring you back. I did what she said, but then I fell sick. Even worse than before. It happened so quickly, I couldn't function, couldn't move. I had these dreams – hallucinations. They were so vivid. I saw your mum…" He chokes. "Bella said the virus was back. She was going to get help. That's the last thing I remember."

I look him in the eye. "She didn't get help. She poisoned you. Bella isn't what she seems. She targeted you because she knew you were Mum's widower. She wanted Mum's graduation designs. She stole them from our attic and used them to launch a label of her own, then she made you shoot her advertising campaign. But you starting asking questions, so she gave you deadly nightshade and left you to die!" My voice breaks. I'll never forget seeing Dad, slumped over the desk in his workshop. It's fixed for ever in my mind.

"Sorry, guys. Time's up." Yasmin's head pokes around

the door. "Mr Jones, you look shattered. Take a break, Freya. You can come back later on today. Give your dad a rest."

Dad is staring into space. I go to stand, but he grips my hand. "Snowdrop, wait." His voice is faint. I have to bend down to hear. "There are things I never told you about the past. Things about your mum. When you come back, I'll tell you everything, I promise. I just hope you'll forgive me when you know the truth."

328

41

A surprise is waiting for me in the hospital foyer.

Sam's lanky frame stands out a mile. I see him loitering in the cafe queue, eyeing up the snacks. My tummy twists. Has he come to give me a piece of his mind?

As I get nearer, he seems to sense me. Before I can tap him on the shoulder, he turns around. The next thing I know, his arms are around me, enveloping me in the world's biggest hug.

All the tears and tension of the past twenty-four hours come flooding out.

"I came as soon as I got your text," Sam says, paying for two hot chocolates and leading me to a table.

"I'm sorry," I start to say, but he shushes me.

"You had other things on your mind." He motions me to drink. "And not just hot interns." I giggle through my tears. "Tell me everything. Don't leave anything out."

I do, starting from when Sam left me at the casting, to what happened at the atelier and Bella's version of events, all the way through to figuring out where Dad was and what had happened to him.

"I worked it out, thanks to you," I say.

"What are friends for?" he says pointedly, then he soothes my guilty conscience with a wink.

"Read this," I say, showing him Naoko's email. I wait as he absorbs it.

"Do you believe it?" he asks, finally. "That Bella's mirror is behind all this? That it's … I dunno … *possessed?*"

I shrug. "I tried to tell you how it whispers. It's impossible to resist."

"Only for some." Sam smirks, then he grows serious. "It controlled your mum. You think it's controlling Bella?"

"Maybe," I say, grimly.

My phone rings in my bag. I reach down and frown. "It's Māra. She's video-calling."

"Who's Māra?"

"Ice Queen from the *Seen* shoot. Except she's not an ice queen. She's really nice. I met her again at the Nightshade casting. She helped after Bella tried to hurt me."

"So take her call."

I press the button to accept.

"Freya!" Māra's hair is flying in her face. Her voice is buffeted by wind. She's outside, somewhere busy. In the background, horns are blowing and sirens wail. "Freya, can you hear me?"

"Just about. Where are you? Are you OK?"

Māra ignores my questions. "Did you go to the atelier? Did you do what we talked about?"

"Yes. But I couldn't do it, I—"

"I thought so." Māra frowns, her lovely face tight and serious. "Freya, they cast me in the show. I found out this morning. It's definitely going ahead."

"I know," I mumble miserably.

"I need to know something," she interrupts. "What were the words? You never said."

"What words?"

"The words you say to the mirror!"

Her urgent tone makes my stomach drop. "Why?"

"There's something you should see."

Māra suddenly disappears. It takes me a second to realize she's flipped her camera around. Now, I'm looking at the view from her perspective. In front of me is a busy roundabout with a massive billboard towering over it. Staring down from the billboard is an enormous poster with a twisting background of vines.

Over the top, bright red letters two-metres high burn their message into my brain.

NIGHTSHADE:
ALL SHALL BE PERFECT

Fear clutches me.

Māra's back. "Could you see it? The billboard, it's causing accidents! There are cars all over the pavement. Drivers are staring at the words, not looking at the road. Everyone is in a trance."

"Are you hurt?"

"I'm fine. But this is scary, Freya. And you know what else?"

"Wait." We're making too much noise in the foyer. Sam and I push our way outside. Māra also moves away from the roundabout, somewhere quieter.

"OK, tell me."

"There's a rumour going around," she says. "At the model apartment, all the girls were talking about it. They're saying the Nightshade collection *perfects* you. I tried to tell them that's impossible, but they don't want to hear it. And they're not the only ones. People have been placing orders before they've even seen the clothes. There are waiting lists a mile long."

Next to me, Sam shakes his head.

"I did an experiment," Māra goes on. "I posted something on social media, just to see. It was nothing – a picture of the book I'm reading. But I added the Nightshade hashtag and it blew up. I got a quarter of a million new followers in one night."

Sam whistles.

"I might know why." I summarize Naoko's story for Māra. "This isn't personal any more," I add. "It's not just about my mum – although the Nightshade show is the last thing she would have wanted. This affects millions of people. Any progress fashion's made – the progress it still needs to make – we can forget about it. In ten days, the Nightshade show will happen. The footage and photos will be shared all over the world, along with Bella's new campaign. Everyone will fall for its so-called 'perfect' message. It's turning the clock back on a global scale."

"We have to fight back," Māra says, but there's no conviction in her voice. She sounds as hopeless as I feel.

"We can't," I say, shaking my head. "The mirror has powers we can't understand, let alone fight. There's nothing we can do."

42

It's afternoon and Sam has gone home. Finally I'm allowed to see Dad again.

He looks up as I open the door. Already his eyes seem brighter – less bloodshot and yellow – although I notice his hands are trembling.

"How are you feeling?" I slip into a chair. "Have you eaten?"

He doesn't answer. His fingers worry a hole in the bed sheet.

"Go easy," Yasmin says, kindly. "He's still got a long way to go."

She leaves us alone.

Dad's shoulders start to shake. "I promised to be honest with you, Freya, about your mum…" His voice breaks. I reach for his hand to steady us both.

"It wasn't an aneurysm, was it?"

Dad shakes his head and shatters my world.

"Why did you lie?"

"Because…" The pause seems to last for ever. Only the soft beep of the monitor breaks the silence. "I didn't want you to hate me, Freya. But you deserve the truth."

Then he tells me. The reason for his silence, the reason behind the secrets.

Another layer in the story of my past.

They met in Tokyo. Dad was a photographer's assistant. Mum was a model on a job. She hated modelling, she told him, hated having no voice. She had so much she wanted to say. He took her for coffee in Harajuku, a buzzy, creative area, full of young people in outlandish clothes. Mum was enchanted. While Dad took photos for his portfolio, she told him about her true passion – fashion design.

They fell in love, became inseparable – but her visa was due to expire. Neither of them wanted to go home. Dad's career was taking off, while Mum's parents were … difficult. Traditional. Dad found out about the fashion course at Kawakubo College and helped Mum with her application. She took a language course, passed the interview. They were both ecstatic when she won a place.

*

Dad pauses the story and I tense, sensing his mood change.

"We didn't plan to have a baby, but when your mum discovered she was pregnant, she was thrilled. We both were."

His forehead creases as he chooses his next words, and I can't help thinking of what Bella said.

Did Mum really care about me? Did she willingly leave me behind?

"We loved you from the moment you were born." Dad's eyes well up. "But times were tough. It was a challenge, juggling work, college, a baby. Money was tight. I took on extra jobs. I was often away. It was hard on both of us, but especially Tess…" He trails off.

"Did you know that Bella worked with Mum, at the college? She was Mum's fitting model."

"She was?" Dad's eyes widen. "I honestly had no idea. I was so busy. I had no time to visit the design studios. Though I knew something wasn't right. Tess … *changed*. She seemed distracted. I put it down to stress. I should have shown more interest. Things between us became … strained."

He looks down. My heart stutters.

"We had an argument, the day she died." Dad shuts his eyes, summoning the memory from where he's locked it deep inside. "It was the evening of the graduation shows. I'd flown back from a trip that day, especially. Tess's tutors thought she was going to hit the big time. I hoped this might be the moment things turned around for us.

When she told me that the show was cancelled – that she'd withdrawn from college – I was angry."

"Did she say why?"

Dad looks away. "She didn't get the chance. I lost my temper, told her she was selfish. After the sacrifices we'd made, it seemed like such a waste."

I move closer, gripping his hand tight.

"She was crying, but I wouldn't listen. Nothing she said made any sense. Then the phone rang; it was a friend. She needed Tess to meet her urgently. Something about a promise? Tess ran straight out of the apartment, even though it was pouring with rain. I couldn't stop her."

"The friend. Was she called Naoko?"

Dad shakes his head. "Her name was Issy."

My heart stops.

"That was the last time I saw Tess." Dad's crying now, huge, jagged sobs that shake the bed. "I called the police when she didn't come home that night. They found her body in the morning, after the storm died down. She'd fallen from a bridge as she cut across the park."

"And did she … did she mean to—" I can't finish.

Dad wraps his arms around me. "No, darling. Your mum loved you very much. She would never have left you, not on purpose. Not in a million years."

I sob into his chest.

"They said it was an accident, although no witnesses came forward. The bridge was slippery, the guard rail was broken – it made sense." Dad buries his face in my hair. "But deep down, I blamed myself."

"No!"

"It's true," he whispers. "It was my fault that Tess was so upset. I should never have said those things. I should have listened to her, supported her. I let her down. Her parents blamed me too, that was obvious. They helped with paperwork, and arranging a memorial service, but after that they barely spoke to me. I'd dragged their daughter into the fashion world. Tess was unhappy and I'd failed to protect her."

"It *wasn't* your fault!" I say, through gritted teeth. "I *know* it wasn't." I can't tell Dad about the mirror. He's too upset, it's too impossible to believe.

"Do you understand why I couldn't tell you the truth?" Dad's voice cracks. "All I wanted was to forget. To get away from the guilt and start again. Tess's parents died soon afterwards, within a year of each other. I think they never recovered from the shock. And after your granny passed away, no one else knew the truth. Calling it an aneurysm was simpler. Nobody asked questions. I hid everything away – my photos of Tess, things the college had given me, anything that reminded me of her. I kept her sketchbooks in the attic, out of sight. It was too painful."

I nod.

Dad pulls back and looks me deep in the eyes. "You're all I have left in the world, Freya. I couldn't risk losing you too. What if you blamed me, the way I blame myself?"

The widowed man was lost
and lonely, eager to forget.
We found him, charmed him, won his trust —
clouding his memories and confounding his
thoughts — convincing him of our love.
Under our spell, he spreads our word with
his artistry and skill. Every image imbued
with my magic — to bait, to snare, to lure.
His weakness is the child, of course,
but that can be contained.
With him as our servant,
the glamour grows.
Our renaissance seems secure.

43

A flood of feelings crashes over me.

First, a wave of relief. So many things make sense now: Dad's reluctance to talk about Mum, his bitterness about the fashion world, his objection to Jas's shoot.

Then, there's a downpour of grief.

Dad's been living with his guilt for years. But how could he have known the pressure Mum was under – from the sinister influence of the mirror?

Finally, there's a tsunami of anger.

Is *Bella* responsible for Mum's death? What *really* happened when Tess ran off to meet Issy? Clearly, Issy decided to break her promise. She didn't destroy the mirror. She kept it for herself.

Did she trick Mum into meeting her? Did the mirror make her do it?

When Tess's show was cancelled, was this some kind of revenge?

I look at Dad, collapsed on to his pillow, and my hands form furious fists. Bella poisoned him. There's no doubt in my mind that she's capable of murder. And how *dare* she imply that Mum took her own life? Mum would never have left me. Naoko said it, Dad said it: Mum *loved* me.

I can't let her get away with this.

Dad's eyes are closed. He looks spent, nothing left to give. I decide to keep my suspicions to myself for now. He's not strong enough to cope. I hold his hand, waiting for his breathing to settle.

In time, perhaps we'll talk.

Right now, Dad needs to heal.

I spend the night on a hard cot bed in the relatives' room in the ICU. The next morning Dad seems brighter, but he's not quite in the clear. The doctors want to run tests on his heart. I spend the day texting Sam and Jake to distract myself and buying so many cups of tea, I'm virtually on first name terms with the cafe staff. It's late afternoon before Dr Rahman officially declares Dad out of danger.

"He still needs to be kept under observation," she tells me. "So I'm afraid I can't discharge him yet. He'll be moved to a ward now. You won't be able to stay. Do you have somewhere you can go?"

I give her Carla's number, although I've already messaged Sam and told him of my plan to go home. With Bella gone, I know I'll feel safe there again. I want to reclaim our house, our space, ready for Dad's return.

Before I leave the hospital, I go to say goodbye to him on his ward. When I get there, I falter.

A police officer is sitting by his bed.

"This is my daughter, Freya," Dad introduces me. "I have her to thank for saving my life after my ... mistake."

I open my mouth, but he shoots me a look: *let me handle this*.

I listen, fists clenched, as Dad mumbles about dodgy herbal supplements, bought from "health food" websites he claims to have forgotten. The officer seems sceptical, but there's not much she can do if Dad insists on this version of events.

As soon as she's gone, I round on him. "Why didn't you tell her about Bella?"

"It's not that simple." He looks away.

"Why? Are you embarrassed?"

"No." He frowns. "Well, I suppose I am a bit. I've been so gullible. I just think involving the police is risky. We'll never prove Bella poisoned me on purpose, and she'll have covered her tracks by now. Plus, she's famous and powerful. Who'd believe me over her?"

I try to interrupt, but Dad goes on. "Better let her think

we're both out of her way. She's dangerous, Freya, surely you see that? It's obvious she'll stop at nothing to get what she wants, and I won't risk her hurting you. I'm alive. We have each other. It's enough."

I can see there's no point arguing.

I take the bus back to Camden, fire raging inside me to think that Bella will get away with what she did. Even deleting her new ad campaign wasn't the tiny triumph I'd hoped. Bella had already made Dad send the retouched files to Victor.

I let myself into the house, stepping over the growing pile of mail on the doormat. After I've fed Kodak, the first thing I do is throw open the windows to rid the house of Bella's sickly scent. *If only it were so easy to stop her toxic plans.* But I have to face reality. Tomorrow is August 24th. In a week's time, Bella and her mirror will get everything they wanted. She'll be fashion's darling, while the mirror will have power and influence like never before.

Its message of perfection will poison the world, faster than the belladonna running through Dad's veins.

I just wish there was something I could do about it.

I wake to a barrage of texts from Sam:

> **Are you awake? It's after 10! Have you logged on yet?**

It takes a moment to work out what he means.

Exam results. They're out today.

My stomach lurches. With Dad being so ill, it had slipped my mind.

> I forgot!
> Where are you? At school?

> *Nah. Seen enough of that place.*
> *Been waiting for you.*
> *I'll come to yours.*
> *We can do it together?*

> Deal.

It takes Sam less than ten minutes to arrive. It's obvious he's nervous from the way he's hopping from foot to foot and running his fingers through his hair.

He makes me go first. I log into my school account, tense. I'd imagined doing this with Dad, going out for lunch to celebrate. Instead I'll be visiting him later, at his hospital bed.

"Have they been posted yet?"

"Looks like it." I click through to my results and wait a lifetime for the page to load.

Yes! I let out my breath. All passes. *And a nine in photography!* I beam at Sam. I've done it. I'm off to college.

"All right, don't get big-headed." He hugs me. "Seriously, though, well done. OK, here goes."

344

He turns the laptop around, so I can't see the screen. As he logs in to his own account, I try to read his face.

"Come on! How did you do?"

Shyly, he turns the screen around.

"You got a nine in art!"

He nods. "And I scraped Maths and English! Only fours, but it's enough!"

"Not enough for sixth form, though." I frown, disappointed.

"I'm not going." He looks at me, a smile dancing on his lips. "I talked to Liam. There's a course where he goes – a diploma in hair and make-up for fashion. With these results, I'll get in."

My mouth falls open. "That's brilliant! What does your dad say?"

Sam clears his throat. "He doesn't know yet."

"You didn't have your talk?"

"I couldn't, could I? Without you."

Guilt pokes me again. "So he still doesn't know anything. About this course. About Liam?"

Sam's silent.

"So when are you going to tell him?"

He looks at me. "Are you doing anything now?"

We head straight to Sam's place without stopping. I abandoned him once before; I won't do it again. I have to be the kind of friend Naoko was for Mum – someone who supports Sam to be true to himself and makes sure his voice is heard.

There's a tense atmosphere in the flat. Carla's in the kitchen. She glances up when we come in. "You're home quickly," she says to Sam. "I heard about your dad, Freya. How's he doing?"

"A bit better, thanks."

"And your results? How did you do?"

"OK."

"Sam?"

In answer, Sam nods towards the living room. A sports commentary drones. We follow him down the hall and he stops outside the door.

"I can't."

"You can," I say, squeezing his hand. "I'll be right beside you. But only if you're ready."

He swallows. "I'm ready." He squeezes my hand back.

Tom is watching cricket with his feet on the coffee table. He frowns when we come in. "What's all this?"

"I got my results," Sam starts. "And ... I did OK. Better than I thought."

"That's great, love!" Carla looks relieved. "Isn't it, Tom?"

Sam picks up the remote. "Dad, can we talk?" His voice is quiet, but firm. "There's something I want to say."

"Oh, yeah?" Tom leans back. "And what might that be?"

Sam looks him in the eye. "It's about me. The truth."

Tom nods and Sam mutes the television. Carla slides on to the sofa next to Tom, her body tense. I don't move a

346

muscle, glued at Sam's side.

"I lied about having food poisoning," Sam begins. "You already know that. But I'm sorry. Really. I haven't been honest with you for a while. I've learned a lot this summer, about what I want and who I am."

Tom is silent. I nod, urging Sam on. He starts at the beginning, with the fashion shoot, the way he felt watching Karim at work. His thrill at transforming me for the casting. As he speaks, goosebumps dot my arms. Sam's passion burns through every word.

"It's what I want to do, Dad. I could be good. I know it."

Tom's face gives nothing away.

Taking a deep breath, I jump in. I could easily talk about how talented Sam is, but there's something else his parents should hear. "Sam's knowledge helped to save my dad's life," I say. "He knew about belladonna, the drug that poisoned Dad. They used to put it in beauty products. It meant I could tell the paramedics in time."

Tom eyes me. "So this interest in fashion, that's your influence, Freya?"

"No," Sam interjects. "It's all me." He pauses. "Dad, there's something else you need to know. Freya's not my girlfriend, she's my mate. My best mate." His voice wobbles. "I'm dating someone else, actually. His … his name is Liam."

A hush falls. Tom is silent. The pause stretches out.

"I'm sorry if you're disappointed." Sam chokes back a sob.

"Disappointed?" Tom's eyes are glistening. "I'm not

347

disappointed, you muppet!" He dabs his face with his sleeve. "I'm proud. That took some guts. But I'm ashamed you couldn't tell me sooner. What do you take me for – a dinosaur?"

"A T. rex!" Lily bursts through the door.

"Maybe a brontosaurus!" Sam giggles through his tears.

Tom pulls Sam into a hug. "I love you, son. I just wanted to help you out, like my dad did for me. I couldn't figure out why you weren't more grateful – clearly your head was somewhere else. Hair and make-up artist, eh?" He ruffles Sam's hair. "It's still painting and decorating, I suppose."

Carla wraps her arms around them both.

"Why's everybody crying?" Lily asks.

"Because they're happy," I say, picking her up.

She makes a face. "Weird."

"So this Liam," Tom says, pulling back to look at Sam. "He's a good lad, is he?"

"I think so." Sam's cheeks are pink.

Tom nods. "So when's he coming round?"

A couple of days later, Dad is discharged from hospital. Dr Rahman is pleased with his progress and he's allowed to recover at home.

Sam comes over to the house to wait with me, bringing flowers from Carla. I put them in a vase on the mantelpiece.

"Aren't you forgetting something?"

Beside the vase, he places the photo of Mum in the silver frame. I smile, admiring his glittery blue nails. Since the talk with his dad, Sam's begun to experiment more. I

348

look at Mum's quirky silver wedding dress, trying not to think about the version in Bella's atelier. In six days' time, the mirror's horrible, exclusive collection will be released into the world.

I'm sorry, Mum. You never wanted this.

The doorbell rings and I run, expecting Dad's cab.

On the doorstep is a man in uniform. "Delivery for Jones. Can you sign?"

"What is it?" Sam joins me.

"Dunno." I shake my head.

The man opens his van and lifts out a huge crate. "Priority airmail. Must have cost a fortune." He heaves the crate into the hall. "Fast-tracked through customs. Enjoy!"

I peer at the label on the crate.

To:
JONES Freya, 5 Pemberton Road,
London, NW1 8JP, UK

From:
MATSUSHIMA Naoko, 5-9-17 Udagawa-cho,
Shibuya-ku, Tokyo, JAPAN

The customs label is in Japanese, with an English translation underneath. I read it and my pulse begins to race:

Consignment Contains:
Clothing.

44

The crate is fastened shut.

I run to get a screwdriver from Dad's toolbox. Sam helps me prise off the lid. The top layers inside are tissue paper, with a note slipped between the sheets.

Dear Freya,

It gives me great pleasure to return your mother's work — her true work, as I think of it. The pieces here were designed and made by Tess, before she found the mirror.

It has been my privilege to take care of them until

now, but they belong with you. Perhaps one day they will
find the audience they deserve.

Your friend,
Naoko

With trembling hands, I reach into the crate. The clothes
have been wrapped beautifully, preserved with such care
that it's easy to imagine that the fabrics are as fresh and
colourful as they would have been all those years ago.

I lift out the first piece: a dress with enormous winged
sleeves. Immediately, I recognize it from the attic
sketchbook. In real life, it's even more stunning – vivid
teal, long and sweeping, with ruched detailing around the
shoulders and peacock feathers that wink in the light.

"Whoa!" Sam breathes beside me.

I take out another piece: a trouser suit in shimmering
fern-green shades, like a forest at sunset. It's cut low at the
back, with a collar riding high around the neck. Jagged
tails fan out at the back of the jacket, one of them longer
than the rest. Dragon-like, it trails the ground, the fabric
forming overlapping scales.

I gape.

Sam lifts up the piece underneath. This one is narrow,
made from stretchy fabric, like a sock. Then I spot the
pockets within.

"I recognize this!" Sam exclaims. "It's the bumpy one! It
just needs the padding!" He roots inside the crate and pulls

351

out beautiful soft inserts which slide into the pockets. The result is a totally different silhouette – one with rounded shoulders, bulbous hips and proudly curving belly.

"What's that?"

An envelope has fallen on to the floor. I snatch it up and open it.

Inside are two Polaroids, both faded with age. In the first, a young woman with short dark hair is sitting at a bench, hemming the teal dress I've just seen. At the same time, she's nursing a tiny baby. A caption is scrawled underneath.

Tess takes inspiration from baby Freya, April 2007

Mum was inspired by me?

My eyes swim, and a lump lodges in my throat. These clothes, this photo – these are the blueprints I've been looking for. Finally, I understand Mum – who she was, what she believed. And I know that I was her muse, just as I am. The two of us were cut from the same cloth.

"What's the other one?" Sam nudges me, gently.

I look at the second Polaroid.

Tess, preparing her graduation collection, March 2008

In the picture, Mum has her back to the camera. She's pinning a tight, narrow gown on to a model who smiles smugly into the lens.

Bella.

"Look!" I point to the background.

Behind Bella is the mirror.

"It really is true."

"Looks like it." Sam shivers. He takes both Polaroids and lays them to one side. Then he nods at the crate. "Why don't you try one on?"

"Me?"

He smiles. "Who else?"

I lift out a garment, nestled right at the bottom of the crate – a dress, silver-grey and heavy – and take it to the bathroom.

Slipping off my jeans and T-shirt, I step carefully into the dress. At first glance, it's just a long, plain column. It hugs my body so tightly, it's difficult to move.

Odd. It's more like something from the Nightshade collection.

Then I notice something. All over the dress are carefully concealed zips, and as I open them, something starts to happen. Shimmering concertina folds burst out, along the neckline, the waist, the hips, even the ankles – setting my body free. I'm like a golden butterfly emerging from a cocoon, or a ray of sunshine bursting through a cloud.

A charge jolts through me.

This dress sums it up. It's Mum's ultimate statement of freedom, revolution, individuality.

I stare at myself in the mirror. I'm a shining work of art.

My fingers itch to take a photograph – *my* photograph. A self-portrait. I've never felt that urge before.

I hold up my phone and face down the lens. No preening. No pouting. No pretending.

Just me.

"Fierce." Sam whistles from the doorway. "I can't believe no one's ever seen these pieces. It's a shame."

At that moment, an idea blooms in my mind, even brighter than my sparkling sculptural dress.

Maybe there's a way to tell the truth, *and* stop Bella and the mirror – all at the same time.

"You're right. It *is* a shame that no one's seen Mum's *real* work." I smile at Sam. "Maybe it doesn't have to stay that way."

Jas flies over within the hour. A quick call and a text with my self-portrait was all it took.

I bring her up to my room, where everything is laid out on the floor. At least twenty individual pieces of clothing, making around twelve looks in total.

Jas kneels, stroking the fabric of a cape like it's a holy relic.

"Let me get this straight. *Belladonna Wilde* knew your mum sixteen years ago, and she's relaunching her career using your mum's student work? *She's* behind Nightshade?"

"More or less." I glance at Sam.

"Bella was the fitting model for Tess White's collection," Sam supplies. He holds out the Polaroid and Jas examines it. "She made the odd suggestion, and thought that made it hers. When Tess left college before her final show, Bella felt cheated. Then her modelling career went downhill, so she tracked down Freya's dad to get it back."

"It's true," I agree. "But the collection that Bella's using for Nightshade – let's just say ... Mum wasn't thinking clearly when she designed it. *This* is the work she really believed in." I gesture at the kaleidoscope of colour and texture all around us. "Mum wanted fashion to empower people. The Nightshade collection ... reduces them."

"Wow." Jas shakes her head. "You know that Nightshade has given *Seen* magazine exclusive rights to launch the new ad campaign across all media after the show?"

I nod. "I've seen the new campaign. It's Bella – totally retouched to look flawless and unreal. But I expect she's paying *Seen* magazine a lot of money to publish the pictures. I'm sure you won't be able to help—"

"No," Jas interrupts. "Fashion's moving forwards. There's no going back. We don't need any more images like *that*. And this is way more important than money. This is about telling the truth. That shot blew me away, Freya." She sighs. "These pieces are *incredible*. Have they really never been shown?"

"Never."

She whistles. "OK, I'm on board. What's the plan?"

I take a deep breath. As I outline my idea, Jas pulls out her phone and makes notes. My nerves jangle. Things are taking shape, becoming real. "What do you think?" I ask, finally. "Can we pull this off?"

"If anyone can, *you* can." Jas's eyes sparkle. "You saw the reaction to your *Seen* cover, right?"

She passes me her phone. On the screen is an update from *Seen* magazine's social media, alongside my cover photo.

"Read the comments," Jas prompts.

> *SEEN magazine:*
> *Check out our Fashion Week special!*
> *#Nightshade #KarimAmariHairandMakeup*
> *#LondonFashionWeek #onestowatch*
> *#selfie #streetcasting #realmodels*
> *#FreyaJonesPhotography*
>
> *16.2k liked this post. Shared 5.3k times*
>
> *Ali_C: Wow. Can't believe this is a selfie!*
> *HTSS123: Awesome shot.*
> *FotoFiend: AMAZING*
> *Row_Eli_P: Who is this girl?*
> *Megz0301: I love this* ♥
> *SP64: Street casting rocks*
> *Sanesla: Great job, Seen mag*
> *VasquezOlivia: Welcome to the 21st Century*

There's more. The numbers are jumping as I read. Another example of the Nightshade effect. It's funny, though. While the likes and comments are nice, that thrill I got when I saw what people were saying about me on Saskia's social media? It's gone.

I don't need other people's approval any more.

Something inside me has changed.

When I took the cover photo, I was terrified. I had no idea what I was doing, or what I wanted to say. But now I know how I want to photograph myself – and it's not about tricks or poses, or trying to be someone I'm not.

I've learned that the best pictures tell stories – and that story is written on my face. Like Jake's chickenpox scar or Karim's daisy tattoo. My wonky nose, my freckles, my big ears. All my so-called flaws make me who I am. I should celebrate them. They're not a weakness; they're a strength.

Jas nudges me. "Earth to Freya? You've gone quiet. What are you thinking?"

I smile.

I'm not the girl I was when summer started. Always hiding, always holding back. I've found my voice and now it's time to use it.

"Let's do this," I say, wrapping my friends in a hug.

The mirror won't get its perfect ending.

I'm going to spread Mum's message – the only way I can.

45

It's the end of August and Hampstead Heath is quiet – only the odd dog walker and a lone yogi, saluting the morning sun.

As I lead the way up Parliament Hill, I look back at my friends. A tingle of gratitude zips through my veins. Jake is there with my tripod and a reflector he's borrowed from a mate. Sam is carrying a rucksack, stuffed with Jenna's make-up kit, and Jas is lugging a wheelie suitcase, crammed to the brim with Mum's clothes. Māra's here too, for moral support. Her role comes later, during the Nightshade show.

But that's Part Two.

Today is Part One.

I hug the camera around my neck – a spare one of Dad's. When I told him why I wanted it, he was happy to lend it to me. He doesn't know the whole picture, though.

Not yet.

We crest the hill and plough on, into the wilder part of the heath. When I decided to shoot Mum's clothes, there was only one place to do it. Not in a studio, with lights and wind machines and all those other tricks, but right here, pure and unfiltered, in one of my favourite spots.

"How about there?" I point to a copse, just beyond the meadow. The trees are ancient, their branches stretching upwards, wild, untamed and free.

"Perfect," Jake agrees.

"Let's not use that word." I smile.

"Good enough, then!" He laughs.

From that moment, the day zooms by. Hours feel like minutes. Time loses meaning. We sink into a sort of flow, each of us doing what we do best.

Jas is amazing. Her eye astounds me, the way she picks out pieces from Mum's collection, combining colours and textures in ways I'd never have imagined. She checks each look with me – "Do you like this? How does it make you feel?" And as she helps me dress, I know I'm in safe hands; respected, empowered. Not exposed.

I'm starting to realize how fun it can be, expressing myself through clothes.

"Ready?" Sam approaches with his brushes.

"Ready." I grin. We've discussed this already. I want

Sam to go for it – to show off his creativity. There's only one condition. I want to feel like me.

He pulls out a compact when he's done.

"Wow," I breathe, staring at myself in the mirror. My hair is pulled back simply, and on my face, Sam's performed the best kind of magic. All the features on my checklist, the stuff I used to hate – nothing is disguised or erased. If anything, Sam's accentuated the things that make me unique. He's brought my Freya-ness to the forefront.

I'm the most *me* I've ever been.

I step into the copse where Jake is setting up my camera like I asked. His jaw drops when he sees me. I'm wearing the sculptural cocoon dress with the concertina folds unfurled. Sunlight bounces off me like a glitter ball. I laugh, enjoying how he's lost for words.

"You remind me of something." Mãra looks at me thoughtfully. "A mirror story I studied, from Japan. The sun goddess, Amaterasu, hid in a cave, casting the world into darkness. But seeing her own reflection in a mirror reminded her of her power. She came out, and the world was full of light again."

"Sounds like Freya!" Jake says and blushes.

Mãra winks at me. "No one's coming. We're good to go."

I don't care. Let everybody see.

I check my frame and focus, aperture and shutter speed. Jake passes me the camera remote control.

My friends fall back as I step in front of the lens, their murmurs of excitement filling me with belief.

My finger is poised on the shutter button. A gust of wind lifts my hair. I stand square on and lift my chin, summoning the spirit of Mum's work.

I am Freya Yuki Jones. Perfectly imperfect.

And I'm claiming this image of mine.

It's almost sunset by the time we've finished. We've roamed the entire length of the heath, shooting hundreds of images, using every piece from Mum's collection in dozens of different ways. I've felt like a warrior, a goddess, a Valkyrie and a queen – and a real photographer above all. In the afternoon, Jas invited some of her street-casting contacts to drop by and we shot Mum's clothes the way she intended – on *real* people, every shape and size and colour. Even Liam turned up at one point and completely rocked Mum's teal winged dress – when he wasn't holding hands with Sam, that is.

I pack up my camera, adrenaline fizzing.

"That was amazing," Jake says softly. "I wish Amy could have seen. It would have shown her that there are loads of ways to be beautiful."

We trek back to Camden. Dad's waiting in his dressing gown, with pizza nobody wants to eat – not until the pictures are downloaded. We crowd round the kitchen table while I hook up my camera to my laptop. Everyone is quiet, even Sam.

The images take ages to come through. The files are huge. It's torture. I can barely look. *What if they're terrible? What if they haven't worked?*

But as the photos stack up, like the pages of a book, my shoulders relax.

They're fine. *More* than fine.

Mum's clothes are vibrant, visionary. The models look so powerful.

My photographs are really, really good.

Sam and Liam whoop. Jas twirls Māra around. Dad ruffles my hair. Jake squeezes my hand.

In the midst of the celebrations, I stare at my face on screen. There's something different about it, something I've never seen before.

Confidence.

In the tilt of my head, the squaring of my shoulders, the look in my eye.

Mum has given me superpowers.

I'm not hiding any more.

He let me down, the widower,
became a liability.
His questions, his paternal love,
they helped him to resist.
My golden girl acted swiftly – she knew
what was at stake. Cutting our losses with
one draught, she left him to his death.
I'm still close, though. I can feel it.
To a flawless world, for ever.
Perfect beauty – on a global scale.
No one can resist me – it's really too
adorable – the tendency to toe the line.
Safety in numbers. Everyone the same.

46

September the first.

The air is heavy with heat. I lie still in bed, composing my thoughts. Yesterday, I was on a high after the amazing photoshoot, but today my gut churns like a whirlpool.

London Fashion Week has started.

The Nightshade show is tonight.

Time for Part Two of my plan.

I roll out of bed, still exhausted. It was late when I finally slept. The others left at ten, but Jake stayed behind. We still had work to do.

First, we salvaged the photos on the memory card. Luckily, all the images were intact – Mum's sketches with her clever, hidden signature, matched to the Nightshade gowns.

Next, we scanned old photos: my picture of Mum on her wedding day, the images from my album. Even the shot outside the spaceship building in Kobe. Turns out, it's a famous fashion museum – Jake and I looked it up.

After those images had imported, I added them to a folder with drawings from the attic sketchbook – the work Mum created with Naoko – along with the shots I took on the heath. The hardest part was editing. We must have spent hours on the slideshow, trying to find the order that worked best. Jake showed me how to add special effects, like panning across a picture or zooming in. We layered an instrumental soundtrack over the top, and between the images, slow, gentle fades.

Finally, we'd finished. My heart beat hard as I pressed play. Jake reached for my hand as we watched the film unfold.

The Story of Tess White.

I snap out of my daydream and check my phone. No word yet from Jake. When Victor assigned him to work with the audio-visual crew on the show, we couldn't believe our luck. In the chaos of show preparations, Bella doesn't seem to have noticed. Even so, I made him promise to text from the venue and keep a low profile, just in case.

I make coffee, reviewing the plan in my head.

Māra's call time is four, for a show time of seven.

365

Nightshade is the last show of the day. "Closing out the first day of Fashion Week is huge," Jas had told me. "Everyone will be there. Security will be tight."

I take a deep breath.

The venue itself is meant to be a mystery, only revealed to guests tonight. But it's not a secret to us, thanks to Jake's insider tip.

The Livingstone Collection.

Here in Camden, just as I'd thought – in the church-turned-gallery where Bella first met Dad. According to Jas, emerging designers usually show their collections in an East-End marquee – but that wasn't good enough for Bella. I can't help feeling she's chosen this venue on purpose, just to rub my nose in it.

Stay calm. Think clearly.

Māra's going to message from backstage. Once she's scoped things out and carried out her task, she'll send us the image we need.

My tummy flutters.

The final part is up to me.

My phone rings, and I pounce on it. "Sam?"

"So … Liam and Karim are on board, one hundred per cent."

"That's great!"

It was Jas who discovered that Raven had approached Karim to help on Nightshade's hair and make-up team. I guess Raven didn't know about the beef between Bella and Karim. When Jas told Karim that Bella was behind the label, he threatened to back out – but Sam convinced him to stay when he called to explain about my plan. Karim and Liam will be important allies … if we manage to get backstage.

Sam's excitement crackles down the line. "Karim said it will be his pleasure to help Bella Wilde get exactly what she deserves."

I grin.

"It's coming together, Freya. We're doing this."

"We are."

I hang up, my mouth dry. Because this is not just about stopping Bella – or even the mirror.

This is about influence. Who deserves it, and how to use it for good.

By three in the afternoon, there's still no word from Jake. I pace the room, praying he's made it to the AV control box, my memory stick in his pocket. The whirlpool in my stomach is a swirling vortex.

At four, I hear from Māra.

> *I'm here. Made the switch!*
> *Going into hair and make-up now.*
> *Pic soon x*

Yes.

My chest feels lighter. Māra's role is crucial. I was racking my brains for ever trying to figure out how to pull off my idea without being seen. Then Māra was called in for her show fitting. As soon as she spotted the long, hooded cloak assigned to Seren Larsson's final look, she called me, and I knew we had a plan. By switching names on the hangers backstage, Māra has claimed Seren's look for herself.

Which means she can sneak the cloak to me.

My pulse is racing, and it's not the coffee.

This is getting real.

Jas messages next, on her way to meet Sam.

> *Just passed the venue.*
> *Bouncers look hardcore!*
> *See you at the cafe in ten?*

It's my cue to go.

I check on Dad, who's napping. He's still tired, but every day he's gaining strength. I leave a note saying I'm with Sam and not to worry. I'm scared he'll try to stop me if he knows what I'm about to do.

The cafe where Sam and Jas are waiting is a retro-style diner, not far from the Nightshade venue. They wave from a booth at the back. As I squeeze on to the seat, Sam's phone pings.

"OK, so according to Māra, *this* is the official hair and make-up look for the Nightshade show."

He shows us his phone. In the selfie Māra has sent, her hair is pulled into a bun and her face is surprisingly bare.

"Natural face? Strange." Jas frowns. "I expected something … *more*."

"At least it's easy." Sam shrugs, getting out a slimmed-down version of his kit. "Ready, Freya?"

I nod. This was Jas's idea. My best chance of getting backstage is to pretend I'm a model in the show.

"There's a side entrance for crew and models," Jas says, now. "So you won't need to use the main entrance or go past the press."

Sam dabs at my skin and I shudder.

"There's still a security guard, obviously," Jas continues. "Just pretend you stepped out to make a call."

I swallow. Jas is wearing a Fashion Week lanyard – an official press pass from *Seen* magazine. I wish I had one of those.

"I suppose I could give it to you," she says, following my gaze. "They sometimes don't check the photos that carefully."

"No, it's too risky," I say. "Better for me to pretend I've left mine inside. And I need you in the audience in case things don't go as planned."

Sam twists my hair up tightly. "I can't use hairspray in here," he says, as a server passes with a tray full of food. "Don't touch it, Freya. You're ready."

I slide off the seat and check myself out in the toilets. It does seem strange that Bella hasn't gone for a more dramatic make-up look, but with my hair scraped back and my face primed and clean, it's true that I look fairly similar to Māra.

"Ready?" Jas asks, when I come back out.

"What about these?" I frown at my jeans.

"Relax." She laughs. "You look like an off-duty model. Here."

She passes me a canvas bag. I already know what's inside – Mum's shimmering silver cocoon dress. I hoist the bag over my shoulder, praying I won't be searched.

"You guys are sure this will work?"

"It was your idea, Freya! No backing out now." Sam hauls me out of the diner and Jas steers me down the street.

"Come on. We've got a fashion show to crash."

47

My stomach lurches as we round the corner, and I spot the white church building with its stately columns.

Despite the earlier secrecy about the Nightshade show's location, it's obvious something big is going on. Sponsorship flags bearing the Fashion Week logo flutter from the arches of the church entrance, a red carpet covers the wide front steps, and even though it's only five-thirty, people have already gathered behind a velvet rope, policed by burly bouncers wearing headsets.

Most of the crowd are dressed in black, but I spot a worrying number of red splashes, just like at the casting. One woman is dressed in scarlet fur from head to toe, despite the heat. I look at Sam – he's noticed too. People conforming to the mirror's vision, primed by Dad's adverts, ready to fall for Nightshade, even before they've seen the show.

"Breathe," Sam reminds me, linking his arm through mine. Jas hands me a pair of sunglasses.

"Standard model accessory."

We get closer. Now, the buzz among the crowd is palpable. Paparazzi are setting up tripods and TV crews are rushing around. A few metres away, a presenter records a piece to camera. Snatches of her patter float towards me on the breeze.

"… most anticipated debut … tickets like gold dust … viral social-media campaign … incredible brand awareness … mysterious designer to be unveiled … pre-orders beating records … billionaire investors on board … soon to roll-out worldwide…" She sighs. "You could call it a *perfect* storm…"

It hits me again, point-blank.

In just a few hours, Bella will have money, adulation and power – not just at the expense of my family, but at the expense of millions of people. The mirror is about to reach the biggest audience it's ever had, as all over the world, people absorb the message that they need to be "perfect" to be happy.

"Time to split up," Jas announces. "I'll go through the main door with the press. The backstage entrance is over there."

She points to an alley running alongside the church. I shudder. The bouncer on the door is the same heavy who threw me out of Bella's atelier.

"Confidence, Freya!" Jas clasps my shoulders. "Act like

you're meant to be there. Nobody will question it." She turns to Sam. "Say you're Karim's assistant. He'll help when you get backstage." She slides her own sunglasses on to her nose and heads towards the crowd, curls bouncing.

"They're ready for us." Sam shows me a message from Liam with a thumbs up. "We're on."

I summon my self-belief, channelling it into my body. I *am* meant to be here. I know the true story behind the Nightshade collection, the terrible things Bella and the mirror have done – to Mum, to Dad, to me. It's on me to right those wrongs and make sure they don't harm anybody else.

I lift my chin and head for the alley, Sam following.

The bouncer looks up from his phone. "Passes."

"We left them inside," Sam shoots back, lightning fast.

"I'm modelling in the show," I mumble. "I stepped out to, um … call my agent."

The bouncer peers closely at my slicked-back hair. My eyelid twitches. I'm grateful for Jas's sunglasses.

"*You* can go through." The bouncer nods at me. "Not you." His beefy arm blocks Sam's way.

"But—"

"Darlings, there you are!" Karim is at the side door, a comb behind one ear. "How many times do I have to tell you? Don't forget your pass!" He tosses a lanyard to Sam, then turns to the bouncer. "He's my assistant."

Before the bouncer can object, Karim pulls us both down a dark corridor, into the belly of the building. I take off my sunglasses and breathe out in relief.

We're in.

"Follow me." Karim strides ahead. "You need a place to hide."

Sam's studying his lanyard. "Wait. This belongs to Seren Larsson! Won't she need it? How will she get in?"

Karim snorts. "Don't worry. When Seren Larsson arrives, everyone will know."

We turn down another corridor with doors leading off it. I guess we must be circling the nave of the church, the gallery space where the show will be held. A few people pass, but they pay no attention, muttering into walkie-talkies as they go. "Producers," Karim whispers. "Stick with me."

"Is Bella here?" I whisper.

"No sign of her yet. But everything's been delegated to the production team. If she's planning a surprise reveal, like you say, my guess is she'll arrive at the last minute."

A hum of noise grows louder as we walk. Finally, Karim stops at a doorway, leading on to a large, faded hall.

"*Voilà!* Backstage."

I shrink from the commotion. Dozens of people are crammed together, busily preparing for the show. The dominant colour in the room, overwhelmingly, is red. Hairdryers roar, drowning out the chat, as models have their hair blown out and slicked back into the same severe style Sam's given me. I scan the room for Victor or Raven, but the buzz of people makes it impossible to see. On the right side of the room, desks have been set up and make-up artists are dabbing with sponges, priming faces with base.

In one corner, I spot Māra reading quietly. She catches sight of me and winks.

At the end of the room, a security guard is standing by a strange white plinth, next to a set of double doors.

"That's the entrance to the runway," Karim explains.

I look to my left. A changing area is lined with portable rails, heaving with fiery-coloured, polythene-wrapped clothes. At the front of each rail, a model's name is written in large letters: *SEREN, ELSA, MAGALI, MĀRA*... Each outfit is numbered according to the order it will appear in the show. Stylists are busy steaming out creases, while assistants are setting out shoes, and, to my bewilderment, carving scratches into the soles.

"To stop the models slipping when they walk," Sam explains.

Karim turns to Sam. "You're better hiding in plain sight." He points to Liam, brushing out a model's hair. "I heard you've got skills. Why don't you assist today, for real?"

"Really?" Sam's face lights up. "I mean, yeah. Whatever. Sure."

"Freya, there's a cloakroom at the end of the hall." Karim points down the corridor. "You can hide there, I'll show you..."

A sudden uproar breaks out. "She's coming!" someone shouts.

I shoot a glance at Sam. *It's Bella, I should go...*

The runway doors fly open. I catch a brief glimpse of a cavernous gallery space and blinding lights beyond.

"Seren Larsson!" Sam gasps.

Karim tuts. "What did I say?"

Seren struts in as if she owns the place. She's wearing a tiny red playsuit, with her eyes ringed in purple and her hair a fuzz of backcombed curls.

"Ugh," Karim groans. "She's come from another show. I'd better undo this mess." He pulls Seren into a chair, Sam hovering at his side. Over his shoulder, Karim mouths at me, "*Go*".

I don't need telling twice.

I fly along the corridor. There's only one door, right at the end. The cloakroom is bigger than I expected, but dark, with only one casement window, framed by floor-length curtains. A stack of suitcases is pushed against the wall. Karim's right. It's a good place to hide for now. I slip inside, and close the door.

Then I freeze.

On the back of the door is a garment bag. A flash of red embroidery spills out.

I spin around.

In the corner of the room there's a dressing table, and on top is a familiar oval frame, carved with twisting vines. Bella's mirror shimmers in the light.

My stomach drops.

Correction. This is not a good hiding place. In fact, it couldn't be much worse.

I've ended up in Bella's private dressing room.

48

Questions hurtle around my brain. What can I do? Where can I go? I can't return to the backstage area, and I can't wander off alone, with all the producers around.

Then I realize something.

The mirror's glass is uncovered, but I don't feel anything. No strange magnetic pull. I move closer. Still nothing. It simply doesn't come.

Strange.

Surely the mirror can't have stopped working?

An idea bounces in my brain. Something has changed, and I know what it is.

It's me.

I used to want to fix myself, but I'm not that person any more.

Perfect isn't powerful. Perfect doesn't exist.

I stare into the glass. Looking back is a face I know well. A face I accept and like. Maybe even love. I listen for the whisper, wait for my features to change.

Nothing happens.

I even say the words, just to be sure. "*All shall be perfect.*"

Still nothing.

Then I grin. A great big goofy grin.

I knew it. Mirror Me has gone.

It's like a weight has lifted from my shoulders. My heart aches suddenly for Bella. I wish she could know how good it feels.

Perhaps she can…

The idea dances through my mind. What if I took the mirror – right now – and destroyed it somehow? Just like Tess asked Issy to do?

A voice in the corridor makes me start.

"It's this way. Everything is set up for you. Would you like my help to—"

"I'm perfectly capable of dressing myself."

Fear stabs me. *It's Bella and Raven.*

I fling myself behind the floral curtain, just as the cloakroom door opens.

"Here we are. We start in fifteen minutes, Ms Wilde. I'll leave you to it."

The door clicks shut and a key turns in the lock.

I daren't move or even breathe. Frozen like a statue behind the curtain, I listen to the rustling of the garment bag, the swish of fabric, the creaking of the floorboards, as Bella starts to dress. Then silence: a pregnant pause, heavy with meaning.

I know exactly what Bella is about to do.

The murmuring begins. I don't need to look. It's easy to imagine the transformation taking place. Once more, for her big moment, Bella is making herself perfect.

The mirror's definition of perfect, that is.

She finishes and there's another sound, a strange one, like the brief whirr of a motor. There's no time to think about what it means. A voice calls out from beyond the cloakroom.

"Doors are closed, people. We have a full house."

There's a knock at the door.

"Ms Wilde?" Raven is back. "It's ten minutes until showtime."

"Come in," Bella barks. "We need to go over the finale."

I hear the sharp intake of breath as Raven enters the room and the sight of flawless Bella strikes her.

"Oh, Ms Wilde, you look…"

"This is what will happen," Bella interrupts, speaking carefully. "The final look of the show is the bride—"

"Naturally," Raven gushes. "And we've cast Seren Larsson in the role; she's very up-and-coming. The plan is that she'll be wearing a cloak, with a hood concealing her face. At the end of the runway, she'll discard the cloak to reveal the gown underneath. I thought it would be *so* dramatic, and you have to admit, it does make sense to showcase that particular dress – it had such wonderful exposure on the cover of *Seen* magazine!" She sighs. "It's the perfect way to close the show…"

"Except," Bella cuts Raven short, "it won't close the show."

"No?"

Bella snorts. "*Seren Larsson* will not be closing my show. The real bridal role is reserved for someone else. Someone who embodies this collection at their core."

"Oh!" Raven finally catches on. "Oh, of course! I'm … um … I'm sure you'll blow them away, Ms Wilde."

"I intend to." Bella's tone is cool.

"It's just—" Raven hesitates.

"What is it?"

"Well … shouldn't we make an announcement first? No photos – once you step on to the runway, I mean? We have security stationed in the auditorium. We can make sure that anyone taking pictures of you is ejected from the building, and their camera or phone destroyed…"

Bella laughs. "Why ever would we do that?"

"Um…" Raven sounds confused. I know how she feels. *Why has Bella changed her tune?* Raven tries again. "I was under the impression that you value your privacy? That you'd rather not be photographed – at least not without consent? And we do have the new, approved campaign images, finished and ready to launch."

"You're absolutely right. That *was* the situation." Smugness permeates Bella's words. "But I'm pleased to say that things have changed."

I don't understand what I'm hearing. Leaning forwards, I risk a peek around the curtain. Bella is encased in the scarlet wedding dress. Her body looks utterly unreal. With her back to Raven, she's staring deeply into the mirror, one hand absent-mindedly stroking its frame.

"With this show, Nightshade's reach will extend far and wide. We'll be very, *very* powerful. In fact, we already are." She hands something to Raven, a small square of card. *A Polaroid.* I spot the camera sitting next to the mirror and realize. *That* was the whirring sound I heard.

"I no longer have any issue with being photographed."

Raven's staring at the card in a daze. "I see."

"Good." Bella smiles. "That will be all."

Raven scurries away.

The voice beyond the cloakroom calls again. "First looks! All models to the fitting area, please! This is your five-minute call!"

I tense. *Five minutes until showtime.*

Five minutes until Sam will come looking for me. With every fibre of my body, I will Bella to leave. Taking a final, lingering look at her own reflection, she lifts up the veil and sets it on her head, pulling the embroidered mesh down over the blank mask of her face.

Then she picks up the mirror and sweeps out of the door. *Thank God. She's gone.*

381

Deep within the building a bass line pounds a menacing beat.

The Nightshade show has started.

"Freya!" Sam's whisper reaches my ears. "Freya, are you in there?"

"Yes!" I rush to the door and crack it open. Sam slips inside. In his arms is the long, red cloak that Māra's swiped from Seren's final look.

"Let's get you ready. We haven't got much time!"

"Sam! Bella was just here!" My heart is pounding with the bass. "And so was the mirror! Something's going on. Bella said 'the situation's changed'. She sounded happy about it." I whirl round. The Polaroid is still on the table where Raven left it. I snatch it up.

"Look!" I turn it round so Sam can see. Bella smirks out at us, resplendently fake.

"She can be photographed again," Sam whispers. "You think the mirror's getting more powerful?"

"It must be. Although it didn't work on me."

"It didn't?" Sam frowns. "Where is it now?"

"Bella took it with her."

He scowls. "To make herself perfect?"

"She did that already." I think for a moment. The answer is obvious, staring me in the face. "Of course. She's going to use it on the models! That's why they're barely wearing make-up. She already knows they're susceptible. She knows they all have huge followings. She's going to make the models "perfect" so they'll step on to the runway

382

and hypnotize the audience. The images will go viral and bewitch anyone who sees them."

Sam nods. "We need to warn Māra. I'll text Liam."

I look at him. "If the mirror's getting more and more powerful, will the plan still work? What if people won't listen? What if we can't get through to them?"

He grimaces. "Don't think like that, Freya. We have to try."

As Sam sends an urgent text to Liam, I scrabble out of my jeans and T-shirt and stash them behind the curtain. Digging into the canvas bag, I pull out Mum's beautiful silvery cocoon dress. Sam helps me step into it. Carefully, we fold each golden concertina until they're hidden behind the zips. Finally, I wrap Seren's cloak around my body until it covers the dress completely.

"There." Sam pulls up the generous hood. "Just keep your head down and try to blend in. You should be OK – it's chaos backstage."

"Second looks!" someone screams outside. The music switches to a driving beat. The energy in the venue is stepping up a gear.

Sam checks the corridor. "We're clear."

I follow him to the backstage area, head down. Sam's right, it's carnage here. With the show in full throttle, producers are screaming, models are pulling off outfits and throwing on new ones, and Raven's team of stylists are running around, primping and prodding the girls before they line up to walk again.

One person stands out amid the mayhem.

At the far end of the room, Bella is waiting by the entrance to the runway: a shrouded guardian in her veil. The mirror stands beside her on the white plinth. I watch as a long line of models forms, waiting for their turn to walk. Before each model heads out on to the runway, Bella steers them in front of the mirror. The girls pause, enraptured. A producer in a headset has to drag some of them away. I'm not close enough to see the transformation happen, but I don't need to. Each model returning from the runway confirms my worst fears. They're a vacant army of Bella clones, all of them dressed in red.

"Whoa," Sam whispers in my ear. "This is beyond weird."

"Bella's guarding the runway. I'll never get past!" My eyes are wide with panic.

"We'll think of something," he says, grim.

"Final looks, everyone!" a woman with a clipboard calls. "Final looks!"

"Freya!" Māra dashes up, making me jump. "You're look number 60. The last model. Here!" She hands me some shoes. I take them and groan. *Heels, again? Could this day get any worse?*

"Did she make you use the mirror?" I peer at Māra. Her eyes seem bright and clear. "It's getting more powerful. Are you OK? How do you feel?"

"I feel fine." She shrugs. "Thanks for the warning, but – it was strange – when I looked into the glass,

nothing happened. It didn't work for me. Not like them."
She glances at the zombified models all around. "I still
mouthed the words, so that Bella wouldn't notice." She
grins. "Maybe I've become immune!"

"I need Looks 50 through to 60!" Clipboard woman
sounds hysterical. "Models, line up!"

"Good luck!" Māra squeezes my arm.

The next thing I know, I'm caught in a wave of models
surging forward. Snippets of their conversation reach my
ears.

"Is that the designer?"

"Does anyone know who she is?"

"What about her mirror? Did you see it?"

"It's amazing."

"It makes me look so beautiful."

"Same. I feel…"

"… perfect!"

"That's it! Perfect."

"We're all perfect."

"Let's take a picture." One model holds up her phone
and they cram their heads together for a selfie. "*All shall
be perfect.*" They murmur the words in unison, eyes shiny
and glazed.

I take my place at the end of the line, more determined
than ever to tear this down. *Everyone has been completely
brainwashed*. Nightshade is nothing but smoke and mirrors.
It's high time people woke up.

"Go!"

Another girl launches on to the runway. I'm nearing the front of the queue. The music builds and my stomach churns. The show is heading towards its climax. It's almost time for me to act.

But there's still one more obstacle to pass.

I shrink into my hood as Bella grabs the girl in front of me and guides her to the mirror. My flesh crawls, seeing the girl's eagerness, the way her mouth moves mechanically, the way her face and body start to morph.

Mesmerized, she steps into the light.

It's my turn.

Bella beckons. The room begins to spin.

"I've got this one." Karim appears between us, steering me away. He pretends to adjust my hood, pushing me towards the double doors. "You're good to go."

But just then—

"Who's taken my final look?" someone wails. "I'm meant to be closing the show, but my outfit isn't here."

I glance behind me. Big mistake. Bella swings from Seren Larsson back to me.

No.

"Wait." Her voice is ice.

"Go!" Headset Man roars over the din.

The doors open. He shoves me in my back.

I find myself out on the runway.

For a second, I freeze.

Flashbulbs explode like popcorn. In front of me, the runway lies glossy and pale like milk. High above my head,

the word *Nightshade* is illuminated in shimmering script. A
red slogan pulses hypnotically underneath.

ALL. SHALL. BE. PERFECT.

The words burn on to my retinas.

I blink, looking for Jas, but the audience is a black hole.
Music vibrates through my body reminding me to move,
but my heels are high, the cloak is long and my silver dress
is tight. I take a step and stumble. Titters rise from the
front row.

An idea pops into my head.

I kick off my shoes. Barefoot is better. Mum would have
done the same. Thinking of her spurs me on. Shoulders
back, I walk with purpose down the runway, the music
cresting as I reach the end.

The track fades, and I stop. The camera flashes peter
out. Everyone is silent, waiting for what comes next. My
eyes roam upwards to the balcony above the hall. A person
is silhouetted in the AV box.

Please let it be Jake.

I push back my hood, and the audience murmurs. Then
I unhook the cloak and drop it to the floor. The murmurs
grow louder, the silver of my column dress startling after
the endless parade of red.

"STOP!"

The voice comes from the entrance to the runway. Bella
has pushed through the doors and is trying to make her

way towards me, but Karim and Liam are there – and Sam too – clamping her arms to hold her back. A handful of models filter out, as if for the final parade. They come to a halt: lost, dazed, confused.

"That person is an intruder!" Bella cries, her veil twisting as she struggles. "Somebody throw her out!"

Holding my nerve, I raise my hand. The signal we've agreed.

"Whatever she says, don't listen!" Bella is struggling violently now. "The Nightshade collection belongs to me!"

With all her strength, she wrestles one arm free and rips the veil from her head. The audience gasps.

"Is that … *Belladonna Wilde?*" someone calls.

Then the runway plunges into darkness.

No.

No!

Stop her!

Don't listen!

Remember, I'm your guide, your friend.

Transform. Conform.

Then spread the word.

Mirror my perfect taste.

49

It feels like years but it can't be more than seconds.

Suddenly there's a flicker, and a bright beam of light shoots out from the AV box. Hundreds of glittering eyes stare – past me, past Bella – at the high gallery wall beyond.

The projector pulls focus and the flicker becomes a solid shape. A title card comes into view, as the opening bars of music sound.

The Story of Tess White

My film begins to play.

First come the photographs from the album in the attic:

Mum as a student in Tokyo, Mum at the fashion museum. The soundtrack weaves the images together, setting Mum up as the focus of the film – just as a caption appears.

> **Tess White studied fashion at Kawakubo College – until her untimely death.**

The audience whispers, intrigued.

> **An original and gifted student, Tess was dedicated to her craft.**

We zoom in on the Polaroid that Naoko sent, of Mum in the studio with me.

> **She even designed her own wedding dress.**

Now we see Mum on her wedding day, her silver dress an echo of the one I'm wearing now.

> **Tess White was ahead of her time.**

We segue into my *Seen* cover: Bella's first copy of Mum's dress. The whispers in the audience grow louder. I can tell people know the shot. They've noticed the similarities and they've recognized me. I hug myself. They're starting to wake up and ask questions.

Another caption appears:

But Tess doubted her talent.
Influenced by others, her graduation
collection was more conventional.

The film jumps to the shots from the atelier: the drawings in the sketchbooks that Bella stole. The camera pans across Mum's designs, zooming in on her signature.

Around me, people shift and sit up. Clearly they're connecting these drawings with the looks they've just seen, walking this very runway. They're doing the maths, wondering about dates, trying to figure out how this could be possible.

The mood of the film changes. The music becomes sombre, serious.

Tess changed her mind about the collection.
She destroyed the clothes.
She did not want them seen.
But someone never forgot.

Now we see the second Polaroid that Naoko sent, of Mum fitting her collection on Bella.

Her fitting model.

The camera zooms in on Issy's face.

The audience shifts, plainly unsettled. They've recognized Bella.

Fifteen years later, Belladonna Wilde tracked down Tess White's sketchbooks. She stole Tess's designs, claiming them as her own.

We shift to my photos of the gowns in the atelier, the same gowns that, just now, walked this very runway.

I hear gasps. Now I know people understand. Bella doesn't deserve credit for this show. I could raise my hand and stop the film right now.

But I don't.

I've only told half the story.

Mum rejected the Nightshade collection. She wouldn't want people to remember her this way. It's time to give her back her voice.

The film plays on.

Tess died before she could share her true vision of fashion for <u>everyone</u>. This is the work she believed in...

Suddenly the film explodes with colour, as we leaf through the sketchbook from the attic. The screen is singing with Mum's incredible, vibrant designs. The audience's gasps give me goosebumps. Mum's ahead-of-her-time talent is simply undeniable.

By the time we reach my pictures from the heath, the atmosphere in the room is feverish. My heart fills with pride as Mum's extraordinary creations fill the screen. A collection full of joy and hope, modelled by real people…

With images captured by me.

I raise my hand to call the spotlight back, ready for my moment. My final transformation. No going back.

This is for you, Mum, I whisper.

My hands move to the hidden fastenings in my dress. In one fluid movement, I pull them loose. As the tight cocoon breaks open, my new self emerges. The golden concertina folds are crumpled like the wings of a newborn butterfly. I coax them into life and they expand like a fan. The fabric holds its shape, light yet strong, like origami. I reach up to the neckline, twisting the sculptural collar up behind my head and neck. It frames my face, a shimmering golden ruff, fit for a sun goddess or a queen.

In the darkness of the hall, there's a flash of light.

Then another, and another.

Suddenly the whole room erupts in flashes as hundreds of lenses point in my direction.

I don't cringe, or flinch, or even blink.

A smile spreads over my face. Slowly, I start to spin, letting the explosions of light bounce off my real and beautiful self.

The music slows. The film has ended.

I come to a standstill with the final frame:

Perfect Imperfection
The vision of Tess White
(1983–2008)

There's a sudden uproar behind me.

I spin around. Bella has managed to break free from Karim and Liam's hold, and she's charging down the runway, her eyes shooting razor-sharp slivers of hatred in my direction.

The hall is silent. The audience holds its breath.

"How dare you?" Her voice simmers with rage. "How dare you take this moment from me!"

"It wasn't yours to take." I hold my head high, meeting her eyes. Her flawless face is almost touching mine but it has no effect on me any more. "You stole this work, you used my dad, and you tried to cover your tracks. But now *everyone* knows Tess White's name and her *real* legacy. It's *her* vision that will live on. Not yours – or rather, your mirror's. It's been using you, *Issy*. Don't you realize—"

Bella lunges and I break off, stumbling backwards. Her hands fly to my throat. We're locked under the spotlight in an awful dance. Nobody comes to help. The audience is frozen, transfixed.

They think it's part of the show.

Then Sam is there, wrenching Bella's hands away – and Karim and Liam too, dragging her back.

"Here, Freya!"

I turn to see Māra striding down the runway. She thrusts

something cold, smooth and solid into my hands.

The mirror.

"No!" Bella screams, fighting Sam's grip. Her face is ashen, her forehead shining with sweat. "Please, Freya, don't do anything reckless."

I waver for a second, seeing her struggle.

Who hasn't wished to be perfect, sometimes?

Is it Bella's fault she fell for the mirror's lies? That she doesn't love herself the way she is?

Jas's words pop into my head: *"Fashion's moving forward. We have to shake things up and break the mould!"*

I think of the amazing photos Dad took of Bella, *before* she had them retouched. The lines on her face, the swell of her belly. The beautiful raw truth.

Decision made.

"You don't need this," I tell Bella, holding the mirror over the edge of the runway. "You only think you do."

Bella whimpers.

I let the mirror fall.

50

The mirror shatters, fragments tinkling across the flagstone floor. On the front row, fashionistas squeal and dust the splinters from their clothes.

I pay no attention. My eyes are glued on Bella.

She's changing.

Not in a puff of smoke, or a flash of lightning. There's no wave of a magic wand. It's more subtle than that. It's probably not obvious unless you're as close to her as me.

But she knows it, and so do I.

Bella's becoming real.

It's in her body – the way she holds her shoulders, the

way her soft flesh tests the seams of her dress. It's in her eyes – lurid emerald muting to natural, everyday green. It's in her face – the faint lines criss-crossing her forehead like a map. It's in the strands of silver, threading her natural brown hair.

I look closer.

It's in other things too, like the dent on her nose, the small raised mole on her neck. The vaccination scar on her upper arm, her chipped incisor tooth.

It's in every one of her so-called imperfections, each with a story behind it. They draw my photographer's eye, making me yearn for my camera.

Bella is truly beautiful.

More than she ever was before.

There's a stunned silence, then all of a sudden, applause thunders through the hall like a stampede. Chairs are scraping as the audience scrambles to its feet.

"*Bravissimo!*" someone shouts. "*Molto bellissima!*"

"*Encore!*"

I look down at the front row. Fashion people are rubbing their eyes, disoriented and dazed, like they've just woken from a deep sleep. Around them, camera phones explode like fireworks.

Bella seems to be in shock.

At first, her expression is vacant, uncomprehending, as if she can't make sense of the congratulations being thrown my way. Then suddenly she stumbles from the runway, barging her way through the still-bewildered crowd. As she pushes open the double doors of the exit, two sturdily-built figures step forward to apprehend her. Behind them, the gallery foyer pulses with flashing blue lights.

The police.

Sam smothers me in a hug. Karim and Liam join in. Māra is whirling round and round. And now, all the other models are tripping down the runway, squinting like moles at the commotion. They're back to their usual selves too: just a posse of teenage girls. I watch as they take in the chaos and slowly start to smile, kicking off their heels and loosening their clothes to join in with Māra's dancing.

I scan the balcony for Jake, but there's no need. He's hoisting himself up beside me.

"Sorry I went AWOL," he whispers. "I had some VIPs to sneak in. I thought they ought to see this."

He points to two people on the balcony – a willowy girl, a man with scruffy hair.

Amy. Dad.

Tears are streaming down my face.

The house lights come on. Ushers attempt to disperse the crowds. Some people are still cheering, while others stand, lost, bewildered, stunned.

A voice rises above the mayhem. "Freya! Freya Jones!"

Jas has elbowed her way to the front row. Her voice rings out, loud and clear.

"Jasmine de Souza, for *Seen* magazine. I believe you're the photographer behind the images we just saw. I'd like to interview you about Tess White's lost archive. What are your thoughts on the celebration of authenticity we've witnessed here tonight?"

A grin splits my face as I answer. "I think there's no going back."

Three months later

"I know I've got the passports somewhere."

Dad stops in the middle of a stream of people to dig in his rucksack. Travellers tut on their way to the security checks.

While Dad searches, Jake turns to me.

"So … I guess this is goodbye."

I smile, hearing him echo the words I said, all those months ago at the railway station. But this time there's no awkward pause, and I *definitely* don't want him to go. He reaches for my hand, pulling me towards him, making my stomach turn somersaults all over again. Sure, I'm excited to be going to Japan. But it means I won't see him for weeks.

"I'll text you every day," he tells me. "Twice at Christmas, if you're lucky."

"What about my birthday?" I grin. I still can't believe I'll turn seventeen in Tokyo, the city where I was born. "Did you know they're forecasting snow?"

"Yes, Freya *Yuki* Jones." Jake's eyes crinkle. "You've mentioned it once or twice."

"Here we go." Dad hands over my passport and boarding pass. "Thanks for the lift, Jake. Sure you don't mind picking us up on the return?"

Jake squeezes my hand. "Happy to, Mr Jones."

"Call me Nick," Dad corrects. "That's an order from your boss."

Jake flushes. I know how pleased he is to have a weekend job with Dad. There was no work for him at Façade after the Nightshade show. Jake reckons it was worth it, though. Amy's slowly getting better. She's having treatment at the clinic and put modelling on hold.

"I'll take good care of The Space while you're away," Jake tells Dad. "We should be up and running in the New Year."

"Good stuff!" Dad grins. "I'm dying to show Lou."

As they make small talk, I smile to myself. It's good to see Dad excited about a project that actually means something. He's sworn off retouching for good, and since his recovery, we've spent every weekend refurbishing his old workshop to start an Image Space – a meeting place for filmmakers and photographers – with a studio and edit suite and even a community darkroom. He's already been in touch with local schools to offer classes – that's how he met Lou. She seems great – definitely down-to-earth – and as far as I know, she doesn't own a single magic mirror.

"One second. I promised to call her before we go through." Dad ducks into the crowd.

"Young love!" Jake giggles.

"He's not exactly *young*."

"Aww, he deserves it, Freya. After everything that's happened."

Bella's name hangs unspoken in the air.

"At least the divorce will be quick," I say. "The lawyer said Bella agreed to everything without a fuss. I think she's hoping it will help her case."

"I'm glad your dad decided to make a statement," Jake says.

"Me too." I nod. Jake told me the real reason he went AWOL for so long on the day of the Nightshade show was because Dad changed his mind about going to the police. Once Jake had showed him my film and told him about my plan to stand up to Bella, Dad said he'd be letting me down if he didn't do the same. It turned out the evidence I'd collected was enough to justify taking Bella in for questioning after the show. According to the police, there's plenty to suggest she had motive to poison Dad, and there might even be grounds for reopening the investigation into Mum's death.

"She never got her comeback," Jake says with satisfaction.

"Not the way she wanted it, anyway." I giggle and slide

my arm around his waist.

It was Mum who got the renaissance in the end – that's one of the reasons for this trip. We're meeting a curator about an exhibition of her work at an art gallery in Tokyo. Bella did get some publicity, though. I grin, remembering how, in the days after the show and before news of her arrest hit, images of Bella at the end of the Nightshade runway circulated round all the fashion press. She was praised for "championing unsung designers", "embracing the ageing process" and "celebrating real women".

She must have hated every minute.

"What about you?" Jake pushes the hair out of my eyes. Not that there's much to hide behind these days; I finally let Sam chop it off. "Any regrets?"

"What about?"

He laughs. "About turning down your own chance of fashion glory."

I roll my eyes. After Jas convinced *Seen* to publish my shoot from the heath, some model agencies got in touch, offering to represent me. I declined. Saskia was horrified, but we talk more these days, and I think she gets it now. I've noticed she's started tagging more of her pictures #nofilter. It makes me smile.

"Send me pictures from Japan," Jake says. "I want to see your face every day."

"You'll just have to follow me," I tease.

I've set up a new account for my photography, and Sam didn't even have to force me. I'm not scared to share my pictures any more – I even post the odd selfie, Freya-style. I guess I'm pretty happy either side of the camera now. I've realized socials aren't the enemy. It's more about how you use them, what you choose to say. That's why I want to study fashion photography after college. Definitions of beauty are getting broader all the time, but as Jas is always reminding me, the job's not over. There's plenty still to do.

"You know what, Freya? I reckon I'd follow you anywhere." Jake's head dips towards mine.

My phone goes off in my pocket. Sighing, I pull it out. Four faces fill the screen.

"Freya! Have a good trip!"

"Are you at the airport?"

"Is Jake with you?"

Māra, Jas and Liam are at Sam's flat, and by the looks of Māra's hair, some kind of shoot is going on. *Experimental* might be the kindest description.

"Have a lovely time, darling." Carla sticks her head into the frame, while Tom waves in the background. Sam's still mortified by how much he underestimated his dad. Tom and Liam get on like a house on fire. And when Sam got a credit in *Seen* magazine for the work he did on my shoot, Tom was so chuffed he offered to take the boys anywhere they wanted to celebrate – although I'm not sure he was expecting to spend the entire afternoon testing eyeshadows in MAC.

"I'll miss you guys." I wave. Māra looks super happy. Her girlfriend's arriving soon. They got their uni places transferred to London, so Māra can model *and* finish her degree.

"Send me photos of Tokyo street-style!" Jas yells. "I might even print them!"

"I'll try!" I laugh. As newly promoted Fashion Editor after Clarissa finally retired, Jas loves having more input into the magazine.

I hang up, my heart full.

"Finally!" Jake pulls me towards him.

We spring apart as Dad comes back. "Sorry I took so long! They've announced the gate. Freya, have you texted Naoko yet?"

"Yes, she's meeting us at Narita." I shiver with excitement. I can't wait to meet my mum's best friend.

"Fly safely, then." Jake shakes Dad's hand. A look passes between them.

"I almost forgot!" Dad passes me a box. "Freya, this is for you." Jake is grinning from ear to ear.

"Oh!" I'm lost for words. I'm staring at a brand-new DSLR camera.

"Call it an early birthday present." Dad's eyes twinkle.

"Thank you!" I wrap him in the world's tightest hug.

"Well, we've got some new memories to make." He kisses my forehead and glances over to the X-ray area. "Why don't I grab us a place in the queue? Catch me up, but don't be long."

"You knew about the camera, didn't you?" I accuse Jake, as Dad heads for the line.

"Maybe…" He pulls me close and whispers in my ear. "I haven't got you a birthday present yet."

"Unforgivable," I whisper back.

"I guess we'll just have to wait until you're back." He looks at the departure board. "Only … twenty-one days, nine hours and … thirty-six minutes to go—"

I kiss him softly on the mouth.

As the shrinking shape of Jake merges with the crowd, I take a mental photograph.

"Ready?" Dad asks.

Carefully, I place my new camera in the tray and slide it towards the X-ray machine.

A new chapter of my life is starting, and who knows what it will bring? One thing I'm sure of: no hiding, or aiming for perfect.

Life isn't some glossy, airbrushed photo. It's messy and complicated and unpredictable. That's what makes it interesting.

My past is falling into focus, my present is full of light.

And I can't wait to frame my future.

Acknowledgements

Thank you to Anne Clark, my wonderful agent, who first saw the potential in my manuscript and helped me find the heart of the story.

To Linas Alsenas, my incredible editor: your enthusiasm is contagious and your ideas are amazing! Thanks for encouraging me to lean into the magic – and for supporting me with Sam's sub-plot.

Thanks to Genevieve Herr, for the insightful edit, to Sarah Dutton for the fabulous copyediting skills, to Johnny Tarajosu and Bethany Mincher for the stunning cover, and to the wider Scholastic team: Eleanor Thomas, Harriet Dunlea, Alice Pagin, Antonia Pelari, Lucy Page and the rights and sales teams. Catherine Bell, thanks for letting me into the fold.

The seeds of *Mirror Me* were sown in Lou Kuenzler's workshop at City Lit – thank you, Lou, and everyone who offered their critique. Thanks also to GEA, especially Emma, Abi, Imogen and my Foundations gang for helping me get the first draft down. Olivia Levez, thanks for your mentorship on the Write Mentor Summer Programme, and to Stuart White and the warm, inclusive Write Mentor organization – thanks for supporting writers everywhere.

I'm lucky to have some fantastic writer friends around me. Special shout-outs to Sue, Annette, Terrie, Fraer, Emma P, Anthony, Lou F, Tess, Nicola, Jasbinder, Melissa, my WM 2020 cohort and my Twitter 23 debuts gang, for all the feedback and encouragement! And to my amazing critique partner, Ali Clack: you help me crank up the confidence and polish my prose. I couldn't do this without you.

April Crichton at La Fetiche patiently answered my questions about fashion design, while Emma Mackie updated me on the world of modelling. Thanks, both! I'll always be grateful that my experiences in fashion were so positive, thanks to my agents – the original teams at Select London and Marilyns Paris/New York – as well as the talented photographers, hair and make-up artists, art directors, editors, designers, stylists and assistants that I was lucky enough to work with (waving at you, Greg Bitterman). Thanks for the good times.

To my lovely colleagues at HTSS Camden, and the Content team at Renaissance Learning, especially Cecelia. Thanks for being excited for me!

A final thank you to my friends and family. Mum and Dad, you brought me up in a home full of books, giving me a love of reading and writing early on. Thanks for the bedtime stories and for encouraging me to do the things that make me happy. I love you.

Helen, Matt, Annie, George – thanks for cheering me on.

To my aunt, Barbara Lane. You've been a constant supporter of my creative whims. It means the world.

Alex Rand, our pep talks kept me going. Are we near the mountain, yet?

Fiona, Rosie, Sam, Andrea, Vicki, Chris, Alys, my Kentish Town kinfolk, and my Bath buddies. I'm lucky to call you my friends.

Simon. You're the best co-pilot I could wish for (to quote M. Rand). Thanks for giving me space to make stuff. Rowan and Meg, you're hilarious and inspiring. I love you so much. I did this for you.